THE

Take Down

ALSO BY MARK ANTHONY

Paper Chasers

Dogism

Lady's Night

THE

Take Down

MARK ANTHONY

St. Martin's Griffin ✖ *New York*

THE TAKE DOWN. Copyright © 2006 by Mark Anthony Holsey. All rights reserved. Printed in the United States of America. No part of this book may be used or reproduced in any manner whatsoever without written permission except in the case of brief quotations embodied in critical articles or reviews. For information, address St. Martin's Press, 175 Fifth Avenue, New York, N.Y. 10010.

ISBN-13: 978-0-7394-7636-9

*This book is dedicated to
my brother Ronald.
You'll always be the big brother
that I look up to!*

ACKNOWLEDGMENTS

There are always numerous people to thank, recognize, and acknowledge. Many people have impacted my life, in both positive and negative ways, and I thank you all from the bottom of my heart. You all know who you are. But to my wife, Sabine, I personally acknowledge you, and I honor you. Thank you for what we share, and as always, thank you for your true love and patience. I will always be a work in progress.

THE

Take

Down

CHAPTER ONE

*a*s I listened to the intense sounds of sex I couldn't help but get turned on by it. It was times like these that made me absolutely love my job. As our men drew closer to the target, the sounds of some serious lovemaking continued to get even louder and more intense, and in the process I got more and more turned on to the point where my panties were actually a little moist from the excitement.

I remember laughing and thinking to myself that whoever the chick was that was on the receiving end of the dick, either she was just the loud screamer type who scream during sex just for the sake of screaming, or she really just couldn't handle the pounding that she was getting.

All of our people on the team were now in the exact positions that they needed to be in and every one of the team members was deathly silent.

"Oh my gawd!!!! OHHHH!!! UGHHH!!!"

That was only part of the screaming sounds that we heard, and it almost became comical to everyone on the team. But no one dared laugh because in every sense of the word, if we laughed our lives could end.

Mixed in with the moaning and screaming of the female, were the loud grunts and commands of the six-foot-four, two-hundred-and-eighty-pound target that we were after.

"G-One to TOC . . . Do you think we should let them finish?" one of the G-Men whispered and asked me through his bone mic that rested on his jaw.

"TOC to G-One . . . Have a heart, it's almost four in the morning. . . . Let him cum and then you guys should go in." I relayed those words to the earpiece listening devices that the entire team was wearing.

I actually had some reasoning as to why I had said what I said. My reasoning was that our target would be much less of a threat if we nabbed him right after an orgasm. And if anything he would at least be in a better mood so to speak, as opposed to us nabbing him without him at least being able to finish what he had started with his little sex kitten.

"Woooo!!! Woooo!!! Woooo!!! Ahhhh!!!"

The chick just wouldn't let up with the screaming . . . But I shouldn't really criticize her because I was still getting turned on by it.

"TOC to G-One . . . On second thought, we gotta get in there and save that broad. Obviously she can't handle *it*," I jokingly said to all of the men. I could hear the small sounds of laughter coming from the others on the team.

I was positioned about five blocks away from where the raid was taking place. I was inside of the Tactical Operations Center, which was the most obscure-looking surveillance cargo van, watching and listening to every detail of the predawn raid that we were conducting.

We were raiding the sprawling seven-thousand-square-foot Queens, New York home of hip-hop's hottest record producer/record mogul/entrepreneur, who was known on the streets and in the music world as Horse. Yeah, his celebrity status had grown to the point where he was one of those infamous one-nickname celebrities, sort of like if you say "Suge" everyone would know that you were referring to Tupac's former Death Row Records label head Marion "Suge" Knight.

Horse, whose real name is Tyrone Hopkins, gained his notoriety, fortune, and prominence by producing hit records for some of the biggest stars in music, and not just rap music, but music across many genres. But unquestionably, his infamous reputation stems from the fact that he is the owner and CEO of Gun Clap Records.

Tyrone "Horse" Hopkins has a very feared reputation and an imposing Hulk Hogan–like body to help further that feared reputation, not to mention the string of violence and murders in the rap music world which haven't been proven but which have Horse and his Gun-Clap Records written all over them.

Horse and all of his homeys across the country had been under surveillance by us, the FBI, for many months now. We also had his phones tapped and we basically knew his every move and all of his habits as well as those of his associates. We knew who visited him on a regular basis, we knew the school that his son went to, along with all of the after-school activities that his son was involved in. We even knew all there was to know about the nanny who helped take care of his son. And to really show you the depth and scope of our investigation, we knew the names of Horse's own schoolteachers, dating back to the time he was in kindergarten!

Quite frankly, when we wanted to go after someone such as Horse, we went after them with everything we had. And like terrorists who plan and plot and wait for years before they strike, we too had planned and plotted and waited for many months before we struck, and there was no better time than the present for us to make our move. We knew that if we moved on him when we did we would be catching Horse with his pants down, literally.

"TOC to all units . . . Move in on three . . ."

As if the broad who couldn't handle the dick was listening to us, she chimed in right on cue and in perfect cadence so that we could time our entry.

"Wooo!!!" she yelled.

One thousand one, I counted.

"Wooo!!!"

One thousand two . . .

"Wooo!!!"

I felt sorry for her because most women don't even reach the point of orgasm, so we women kind of treasure it when we actually reach it. And she sure did sound like she was about to cum, but hey, we had a job to do.

One thousand three . . .

"FBI!!! Get your hands in the air! I wanna see your hands!" one of the agents commanded after bursting into Horse's bedroom.

"What da fuck?" Horse hollered back, as he obviously was shocked by our unwanted presence.

I could hear all that was going on inside the house but it took a minute for us to get the camera in position, the Court TV camera that filmed and documented the entire raid while simultaneously transmitting back to our surveillance van.

"Get your hands in the fucking air and step away from the bed!!!"

The camera was finally in place and again I couldn't help but be amused and think about how this job had to be the best in the world. From the viewpoint of the camera, it looked as if Horse and his rap-video-looking cutie had just been doing it doggy-style when we barged in on them. Her back was facing Horse and she lay face-first on the king-size water bed with her hands outstretched in order to follow the commands of the gun-toting federal agents.

Horse was sweaty and butt-ass naked with his knees on the bed and his bodybuilder chest facing the girl he had been screwing. And although he tried to talk tough, he made sure that he followed orders and kept his hands hoisted in the air where the agents could see them.

"Everybody slowly step away from the bed and keep your hands in the air where we can see them!" the agents screamed.

The petite, young-looking cutie spoke up.

"Can I at least put some goddamn clothes on?" she stated as she got up from the bed, totally disrespecting all authority and proceeded to walk toward her clothes.

One of the agents quickly grabbed her by the arm and slammed her up against the wall and handcuffed her as she screamed in pain.

"You better get your fucking hands off of me!!! I swear to God I will kill you if you don't get your hands off of me!

Ahhh! These cuffs are too tight! Loosen these goddamn handcuffs, bitch!"

All of us in the TOC couldn't help but laugh as one of the other female agents who was sitting next to me said, "Jessica, would you listen to all of that mouth and attitude coming from that chick? A minute ago she was screaming for dear life as if someone was killing her 'cause she couldn't handle the dick. Now she's talking about *she'll kill somebody . . .*"

"Y'all don't gotta be handling my girl all rough like that!" Horse barked. "Do y'all got a fucking warrant? Let me see some papers from a judge or something! Y'all can't just walk up in my shit like this!"

Not only did we have authorization to enter Horse's home, but we had obtained that authorization some time ago. And that was how on a prior occasion we had installed listening and monitoring devices throughout the home; we had studied the alarm system so that we would know how to deactivate it upon entry.

The biggest agent, in terms of physical size, that we had on our team grabbed Horse by the wrist and proceeded to handcuff him.

"Jessica, damn, *girrrl!* Now I see why that broad was screaming and carrying on the way she was," one of the other black female agents stated in her *sista from the hood* kind of tone.

As Horse's manhood came into full view on the screen, I replied, "Yeah girrrl, I see too! And I also see why the hell they call him Horse," I added while slapping my coworker five.

"TOC to all units . . . Hurry and put some clothes on the

suspects," one of the male supervising special agents in the TOC ordered.

"G-One to TOC, copy."

I couldn't believe how insecure these men that I worked with were. They didn't rush to give an order for the cute rap-video-looking broad to be clothed. But as soon as they saw the size of Horse's manhood they immediately started calling and ordering for the suspects to be clothed.

"G-Five to all units . . . jackpot!"

At the time I didn't exactly understand what G-5 was talking about but apparently he was trying to convey that he had located what we knew was inside the home, that being a stash of cocaine, three pounds of marijuana, and more importantly a .45-caliber handgun, the same handgun that had been used in the murder of rival West Coast superstar rapper Frank Nitty.

While we conducted the predawn raid on Horse's home, we were also simultaneously conducting a raid on the Midtown offices of Gun Clap Records. During that raid we seized computers, file cabinets, pictures, telephones, and everything else that looked important.

We wanted to send a powerful message to the entire hip-hop community, but more importantly we wanted to send a message to Horse and his silent partner Tyrell "Supreme" Morgan. And that message was this: *the FBI is not to be fucked with 'cause we know how to shut shit down if we have to!*

CHAPTER TWO

*b*y the time the media got wind of the raids that we had conducted, there was a virtual media circus. So to accommodate the media, the assistant U.S. attorney decided to hold an 11 A.M. press conference to give the details of exactly what had transpired during the night of the raids and why. The press conference was packed wall to wall with cameramen, photographers, and news reporters as well as numerous law enforcement officials and personnel.

What was ironic was that I was helping to engineer the investigation into Gun Clap Records, and yet I could not be present at the news conference to share in the glory and recognition. See, I was deep undercover and it was not the time to have my cover blown. There was still a whole lot of work to be done and this raid of Horse and his record label was only the tip of the iceberg.

As they say in the streets, my *government name* is Paula Winslow but my undercover name is Jessica Jackson. I'm a twenty-five-year-old African-American female FBI agent. My job is my life, and my life is my job. In fact, my undercover role is so real to me that it has gotten to the point where I instinctively don't even respond to the name Paula anymore. All of my friends and coworkers call me Jessica or Jessie for short.

Two years ago I was transferred to an FBI office in Manhattan. Prior to being transferred to New York City, I had spent my entire short career in the Midwest, St. Louis, Missouri to be exact. I had handled money laundering investigations, bank robberies, kidnappings, and all of the other types of investigations that the FBI conducts. From day one I loved my job, but the thing was I was in Missouri! The middle of nowhere and I wanted out of Missouri in the worst way. I hadn't joined the FBI to be holed up in a bunch of small-ass hick towns in the Midwest.

A lot of agents had joined the FBI because they wanted to make a mark. They wanted to make a difference in the world. For me, at the end of the day I could have cared less about making a mark or making a difference. I was motivated by one thing, and one thing only, and that was making money by any means necessary.

Greed might be a better word to describe my obsessive ambitious motivations. If you were to open me up, what you would find is a hustler in every sense of the word. And my job as an FBI agent, well that was my hustle and I was determined to get rich off of it. I wanted to be *that bitch* that got rich even if it meant that I had to be corrupt in the process. To get rich off my FBI hustle I knew that I had to get my ass to either one of these three cities: New York, Los Angeles, or Miami. The

problem with that was every FBI agent and their grandmother wanted to get transferred to a city like the Big Apple
or Hollywood.

Fortunately for me, as fate would have it, while I was still
in St. Louis and with only two years of experience under my
belt, my supervisors and superiors approached me and spoke
to me about the possibility of transferring to New York and
putting me on a very big case.

"Paula," my immediate supervisor said to me, "this investigation has the potential to be bigger than the Donnie Brasco
investigation. Donnie Brasco helped put a dent in the mob,
but what we have the potential to do is take down both hip-
hop and the mob at the same time!"

As I listened attentively to both my supervisor and his
boss, my supervisor's boss began to break down for me the
background details of an investigation that the New York City
office was currently undertaking. He explained that the FBI's
organized-crime unit had secretly infiltrated the Calvino
crime family and during their investigation had been able to
determine that the Calvinos had been supplying Tyrell
"Supreme" Morgan with illegal narcotics since his release
from federal prison in 1996. The Calvinos were Supreme's *connect,* as they say in the streets.

He went on to explain exactly who Supreme was, just how
long Supreme's rap sheet was, and how the FBI's organized-
crime unit had real good reason to believe that Supreme was
able to illegally bankroll Gun Clap Records with money that
Calvino soldiers needed to be laundered.

My heart rate picked up. I was quickly becoming anxious
with anticipation because this was sounding like a dream in-

vestigation that I knew I would be able to excel on. At the same time, I knew I would be able to somehow exploit the investigation to my financial gain.

"Paula, feelers went out to all of the field offices across the country, specifically asking for a list of recommended female agents with the skill and ability to go to New York and take part in the organized-crime unit's investigation that is already underway. More specifically, they're looking for someone who would be able to infiltrate Gun Clap Records and get the concrete evidence that we need to more definitively tie the Calvinos dirty money to Gun Clap Records," my supervisor's boss concluded. "We need someone who can wear a wire and get close enough to Supreme or Horse and get them to incriminate themselves by admitting to the money-laundering suspicions on tape, and the Bureau's feeling is that it won't happen unless we bring in a female agent to get close to these two. It just won't work with a male agent."

There was a brief pause where nobody said anything and I thought silently for a moment. I knew that my supervisors wouldn't have even come to me if they didn't believe in me and since I knew that obviously other female agents were being considered, I wanted to sell myself so that I could be the agent that was chosen for the assignment.

"Jessica Jackson!" I blurted out.

"Jessica Jackson?"

"Yeah, that will be my undercover name . . . Paula Winslow will cease to exist." I smiled as I overtly began selling my boss on a plan.

I continued on, "Jessica Jackson . . . and the code name

for my part of the undercover operation will be *White Choco-late.*"

"Paula, you're losing me," my boss stated.

"Listen, I don't know what other candidates are on the list, but I'm your girl! I know the hip-hop world. My fiancé, the cop, he moonlights as a bodyguard for all of the top Midwest hip-hop artists, he promotes hip-hop events, and I . . ."

"Paula, that is exactly why your name was on the top of the list. And not for nothing, Paula, you are drop-dead gorgeous and your looks would be the perfect distraction that could help you get these guys to trust you. But, Paula, these guys are hardened, violent criminals. Supreme ran one of the most vio-lent drug gangs in the eighties. Even if you were chosen for the assignment, I am telling you to really consider all of the dangers and other ramifications that would go along with this assignment."

I chimed in, "Listen, the hip-hop world is all about the money, the bling-bling, and the women. If I'm added to the operation, my name would be Jessica Jackson and White Chocolate, well that . . ."

I sold my superiors on this plan to send me to New York where I would start a modeling agency called White Choco-late Models Inc. White Chocolate Models would be a legiti-mately run company, funded with government money, but of course it would be a front organization to allow me to develop my necessary contacts in the hip-hop world which would en-able me to make some headway into my specific undercover assignment.

I soon began overselling my qualifications as I stated that

if I was added to the investigation I would be able to top the Donnie Brasco investigation.

See, Donnie Brasco had gone deep undercover as an FBI agent and at the time he was the first agent in FBI history to ever infiltrate the mob as deeply as he'd penetrated it. And because of his investigation, law enforcement agencies all across the country were able to root out and get a foothold on organized crime in a way that had never seemed possible.

"Why are you so overconfident that you can pull this off? Donnie Brasco was a major piece of work performed by one of the best agents ever in the Bureau . . . What exactly do you mean that you can top Brasco?" my salt-and-pepper-haired boss asked me.

"I can top it because as successful as Donnie Brasco was, you even just admitted that he'd only put a dent into the mob, he didn't get you the mob's top man. Hell, he didn't even get you the mob's top family in New York at the time. . . . And what I'm saying is that if I get a shot, if you can pull strings for me to get this transfer done and added to this investigation, I am guaranteeing you that I will not only get you the proof that Gun Clap Records was founded with dirty money that the Calvinos needed to launder, but I will get you Paulie Calvino, the head of the Calvino crime family. New York and the country's largest and most dangerous crime family."

I remained silent after I spoke and was hoping that I hadn't talked myself out of consideration for the transfer. I could tell that my boss was probably thinking that I was just some fantasy-thinking, bored-as-hell FBI agent that wanted out of the slow St. Louis office and was willing to drum up any far-fetched pitch just to get a transfer. But instinctively I knew that I had to continue to sell myself.

"Boss, I can see the wheels spinning in your head, and I can even see the smiles and smirks starting to form at your skin lines . . . But please trust me on this. I am not some fantasy thrill-seeking agent who just wants a transfer to New York. It's deeper than that to me. I *know* that I can do this! And I know that you're not seeking any recognition, but if I am able to pull this off don't you understand that everyone will know where my recommendation came from?"

"And if you screw up out there, being overambitious, guess who Washington and New York are going to look at? Me! My ass and my reputation will be on the line just as much as your career would be on the line."

"White Chocolate?" my boss stated with a whole lot of oddity in his voice.

"Yeah see, this is the thing. You don't go after these hip-hop guys by going through the back door, or through the side door or even through the roof for that matter. Those days of investigating like that are long gone. You come at them in the most indirect way but a way that is as natural to them as putting on their pants or taking a shit. And see, that is where the White Chocolate modeling agency will come in. See, what I would need to do is . . ."

That day and on several other occasions I continued to sell my boss on my qualifications and on the idea that I had. And over time he began to buy everything that I sold to him. He bought what I was selling simply because I had backed off and I hadn't given him too much to digest at one time. It's like if I give someone a slice of pizza, and they enjoy the slice then chances are they will want another slice. And when they finish that other slice they will probably ask for another and then another and so on until the whole pizza pie is completely eaten up. But if I ram the whole goddamn pizza pie down their throat at one time then they will forever be turned off by pizza.

So after a couple of months of continuing to sell my qualifications and pitching my idea to my superior and then to his superiors, the whole Bureau had bought into my idea and my skills. The fact that I look much like the actress Halle Berry— I'm sure that somewhere along the line that also helped influence my male bosses' decision to let me go deep undercover in New York. But hey, women have to use what we got in order to get what we want.

In further detailing my plan I had explained how I didn't think it would be smart to be assigned to the FBI's Organized Crime Task Force. I wanted free rein to develop my own contacts and that in doing so I would be more effective. I might have been young with limited experience, but I was sharp as a whip and smart as hell.

Unfortunately for me, that was where the Bureau had to draw the line. They were cool with the Jessica Jackson name and the White Chocolate Models but they made it clear to me that there were already highly experienced lead agents on the case from the organized-crime unit who had made major headway and that I was simply going to be brought in to further assist the work of those agents. I wasn't going to be a lead agent or some dynamo on the loose with no reins who could potentially screw everything up. My role and tasks were clear: get close to Horse and Supreme and get the concrete indisputable evidence that the FBI needed to prove that Gun Clap Records was knowingly started and funded with laundered mob money.

To passify my bosses and to get put on the investigation, I knew that I had to pretend to follow the lead and the directives of the FBI and that of the other senior agents on the case. But I had a lot of cards in my hand that I hadn't told my superiors about because I knew that they would not have had the foresight to see my vision. But the cards that I was planning to play in the White Chocolate undercover operation were gonna be played so I could advance my own personal hustling agenda, and those cards were an ace of spades that went by the name of Tyrone "Horse" Hopkins and an ace of diamonds that went by the name of Angela Calvino, the daughter of Mafia don, Paulie Calvino.

After I'd dreamed up the plan for White Chocolate Models I began to proactively study the New York hip-hop world and the New York Mafia world. One, a white-Italian-dominated world, and the other, a black-dominated world, and I knew that being half-black and half-white I was the perfect person to find out exactly how these two worlds came to be connected. But something kept telling me that despite what my superiors and lead agents wanted from me, that if I wanted to really get this investigation on and poppin' and to get paid off of it that it would be smarter for me to secretly create a brand new union between the two worlds of hip-hop and the mob.

Unfortunately I knew that if I committed to this transfer that my personal life and my relationship with my family and especially my relationship with my fiancé was gonna suffer big time. But I was willing to make that personal sacrifice because I knew all that I stood to gain if I were to freak this investigation to my advantage.

CHAPTER THREE

*i*n no time Horse had managed to make his bail. He had put up $2.5 million of his own money in order to regain his freedom. He was a free man but the federal government was gonna do everything within our power to make sure that we kept the pressure on him until his trial.

I stared at the television screen and I watched Horse spin everything that he had been accused of. He had one of the most powerful public relations firms working in his corner and in the upcoming weeks and months I was sure that they would earn every penny that Horse would pay them.

"They got nada. Naaada...Nothing! None of these charges will stick. I was basically set up and framed. But it's okay 'cause I got a strong legal team behind me and all I can say is that when we get our day in court, everyone will see for themselves that I'm innocent," Horse confidently and emphatically stated with much charisma to the media as he held his own damage-control press conference.

"So Horse, how do you explain the fact that they found the murder weapon in your home?" one of the reporters asked.

Horse was silent as his lawyer whispered something into his ear.

"All I can say is that everything comes out in the wash . . ." Horse replied.

"So are you insinuating that the government framed you on all of the charges?"

Horse smiled and commented, "All I'm saying is that I wanna get back to making hit records. I make hit records and I make a lot of money. Everything I got I've worked my ass off to get and . . ."

One of the reporters interrupted Horse while he was speaking. "Horse, what about the government's allegations that Gun Clap Records was started with 'mobbed up drug money'?"

"What about it?" Horse replied in his true-to-form cocky manner.

"Do you deny it? Is there any truth to it?"

"Look, this is the thing: when people can't explain my success, when they don't wanna attribute my success to hard work, then they try to come up with all kinds of myths to explain what it is that they cannot seem to logically understand."

"So you're denying the allegations that Gun Clap Records was founded with mob money?"

Horse smiled and stated, "I'm saying that I've worked twenty-two hours a day, every day for as long as I can remember. While the rest of ya'll are sleeping, I'm in the studio making hit records and when I leave the studio I'm in my office grinding it out every day. I don't sleep! I worked my ass off for what I got. Everybody in my company has worked their asses off to help build Gun Clap to be where we are today, and to insinuate anything less than that would be an insult to my whole team. All I know is that Gun Clap was founded on hard work, it was founded on the principle that it's okay to party hard and to play hard, just as long as you work hard. . . . So you best believe that ya'll are gonna keep seeing me flying in Lear jets and driving around in a Rolls-Royce or a Maybach or whatever is hot. I mean it's only right, ya' dig?" Horse said, sounding like a braggadocio.

At that point Horse's lawyer whispered something else into his ear.

"Listen, I wanna thank ya'll for coming out, and again I wanna state and make it perfectly clear that I'm innocent of all these charges that have been brought against me. And on the advice of my lawyers, I won't be answering any more questions today, thank you . . ." Horse ended and was quickly flanked by his entourage which included his ten-year-old son, Darius.

"Horse, what about your affiliation with Supreme? I mean he was once convicted of drug trafficking. Do you have any comments on that?" a reporter blurted out.

Stopping dead in his tracks and freeing himself from his entourage, Horse spun to answer that reporter's question. "Yeah, I can comment on that. I've known Supreme all my life. That's my nigga fo' sho and he'll always be my nigga. Understand this, if I choose to hang with 'Preme or anyone else for that matter, then that's who I'm gonna hang with. I'm a street nigga! All my life I've been a street nigga. I'm from the bottom but I came up! Ya' dig? Yeah, I might have made some hit records for people that are mainstream or for cats that crossed over, but at the end of the day I'm a street nigga born and raised in Southside Jamaica, Queens. Street niggas is who I trust and who I know. . . . Ya'll can take this to the bank, whether I'm free or locked behind bars for twenty years, until my casket drops I'm always rolling with Supreme and there ain't no man or woman alive who's gonna regulate who the fuck I associate with!"

See those were Horse's words to the media and to the public. But behind closed doors when he had been interrogated, even with his lawyer present, it was a completely different story. Horse was scared like a bitch. He feared that his empire was gonna be taken away from him right from underneath his feet. He also insanely feared that his son, his most prized possession and future heir to the Gun Clap throne might also be taken from his custody, but in the public's eye he never let anybody see him sweat.

As soon as the press conference was over I immediately placed a call to Gun Clap Records. I knew that Horse wasn't there but I wanted to make everything appear to Horse that I was still in his corner.

"Gun Clap Records, how can I help you?" the receptionist answered, sounding very exhausted.

"Hey Tamika, this is Jessica from White Chocolate Models . . . Listen, I know that everything must be crazy over there with all the drama that's been going on but I just wanted to leave a message for Horse . . . Can you tell him to call me as soon as he gets a chance?"

"Okay, I'll give him the message."

"Tamika, did he turn off his cell phone or something?" I asked, trying to sound sincere and concerned at the same time.

"Look, I really can't comment on anything right now. It is a zoo up in here. We're still waiting to get our computers and everything back that was confiscated by the feds. But I will make a note to tell him that you called."

"Okay, thank you."

The truth of the matter was that I knew that Horse had turned off his cell phone. In fact everyone associated with Horse had been ordered to turn off their cell phones and to turn off their two-way pagers. The FBI had been monitoring all of the communications that were going on between the two-way pagers and the cell phones, and someone in Horse's camp must have suspected that we were eavesdropping on them.

In a matter of days we had gone from having so much access to the conversations of those associated with Horse to virtually having no conversations to monitor whatsoever.

Horse also had security experts dispatched to his offices, his homes, the homes of his associates, his cars, and all of his associate's cars in an effort to look for and remove all of the bugs that the FBI had strategically placed.

It was at that point that I started to second-guess myself and I began wondering if I had moved too quickly. See, it had been on my word that the raids had been ordered. I just felt that it had been time to put the pressure on Horse and my gut told me that if we applied the right pressure to him he would fold. But what I hadn't calculated was that he would be smart enough to discard his phones and look for bugs.

I knew that I had to rely on my instincts and trust that the investigation would continue to go the way that I wanted it to. So with Horse now virtually off the radar screen, I decided to work the other side of my investigation until I could get in touch with him. In fact, I knew that it was time to really try and accelerate that other side of the investigation.

After I hung up with the receptionist at Gun Clap, I placed a call to Angela Calvino just to chat her up and to see how she was doing.

The way I had met Angela was similar to the way in which I had met Horse, and that was by religiously hanging around all of the routine places that they hung out and cautiously looking for opportunities to genuinely get to know them without appearing suspicious or coming across like a groupie or an annoying hound.

For a few months straight I had been purposely going to the same day spa that Angela had been going to on the exact same days and times as she. I also had been going to some of the same Manhattan and Long Island nightclubs that she went to.

Angela had also tried her hand in the modeling business, which was something that I knew about her way before I had decided to leave the FBI office in St. Louis. Through the modeling business she had met a model who ditched modeling for the record industry and subsequently went on to make millions of dollars as a singer. Angela had always beaten herself up for not having been the one to manage the young lady's career, and she vowed to never let another opportunity like that pass her by. So as she worked in the modeling industry she did so always with the hopes of finding that model that could be the next Britney Spears or Christina Aguilera.

"Hello . . ."

"Hi Angela, this is Jessica. Are you busy right now?"

"No, I can talk. What's up hon?" Angela replied. She sounded as if she was in a good mood, but if there was one thing about Angela it was that she was one moody blond-haired beautiful bitch that thought the world absolutely revolved around her.

"How would you like to meet Tyrone Hopkins?"

After a slight pause Angela responded very bluntly. "Who the fuck is Tyrone Hopkins and why would I want to meet him?"

"Horse? Angela, come on, you never heard of the record producer named Horse? Well his real name is Tyrone Hopkins."

"Oh, okay. Yeah, he's been all over the news lately. Why would I wanna meet him? No offense but he seems like nigger trash."

"Angela, come on, think with me. What do you always say is one of your biggest regrets?"

"Jessica, I don't have all day. Would you hurry up and get to the goddamn point of your call?"

That was Angela's style of always trying to be the one in control. Usually she didn't mean anything by the way she spoke to people, she was just brash by nature and if you didn't know her you could easily take it as her being rude. I knew Angela's ways because I had studied them. So I knew how to respond to her.

"No, Angela slow up a minute . . . Just think. You always talk about how you let that model get away from you and sell all of those records over in Great Britain or Australia or wherever the fuck she lives. Now here I am telling you that I can introduce you to Horse and you can't make the connection."

There was a brief pause in the conversation as Angela thought hard about what I was saying.

"Yeah, Jessica, I can't make a connection with what you're saying, I . . ."

Trying to appear disgusted with her, I cut her off and blurted out an Italian phrase, "Madone!"

"What the fuck is your problem?" Angela asked. "All I'm saying is I can't make a connection because if I'm gonna manage somebody or make someone's career it's gonna be in pop music. Not with that gangsta rap nigger-music shit!"

"Angela, so what are you saying? That you don't like rap music? I hope not, because it's not even really about the music."

"No, that's not what I'm saying. I'm just telling you that I would rather—"

"Look, Angela I'm gonna set this up and I'll call you. Just please be ready to move at the drop of a hat when I call," I said as I again cut her off in the middle of her words. I was showing a bit of disrespect toward her, which is something she wasn't used to.

"Jessica, what the fuck? Oh, I take fucking orders from you now? You've got some pair of balls, Jessica!"

I purposely wanted to push Angela's buttons and I was succeeding. But I had to get her to see where I was coming from without sounding like I was up to something that could possibly hurt her. And I knew that the best way to get someone to see your point was by making them feel like they were an idiot for not seeing what seemed so obvious.

"All right, Angela, I'll be totally honest with you."

"Thank fucking God! You know you were really starting to piss me off."

I sort of laughed into the phone.

"Jessica, this is not funny! You're lucky I like you because I don't just let anyone call me and joke and laugh when there isn't anything funny. I don't have time for that shit," Angela stated with her classic New York–Italian street accent.

"Angela, the other day . . . Um, I don't know . . . Maybe a month or so ago when everybody was at that club out in Island Park . . . What is the name of that club? You know, the one on Long Island . . . *Spratz on the Water*. Now think back . . . Who was everyone going crazy over? Remember the guy from Howard Beach? The rapper, White Lines? Angela, he is a million-dollar meal ticket! The guy could be bigger than Eminem!"

"Holy shit! Jessica, you are so right!" Angela stated through the phone, sounding as if she had just received a revelation from God.

"You see what I'm saying, Angie? Who gives a shit if it's pop music, rap music, country music, or whatever kind of music? At the end of the day what it boils down to is will the music sell five million copies or not?"

Seeing exactly where I was coming from, Angela jumped right back in. "Yeah, Jessica, and when you think about it, Eminem sells more records than the biggest pop and country acts combined!"

"Exactly! And White Lines would have much more street credibility than someone like Eminem. Plus, as far as I'm concerned, he really sounds good. Can you imagine a white boy rapper with street credibility? He'll sell ten million records in his first week! And Angela, you'll be managing him, making ten percent at least, off of everything that he earns . . . And when you need models for his many music videos, who are you gonna call? Do you see my vision?"

"Jessica, when can you set this up?"

"Well, like you said earlier, Horse has so much going on right now with his legal issues, but I called him earlier and I'm waiting for him to get back to me. So when he calls me I'll set things in motion."

"Okay, let me ask you something and also tell you something. Number one, don't you dare fucking tell him who my father is! Let me do that . . . And number two, how do you know him so well that you can just call meetings with him?"

"Angela, I don't run my mouth to people. That is the first thing . . . So don't worry about me talking about your father. I mean no disrespect, but do you ever hear me mention your father's name?"

Jessica cut me off and stated, "No, no, no, don't get me wrong, it's just that I don't want to get by because of who my father is. I mean sure, he's a great man but I want to make my own way in life."

"Angie, that's not a problem . . . But to answer your other question, I met Horse some time ago and he's used my agency a couple of times when he needed models for his artists' music videos or photo shoots. . . . Remember I was telling you that I own White Chocolate Models?"

"Right, that's right, that's right. I forgot about that."

"So I'll get back to you on that."

"Okay, do that . . . And Jessica, keep this quiet. Keep it between me and you. Don't talk to nobody about White Lines. Let me take it from here, okay?"

I assured Angie that her last wish would be my command. She had taken my bait. Now I had to get in touch with Horse and make sure that I sold him on the meeting so that I could put things in motion and reel everyone in.

There was no better job in the world than my job. I was getting paid to lie and be somebody that I wasn't. And in the process I was living out a life only seen in the movies. But this was no movie. I knew that I had to be extremely careful because all it would have taken was one false move and my life could have been snuffed out very quickly!

CHAPTER FOUR

*i*f there is one thing that the criminal underworld hates it is a snitch. A rat, a canary, a stool-pigeon, whatever adjective you want to use in order to describe people who give information to the authorities—they are the scum of the earth. What is so funny and ironic is that there are literally thousands of so-called rats, and some of them literally get paid to talk and others do it just to get or keep their asses out of a sling. Regardless of their motives for ratting out others, snitches help people like me, as well as local law enforcement to do our jobs each and every day. In fact we wouldn't be able to do our jobs as effectively if it weren't for the rats in the underworld.

When Horse got raided, most of the information that we had compiled had come about as a result of my undercover investigation and our wiretaps and surveillance. But we did have some inside help. One of the lead agents had a well-connected confidential informant who went by the name of Chris Mims. Chris had worked security for most, if not all of the big names in hip-hop. He had full access to what went on inside hotel rooms, tour buses, and record industry closed-door meetings. Chris had been cooperating with law enforcement for about two years. He had been caught with an illegal handgun, which in New York State gets you a mandatory one-year jail sentence. And in order to avoid jail time, yup, you guessed it, he agreed to cooperate with authorities and help supply us with information when we needed it. That was a real punk move on his part, because a year in jail is nothing, especially if he was supposed to be really street.

The problem with Chris was that he could always give precise information as to why something happened or when something was gonna happen but he could never supply us with that damaging incriminating information or tip that we needed. And that is why my investigation was so important. See, after I'd come into the picture, we were able to get closer to our subjects and know their movements and what they were talking about. We were able to put pieces of a puzzle together and having someone like Chris around to supply us with that puzzle piece was vital to our obtaining legal permission to get things like wiretaps.

In fact, Chris was the one that told us with guaranteed certainty that Horse would have the illegal handgun in his home when we raided it. He also told us that whenever Gun Clap artists went on tour that Horse would supply them with weed and cocaine for the trip. It was sort of like a bonus that he would give them, and Chris knew that the *bonus* cocaine and weed would be in the house.

As I would later find out, the toughest thing about dealing with a confidential informant is that they have the ability to sit on both sides of the fence. They can supply you with false information that could make you look like an absolute fool if you used the information to conduct a search or make an arrest. Informants sitting on both sides of the fence could also potentially be dangerous and life threatening to law enforcement if the informant decided to tell his criminal cronies who in fact it was that was investigating them.

The lead special agent in charge of the White Chocolate operation had made a decision very early on to not let any of the confidential informants know who I was. The agent in charge had made it clear that if and when Jessica Jackson became too visible on the criminal radar to the point where informants began to question agents as to who I was, that all of the agents were to be mute on the subject and act as if I was just some sophisticated good-looking black broad who owned an up-and-coming modeling agency.

I knew of all the other confidential informants that were being used as part of the White Chocolate investigation, but it was just something about Chris Mims that I didn't trust. Something about him just didn't sit right with me. I mean yes, he did fit the typical big, black, muscle-bound bodyguard image. But my distrust of him had nothing to do with his image or his physical appearance. It had more to do with a gut instinct that I had about him.

He's just like the other informants, I told myself, as I tried to dismiss my reservations about Chris. I wanted to clear my mind of any wavering doubts because I was ready to follow up with another phone call to Horse and I wanted to make sure that I was speaking to him with a clear head. It had been forty-eight hours since I last called his office and he had not returned my phone call. From tracking all of Horse's movements I knew that he would usually arrive at his Midtown Manhattan office at about 11 A.M. every morning. So when 11:15 rolled around I didn't waste any time in calling him.

I dialed the office number and I got Tamika on the phone once again.

Trying to sound as polite and sophisticated as ever so that I would be taken more seriously, I said, "Yes, hi, Tamika. It's me again, Jessica. Listen, Horse never got back in touch with me and I was wondering—"

Tamika cut me off in midsentence. "Jessica, I gave him the message. You'll just have to be patient with him but he'll get back to you. And if not, his assistant will definitely follow up with you."

I couldn't stand Horse's arrogant-ass assistant and I needed to get this meeting thing with Angela in motion ASAP.

"Tamika," I whispered into the phone as if I was about to tell her a secret, "look, this is between me and you but I am really trying to set something important up with Horse. I have never asked you for anything and I have never given you a hard time. But if you put me through to him right now, I'll make sure that a two-hundred-and-fifty-dollar gift certificate gets delivered to you this afternoon."

With typical black girl attitude, Tamika sucked her teeth, and although I couldn't see her through the phone I could tell that she was also probably rolling her eyes and twisting her neck.

"Okay Jessica, hold on," Tamika replied as she noticeably breathed a sigh of disgust into the phone.

So much for thank you for the gift certificate, I thought to myself as I waited on the other end of the phone desperately hoping that Tamika would put me through to Horse. As I waited on hold for about two minutes I began to practice rolling my eyes and twisting my neck and sucking my teeth in the way that I envisioned Tamika to have done it. It became comical and I almost burst out laughing at the wrong time.

"This is Horse. Get at me!" Horse stated as he'd finally come to the phone and took me off hold.

"Horse, hi, how are you? This is Jessica," I said in my rosiest voice.

"Oh, what's good ma'?"

"Well I wanted—"

"Yo, I didn't forget about that money. We're gonna get it to you. It's just that it's been real crazy over here, a whole lot of drama. Ya heard?"

Horse was referring to money that Gun Clap records owed White Chocolate Models for some print work that some of our models had done for his artist that went by the name of S&S.

"No, I'm not calling you because of that. Take your time with that. I know you're good for the money. . . . Listen, Horse, I know that things must be crazy for you with everything that has been going on, but I think I can show you something that could totally take all of this negative attention away from Gun Clap."

Horse laughed. "What the hell are you talking about ma'?"

"Well, first of all, you know from the time I met you in the bowling alley in Chelsea Piers that I have never asked you for nothing. I never asked you for a handout, never. And when you found out what I do for a living it was *you* that asked me if my company could get you some girls for your videos . . ."

"True dat, okay so what are you getting at?"

"Well now I do need a favor from you. Do you know Paulie Calvino?"

"Paulie Calvino the Mafia boss? That Paulie Calvino?"

"Yes, him."

"Nah, I mean I know of him. Just like I'm sure he knows of me, but I never personally met him. That's 'Preme's man though. But why you ask?"

"Well me and Paulie Calvino's daughter are good friends and she is managing this guy from Howard Beach. He rhymes and I think he is pretty good. Matter of fact, I know he is good. Eminem type of good."

"Ha! Ha! Ha ha ha! Whoa! Are you for real? Jessica there ain't no fucking rappers coming out of Howard Beach. This *nigga* is a white boy?"

"Yes he's white but—"

Horse cut me off. "Jessica, on the strength, no disrespect but I'm not looking for no *Vanilla Ice* rappers that—"

I knew where Horse was going so I interrupted him just as he had rudely interrupted me. "Horse, like I said, I haven't ever asked you for anything, I'm just asking you now if you can give me and Paulie's daughter about fifteen minutes of your time. Hear the kid out and see what you think, that's it. If you don't think he's any good then fuck it, she'll shop him to another label. But I promise you that he is not a gimmick Vanilla Ice kind of rapper."

"A'ight that's cool. I'll give you the benefit of the doubt. So what name does dude rhyme under?"

"White Lines."

"A'ight, I'm feeling that. So you said the kid can really rhyme?"

I was excited that Horse was rolling with the idea, but I didn't want that excitement to come across to him.

"Horse, I wouldn't waste your time if he wasn't. I know you get a million people coming to you with demo tapes and whatnot. But what's funny is that I saw this kid at a club out in Island Park . . ."

"Where the fuck is that?" Horse questioned.

"That's on Long Island, not too far from Rockville Center, over in that area. . . . But anyway, I see this young Italian kid performing and he really sounds good. And I was thinking to myself how rappers are always talking about their 'street credibility' and how 'they live what they rap about', and I'm saying to myself, this kid looks like he has street credibility. He would be a perfect fit for Gun Clap."

Horse paused, and then he laughed.

"So the kid is nice with the mic, and he has street credibility? This is a white boy? Okay so what's in it for you?"

"Nothing is in it for me. Of course if he gets signed and becomes bigger than Eminem I just want you to call me and let me supply the girls for the video shoots, the posters, the stickers, the album covers and all of that," I said as I laughed through the phone, trying to break the ice.

"A'ight so listen. If this kid is that nice, bring him through tomorrow at one thirty and I wanna hear him spit . . . But yo, I got first dibs on this cat, right?"

"Yes, nobody even knows that he exists."

"Cool, keep it that way. So come through tomorrow."

"Okay, thanks love."

Just as Horse was about to hang up the phone I caught his attention one more time. "Horse! Before you go . . ."

"Yeah what's up?"

"I was just wondering if we could also maybe hang out together one night . . . You know, maybe go to the club and just have a good time or something?"

"Who? Me and you?"

"Yeah, me and you . . . You could bring some of your friends too if you want and I could bring some of my girlfriends and we could have a good time. . . . Or me and you could chill alone together if you want?"

Horse was silent. He didn't respond.

"What? You don't wanna be seen in public with my sexy ass or something?" I playfully asked as I broke the awkward silence.

"Oh nah ma'. It's all good. I mean, you know, anything could happen, you kna'imean?"

I smiled and I giggled a little in order to break the ice. Then I chimed in with my seductive puppy-dog voice that I knew Horse or any man for that matter would fall for. "Horse? Are you turning down my offer, sweetie?"

Horse laughed on the other end.

"What's so funny, love?" I asked.

Calling people "love" was a bad habit that I'd had for years, but it was sort of appropriate to use it in this case.

"Nah, I just didn't expect that to come from you that's all . . . But yeah, we can hang out. Umh, damn. Yo, hold on a minute, I gotta take this call."

As I waited on hold, I knew that I had just scored big time with Horse.

. . .

Sorry I put you on hold, I gotta go, but listen, take down my new cell number real quick. And don't give that shit out either!" Horse emphatically stated.

"Horse, you know I wouldn't do that," I assured. "What's the number?" I asked as I stood handy with my pen and took down the digits.

"Just call me and we'll work something out. A'ight?"

"Okay good. So I'll come by tomorrow around one or one thirty."

"Fo'sho," Horse replied as we both hung up.

CHAPTER FIVE

*t*he thing about doing any kind of undercover investigation is that you have to allow yourself to never feel any kind of pressure. Pressure in undercover work only leads to you coming across as too eager or like you have some kind of agenda. And when that happens you start to raise red flags among the people that you are investigating. Ideally you just want to go with the flow. You never want to ask too many questions but you always wanna be observing people, places, faces, times, cars, addresses, and how certain individuals interact with others. And in my case I could only rarely wear a wire or take any kind of notes or anything because I was fearful that something like that would later come back to haunt me if I ever got caught or if any evidence of notes ever ended up in the wrong hands.

Much later that night, hours after I had confirmed things with Horse, I called Angela to tell her what had transpired. I purposely called her when it was nearing twelve midnight because I wanted to make it seem as if it had almost slipped my mind to tell her. Again, like I said, I didn't want to ever appear too eager or too anxious.

Angela picked up her cell phone and I didn't even acknowledge her hello with a hello of my own. I just got right to the point.

"Angie, listen . . . I totally forgot to call you back earlier. But I'm glad that I caught you before you went to sleep or something. Okay tomorrow at one P.M. I set up a meeting for you—and Angie, whatever you do, please be on time."

"Jessica! I can't fucking believe you!"

"Angie, I told you I would get it done. Now don't make me look bad by not showing up."

"Don't *fucking* make *you* look bad? How are you gonna tell me at midnight that I have a meeting at one o'clock the next afternoon? I should be asking if you are trying to make me look bad. My goddamn hair isn't done, I haven't spoken to White Lines. And what am I going to wear, Jessica?" Angie asked, as she came across as the spoiled, obnoxious, foul-mouth power-obsessed brat that she was.

"Angela, do you wanna meet with him or not?"

"Of course I fucking wanna meet with him! That's not the point, Jessica! The point is how you totally mishandled this!"

"My god, Angela!" I said with a lot of ghetto attitude that I managed to muster up, coming across as if I was getting deeply disgusted.

"Where am I meeting him at, Jessica? What's the address?"

I proceeded to give Angie the Times Square address of Gun Clap Records, and I told her that I would escort her to the meeting. I also told her to dress sexy and to make sure that

White Lines was prepared and on time. I made sure that I didn't tell her that I had in fact told Horse that her father was Paulie Calvino because she would have absolutely blown her top and lost it.

Initially when all of the details regarding the White Chocolate undercover investigation were put into place I wasn't given that much autonomy to act on my own. I had to strictly report every move I made to the lead field agent of the Organized Crime Task Force. But as I got closer to Horse I was given more and more flexibility and autonomy. But that autonomy was given to me not so I could abuse any type of privileges. Instead, it was given to me so that I could always come across as legit and not have the slightest inkling of a scent of law enforcement on me.

Therefore I had to personally make sure to file all of the necessary paperwork like payroll taxes and any other similar filing requirements associated with White Chocolate Modeling Agency, so just in case anyone checked we would always come across as a real company. I had to get real office space in Manhattan, I had to hire temporary workers to form a staff, I had to call the phone company and place an order for phone service, and among many other things, I had to open a corporate checking account and a Jessica Jackson personal checking account.

All of that had to be done without the assistance of the FBI. Of course the FBI funded my operation but it was not like it was an open checkbook with unlimited funds. Everything was budgeted out and I had to strictly stay within that budget.

So any money that I made from the modeling agency was funneled back into the business in order to help me stay under budget. When and if I were to go over budget or need approval for large ticket items, I would have to take that to my lead agent, who in turn would have to take that to his boss, who might have to take that to his boss at FBI headquarters. And the last thing that I or anyone else involved in the operation wanted was headquarters monitoring us or sticking their noses in our business. The unwritten rule was to stay out of sight and out of mind, and I knew that, so therefore I made sure to stay within my budget and never ask for anything unless I truly needed it.

Also included in my budget were my living expenses, which included money for housing, a car allowance, and entertainment funds. Being that I was half-black and half-white I knew that I could pretty much fit into any type of neighborhood. I had thought about trying to find a place close to Supreme or close to Horse but I didn't want to bring suspicion to myself so I decided to rent an immaculate house located on 86th Street and 157th Avenue in Howard Beach, Queens. The predominantly Italian neighborhood of Howard Beach is as Italian as they come, with immaculately manicured lawns, sprawling houses that look like mini mansions with brickwork to die for, and a bustling and buzzing shopping and business district that runs right through Howard Beach's major thoroughfare known as Cross Bay Blvd. Basically, Howard Beach is like bringing the best of the best that suburban life has to offer and placing it in the city. And part of its appeal is that in only ten to fifteen minutes after leaving Howard Beach, a person could be in either Brooklyn, Staten Island, Manhattan, or Long Island.

The urban/suburban contrast of Howard Beach is also one of the reasons that it is the neighborhood of choice for many of New York's Mafia soldiers, captains, and bosses. And yes, it is also the home of Paulie Calvino.

Angela lived at home with her father, mother, and two of her brothers. They lived on 84th Street and 160th Avenue, which was less than a minute away from where I lived. I had made plans to meet Angela at her house at 11:30 in the morning. I made sure that I arrived on time in my silver 745 BMW.

Although I actually had access to Angela's home telephone number, she had never personally given it to me so I called her on her cell phone.

"Hi, Angela, I'm just letting you know that I'm sitting outside in front of your house," I said as I purposely wanted to be as cordial as possible.

"Okay, give me about five minutes."

"Okay, no problem."

I knew that women like Angela loved to be spoiled and catered to. They loved being the center of attention and being waited on. And one thing that they really love is being driven around in nice cars. They love to ride shotgun and have their best friend drive them as if their best friend is their chauffeur or something. So as soon as Angela stepped out of her front door I decided to cater to her ego.

I immediately exited my car and walked up to her and took the bag that she had in her hands and placed it inside the trunk of my car. After that I ran around to the front passenger door and I opened it for Angela and waited for her to get in before I closed it behind her.

"Angela, you look gorgeous. I love that skirt, and those shoes! I love those, what is that, Prada?"

"Yes, it's Prada . . ." Angela nonchalantly replied without the slightest hint of a thank you, as she looked in the mirror that was located on the sun visor.

"So, what are you hinting at? That my hair doesn't look nice?"

"No, I'm not hinting at that at all," I replied.

"Well, for Christ's sake, I get in your car and you don't say nothing about my hair, my makeup, my nails, what am I supposed to think, Jessica?" Angela replied with all seriousness.

I was about to compliment her hair but as soon as I opened my mouth I was rudely interrupted.

"Look, just forget about it. We have to pick up White Lines, he lives on the other side."

The other side referred to the other side of Jamaica Bay which also ran through Howard Beach. The other side was also known as Old Howard Beach, simply because that is where most of the older houses in the community were located.

Before long, we were outside White Lines's house. His real name was Joseph Barone but everybody called him Joey. And as we prepared to pull up in front of his mom's crib Angela called him on his phone.

"Hey hon, we're right down the block . . . Are you ready? Okay come outside."

Angela hung up the phone and before long, White Lines appeared. He had his hair cut short and as he locked the front door of his house he placed a dark blue Yankee fitted baseball cap over his head. He had on a white throwback jersey, dark blue jeans, and some tan construction Timberland boots that were loosely laced.

As he made it to the car he walked around to Angela's side of the car and reached his head in through the open window and gave her a kiss on the cheek. As he got in the backseat of the car, I noticed that he didn't have the typical street Italian accent. If anything he sounded more like a homeboy from Harlem.

"Joey, did you ever meet Jessica?" Angela asked.

"Nah, I didn't, my bad, how you doin' ma'?" he asked. I wanted to burst out laughing because a picture of the comedian Jamie Kennedy doing an impression of a white boy rapper from California formed in my mind.

I actually bit my tongue to stop myself from laughing. And I reminded both Angela and Jessica that I had in fact met Joey at the club Spratz on the Water.

Joey couldn't remember meeting me but as we maneuvered our way to Manhattan he quickly changed subjects and of course he complimented Angela on her hair and how good she looked.

"*Thank you, Joey,*" Angela emphatically said. "Can you believe Jessica had the nerve to say that I look like a piece of shit?" Angela asked, and I am convinced that she was convinced that I had in fact said that though I had never said such a thing.

"Aweee, Jessieee! Come on, this girl is fucking beautiful over here!" Joey replied, finally showing his Italian heritage.

I kept mute on the point and before I could speak, Joey

spoke up again. "So Angela, I'm actually gonna spit for Horse? This is fucking unreal! Fucking unbelievable!"

Angela chimed in, "Just go in there and impress him, Joey. Do what you do best and I'll take care of the rest. I know how to talk the same talk as people like Horse. I know that I can do a helluva better job than that asshole prick wannabe manager that you just fired . . . You did fire him, right? You did tell him that I was managing you now, right?"

This was news to me, as I quietly listened in.

"Oh Angie, fuggedaboutit! I just mentioned your name and he understood. You know what I mean? Bada-bing, there was no discussion. It was a done deal. It's a beautiful thing!" Joey said as he brought his fingers to his mouth and gestured out a kiss.

Before long we had reached Times Square and I offered to let Angela and Joey out in front of the building while I was gonna go and park the car. To my surprise, Angela said that she would rather us all walk in together. So after parking in one of the most expensive parking garages in the world, we made our way to the large office building.

For the sake of Angela's ego, I had never asked her to comment on how I looked. But I knew that I looked sexy as hell. *Who wouldn't love this job?* I thought to myself as the three of us entered the lobby. I had to pinch myself and actually realize that I was getting paid a salary to do this job, and in a few minutes I would be sitting down with a multimillionaire discussing the possibility of signing a future rap star to a record deal.

We got our visitor passes from the security guard who was situated in the lobby of the building and we were allowed to get on the elevator, but that was only after he'd called up to the record company to verify that it was okay to let us come up to the label's office.

As the doors of the elevator opened to our floor, we were greeted by the loud sound of rapid gunfire that literally scared the shit out of the three of us. Thank God the gunfire was not coming from a real gun, but instead from the blaring sound system that bounced off the walls in the receptionist's area on the twentieth floor.

After realizing that we weren't being shot at, we walked toward the large platinum Gun Clap Records logo that was hanging above the receptionist's desk. I tried my best to yell over the loud music and explain to the receptionist that the three of us were there to see Horse.

"Hi . . . Hello! We have a one o'clock appointment with Horse . . ." I screamed at the top of my lungs.

The receptionist, who didn't look like a girl from the ghetto, but like she had the ability to create a bad attitude in an instant, just looked me right in my face and didn't say a word.

"Hellooo?" I spoke even louder, this time with a sarcastic attitude in my voice. Thank God the loud music had finally been lowered to a human ingestible level.

"Hi, I don't know if you heard me over the loud music but I was trying to tell you that we have a one o'clock appointment with Horse . . ." I said as I smiled, feeling a bit relieved.

Angela looked at me and shook her head. White Lines just looked around at the gold and platinum album plaques that were lined all along the walls.

"I heard what the fuck you said!" the pretty receptionist stated.

Her attitude caught all of us off guard, but she had definitely succeeded in getting our attention.

"Excuse me?" I questioned.

The receptionist stood up from her chair, and I wondered if this was the rude girl Tamika who I had spoken to when I called the office.

"You heard me! I wasn't told nothing about no one o'clock appointment. So I suggest that you and your two *white-bread-ass* friends turn the fuck around and press that elevator button and get the hell up outta this muthafucka!"

The receptionist was clearly trying to intimidate us. Being who I was by nature I wasn't easily intimidated. Neither was Angela.

"Look, I don't know what your fuckin' problem is," Angela spoke up and barked, "but obviously you don't know who the hell you're talking to! Speak to me with disrespect like that one more time and I swear on my brother's grave that I will come around that desk and beat the living shit out of your black ghetto ass!"

That was definitely not what the receptionist was expecting to hear. And she looked at us for about a minute straight with a deathly stare. No one spoke a word and then finally the receptionist picked up the phone and spoke into it very low so that we couldn't hear what she said. She put the phone down and didn't say anything to us at all. And I didn't know what to think.

"Miss, are we going to see Horse? We really don't have all day."

As I was speaking my words, a tall heavyset man opened

one of two doors that led from the office lobby into the main office quarters.

"Ya'll can come wit' me," he said.

We followed right behind him without speaking. He took us into a large conference room and we sat down and waited.

"What the fuck was that black bitch's problem?" Angela asked.

"Angie, listen to me. If you go into any hip-hop record company, you'll be greeted and treated the exact same way. It's fucking unreal the balls of the people at these companies," White Lines stated as if he was speaking from experience.

Finally a well-dressed young lady came in and introduced herself as Horse's assistant and told us unapologetically that we would not be able to meet with Horse but if we would like, we could speak with one of the senior A&R executives.

"Why can't we meet with him? He personally gave me this appointment time yesterday," I said, sounding kind of desperate and hoping that I wasn't blowing my contact with Angela. I knew that I had to take control of the situation before Angela or White Lines spoke up. Especially considering that the assistant was not even attempting to answer my question.

"Look, I'm very busy so tell me what ya'll wanna do," the assistant said.

"Okay, we'll meet with the A&R," I said, hoping to salvage the trip to Manhattan. I was also desperately wondering what had happened to Horse and why he hadn't at least called to tell me that he wasn't going to be able to make it. I was very tempted to call him on his cell phone but I opted not to out of fear of coming across as anxious or overly eager.

So we followed Horse's assistant through the surprisingly

immaculately clean offices. All the while I was studiously taking in everything I saw and trying to pick up on anything that
I could pick up on.

"G-Baby, they claim that they had a meeting with Horse,
but I didn't know anything about it. Can you hear them out
and handle this for me?" the assistant asked.

"I gotchu ma' ma'," G-Baby replied.

While slightly cocking his head and twisting his lips,
G-Baby asked how he could help us.

"You know, Jessica, this is fucking bullshit! You told me
that we were gonna meet with Horse, not some arrogant-ass
flunky! Let's get outta here. Take me home right now, Jessica!"
Angela barked, as she had obviously lost her temper. Now I
was really beginning to sweat.

"Okay hold on. G-Baby is it?"

"Yeah that's my name, and yo, on the real, I'm doing y'all a
favor so I don't appreciate being called nobody's flunky!"

"Listen, G-Baby, I'm sorry about that and I know you don't
have all day and neither do we. I just want you to hear this guy
rhyme and after you hear him rhyme I want you to tell me if
this is not only the best white rapper you have ever heard, but
one of the best *rappers* that you've ever heard. Period!"

"Yeah a'ight. Go ahead, let me hear you spit something,"
G-Baby reluctantly said.

Thank God that White Lines wasn't shy and that he was prepared. As he recited his rhymes, I could see G-Baby actually sitting up and taking notice. And when White Lines had finished,
G-Baby simply and calmly stated, "Kick another rhyme for me."

When White Lines was done with that second rhyme,
G-Baby said it again, "Kick another one for me."

White Lines complied. "Kick it again, another rhyme."

At this point, G-Baby was really into what he was hearing, and I know that this talented kid from Howard Beach was the last thing that he actually expected to hear.

"Spit some more shit!" G-Baby commanded.

As time went on, we realized that we had been in G-Baby's office for close to forty-five minutes. And he definitely knew what he had in front of him. Whether he originally took us seriously or not, through his body language he let us know that he was definitely interested in what he was hearing and seeing.

"So what's your situation? Are you signed to anybody, are you looking to get signed or what?" G-Baby asked.

Angela jumped in and took over the discussion from that point on.

We eventually left the building, not with a contract in hand, but we did leave with some serious consideration on our side coming from G-Baby and Gun Clap Records.

The three of us exited the office building and I know that everyone was feeling good. G-Baby had promised to get back in touch with us, and I really believed him. I just kept wondering what had happened to Horse.

Ironically as we crossed the street and made our way to the parking garage, a young lady came over to me and asked if I was Jessica Jackson. Actually I don't know if calling her a young *lady* is the correct term to use, because although she was young, about twenty-four years old or so, as rough and masculine as she looked, it made it hard to call her a lady. She looked more like a butch.

"Yes, I'm Jessica. Is there some sort of problem?"

"Nah, were you just in the building looking for Horse?" the

butch asked in her saggy jeans and white wife-beater with very saggy, uninviting-looking titties.

"Yes I was but he—"

"Yeah, he's there now, he wanted to speak to you real quick. Can you come back wit' me to see him?"

Feeling a bit relieved because we would in fact finally get to see Horse, I smiled and said to Angela and White Lines, "See something must have come up... I knew that he wouldn't just give me his word like that and then not show unless he had a good reason. He was probably running late or something... Come on, let's go back and see him real quick."

"Nah, yo hol' up. All of ya'll can't fucking come! Only you, the rest of ya'll just fall back a minute. We'll be right back." the butch said in her masculine-sounding voice.

Immediately my radar went up. I didn't know what to think. Something didn't seem right. I started to call Horse on his cell phone but that would have been dumb considering that I was right down the block from his office and he was supposedly waiting for me to come up.

Why didn't he just call me on my cell phone? I thought to myself. *Maybe G-Baby didn't really like White Lines and he relayed that to Horse and Horse wants to break the news to me and let me tell Angela.* I didn't know.

I didn't have much time to think and I didn't want Angela getting annoyed so I quickly spoke up, "Here, Joey, take the parking stub and get the car and the two of you can meet me in front of the building... By the time you pull around I should be done."

Angela butted in with words that sounded like she was

highly annoyed. But she was cut off by the butch who told her that Horse didn't have all day and that I had to hurry up.

As Joey and Angela headed for the parking garage, the butch and I quickly crossed Seventh Avenue. I was walking in my Manolo high-heel shoes and I couldn't walk as fast as the Timberland-boot-wearing *gangster girl*. Just as we reached the office building the butch stated that we weren't going into the building but instead we had to go into Sbaro's restaurant.

"Sbaro's?" I asked with a puzzled look on my face.

"Yeah, we're not eating anything, we just gotta see somebody."

My law enforcement instincts took over at that point and I knew that something was definitely up.

"Um, what is your name?" I asked.

"Trina."

"Trina, I think I'll just wait out here on Seventh Avenue. It's too crowded in there," I said, stopping dead in my tracks.

"Jessica, what the hell is wrong with you? Bring your ass on!"

The butch looked disgusted but I had no idea where she was bringing me. She immediately got on her cell phone and began dialing.

"Yeah, she said she ain't coming in . . . How the fuck do I know? You speak to this bitch! 'Cause she's getting on my nerves! Word . . . Look, if you don't speak to her I'm bouncing and leaving her right the fuck here!"

I had no idea who she was talking to but I took the phone as the butch handed it to me.

"Hello?"

"Hi, Jessica, this is Cynthia, I had met you at a video shoot a few months back. . . . You probably don't remember me but we definitely did meet. Anyway, the only reason that we wanted you to go inside Sbaro's is that we got twenty-five-thousand dollars for you but it's all in cash. And it's better to deal with that kind of cash in a very crowded spot in case somebody tries to rob us or something like that," Cynthia stated in a whispering kind of tone.

"Cynthia, I really don't remember you. But what I don't understand is why the need for all of that cash?"

"Didn't you hear on the news about how Gun Clap got raided and all of that? Well the Gun Clap bank accounts are still frozen and we can't wire money or write checks or anything."

I was ready to ask Cynthia, if the Gun Clap bank accounts were closed then how did they get access to so much cash? But the rule of investigations is do not ask too many questions and do not seem overanxious, and at the same time I knew that I couldn't be too cautious or too apprehensive because after all, why would someone such as myself, *a modeling entrepreneur* not want to take the cash payment that was due me?

"Okay, Cynthia, no problem . . . Yes . . . Okay . . . All right, I'll put her back on the phone."

I handed the phone back to the butch and she spoke two words into the phone and then hung up. After which I followed her as she walked upstairs to the second level of Sbaro's and headed toward the bathroom.

My heart was racing because I didn't know what was up, but common sense told me that I wasn't getting ready to see Horse.

The butch knocked on the bathroom door two times and then paused and knocked two more times. The door opened and I saw another butch-looking female standing inside the bathroom holding a backpack.

"Come in real quick and count the money to make sure it's all there," the first butch said as the second butch held open the backpack to show me that there was indeed a large sum of money inside the bag.

"No, I trust you. I know that it's all there. Cynthia told me it was twenty-five grand and I know—"

"Bitch, get the fuck in the bathroom!" the first butch said as she cut me off in the middle of my statement and pushed me into the bathroom.

The second butch locked the bathroom door so that no one else could come inside. And before I knew what was going on I had the barrel of a chrome .45 handgun jammed inside my mouth by the first Timberland-wearing saggy-jeans butch. The gun had been jammed so hard inside my mouth that it felt like one of my teeth had been knocked loose and it also felt like the gun was touching my tonsils.

"If you scream I'll leave your brains right here up against this bathroom wall! Matter of fact they'll be using your brains on the muthafucking pizzas downstairs."

With my heart racing a mile a minute, the only thing I was thinking about was my family who lived out on the West Coast in California, as well as my fiancé who was still in St. Louis and had begged me not to come to New York for this assignment. I held my hands up in the air to show surrender. I couldn't talk because the gun was still in my mouth and gagging me.

"Bitch, I'm gonna ask you this one time and you better fucking tell me the truth!"

The only thing I could do was keep my eyes wide open and

I quickly nodded my head up and down to indicate that I would tell the truth.

"Are you a fucking federal agent?"

My heart literally dropped to my toes, but I had to quickly gain composure, and I immediately thought back to how we were trained in the academy to spot a liar, and I made sure not to make any of those liar mistakes.

"I shook my head from side to side and I tried to speak the word *no,* but with the barrel of a gun jammed in my mouth it wasn't that easy to do.

The next thing I knew, I was slapped across the face with the barrel of the gun and I immediately fell to the ground. And at the point the second butch approached me and stood over me and pointed a gun to my head and cocked it.

"Please don't kill me!" I sincerely begged for my life.

"I should kill this bitch right now! I know she's a fucking cop or some shit! I can smell it on her Halle Berry–lookin' ass!" the second butch stated.

At that point my cell phone began to ring.

"Don't answer that shit! 'Cause you got about two seconds to explain how the fuck Horse got raided!"

My eyes got even wider as I knew somehow my cover must have been blown.

"One!"

I pleaded, "Okay, no, no, please, please, just let me talk for a second . . . Please," I begged. Feeling like I was ready to literally crap in my pants.

My cell phone began ringing again.

"Don't fucking answer that phone! Bitch, you got one more second . . . You better tell me something!"

"Look! I'm not a cop, I'm not an FBI agent, or anything like that!" I said as I was breathing real heavy and practically hyperventilating. "I don't know where all of this is coming from. All I do is run my modeling agency . . ." I said as I lay with my back on the hard tiled bathroom floor. I was about to force myself to cry, just to make it look good. But at the same time I wanted to cry because these two chicks looked like they meant business.

"Two!"

"Wait! Wait please! Oh God no!" I screamed as I held my hands up, preparing to fend off the hot slug that I was anticipating receiving.

My cell phone began ringing again, and I was sure that it was Angela wondering what was taking me so long to come out of Horse's office.

"I can prove to you right now that I'm not a cop!" I stated in a desperate attempt to save my life. "Look inside my bag and tell me what's in there."

The butch kept the gun cocked to my head and nodded for the other woman to look inside my bag. I prayed like hell that somebody might try to come inside the bathroom but that just wasn't happening. Then I thought that whoever had ordered this job on me must have covered themselves and they probably had somebody camped outside the bathroom preventing others from coming inside.

"Yo, this bitch got like an ounce of fucking coke in her bag!" the butch yelled.

"Look, I'm telling you I'm not a cop! Cops can't do drugs! I'll snort that shit right here in front of y'all to prove I'm not a cop . . ."

The butch placed some of the coke on her tongue to verify that it was indeed cocaine.

"Yeah the shit is real," she confirmed.

The other butch with the gun to my head wouldn't relent.

"So fucking what! Cops do muthafucking drugs! Y'all are the law! Y'all do everything else illegal!"

Now I didn't know what to do.

"Yo, let her snort this shit," the butch stated, as they both made sure not to call each other by name.

"Sit the fuck up!" I was ordered.

As they handed me the coke and asked me to snort it, one of the girls placed a call on her cell phone.

I quickly put some of the coke on my pinky fingernail and snorted it up my nose. I could hear the girl on the phone saying that she thought I was clean.

I began to feel a bit more relieved but I knew that I wasn't in the clear just yet, as I was ordered to snort some more of the coke.

"Bitch, if you're lying to me, I swear to God that I will find you and kill you! You hear me?" the lady asked as she pressed the gun against my temple.

I quickly nodded my head and snorted some more coke. My cell phone began ringing again.

"Okay, yeah . . . A'ight. No doubt. . . . One!" the other butch said as she spoke into her cell phone, sounding more and more like a man.

"Pull your skirt down!" the second butch ordered.

"What?"

"Pull your skirt and panties down!"

"I'm not a cop! Please believe me. I'm not wearing a wire," I desperately stated, thinking that was the only reason that I could have been asked to pull my skirt and panties down.

"I said pull your goddamn skirt and panties off!" the butch yelled as she ripped open my shirt.

At that point I began crying but I complied and pulled off my skirt and panties and I remember thinking that all of the so-called glitz and glamour of my job had quickly faded. The reality of my actual job set in big time. The reality was that I was dealing with hardened criminals with rap sheets lengthier than a football field. Yes, they may have been successful people with money but I was in the belly of their world and I was beginning to feel their wrath.

Fortunately, I had been smart enough to anticipate what I would do as a last resort in a situation like this one. See, I knew that I could not have a badge or any kind of FBI credentials on me. I knew that I could not always have some type of recording device on me. And I knew that I couldn't carry a gun with me at all times because that would make me look suspicious and in a situation like I was presently in, it would have gotten me killed. But I knew that if I always carried an ounce of cocaine on me, that as a last resort, when and if I was confronted like I presently was I would snort the cocaine in order to prove that I wasn't squeaky clean. My status as an agent would be doubted.

"Look at that pretty *light-skinned* pussy!" one of the butches stated.

My heart began racing again. I now knew that these two women, if you could call them that, were not just looking for a wire. Sticking her middle finger in her mouth and taking it out and sticking it between my legs, the dyke-butch came close to my face and kissed me on my lips while she placed her finger inside me. Besides gasping from the pain that her finger caused, I showed no emotion and I was thoroughly disgusted as I was being *raped* by another woman.

"Hell nah, she ain't a fucking cop!" the butch said, as she laughed and then licked on the finger that she had just had inside of me. She stuck her finger back inside of me and said, "If she was a cop, she wouldn't let me play with her like this . . ."

A tear rolled down my eyes, as I was now in a hugely tough position. I now knew that Horse had backed out of the meeting because he must have somehow been tipped to the fact that I was an agent, *but tipped off by who?* I was feeling like the investigation might either be stalled or have to end because if I reported this to my lead agent he would have pulled me from the investigation and rained down fire from heaven on Horse and his people, something that would have brought me a sense of vindication for what I was presently going through, but I would have felt like a complete failure. Also what about the cocaine that I had snorted, the Bureau knew nothing about me carrying that cocaine and they definitely wouldn't have backed me and sanctioned that. They would have had to uphold their rules for the sake of the integrity of the FBI, and therefore probably would have suspended me or even fired me.

Those were the thoughts that ran through my head. My cell phone continued to ring off the hook and I knew it was Angela but I couldn't answer it. I couldn't answer it because I was now being raped by two butches who had ordered me to the floor and simultaneously probed my vagina and my anus.

"Yeah she ain't no cop! Not with this pretty pussy she ain't."

"Jessica, you're gonna cum for me, okay?" the butch said as she removed her stained white wife-beater and exposed her unsightly *National Geographic*-looking saggy breasts. "After you cum you can put on your clothes and go," she added.

I was then instructed to close my eyes and just relax and I was assured that I wouldn't be killed.

CHAPTER SIX

*a*fter I had been attacked in the bathroom, the two dykes left me on the floor to fend for myself. I had a million and one things flowing through my head and as I made it to my feet I gathered my things and made it into one of the bathroom stalls. A frightened, disgusted, hysterical wreck is probably the best way to describe how I felt as I sat on the toilet bowl and tried to gather my senses.

I remember thinking to myself that I was definitely gonna get my own vindication—I didn't need the Bureau to back me, I was originally from Compton, and although I was a pretty girl, I had a hustler mentality that was laced with a hood mentality. I knew what being street was all about and I knew that if they suspected me of being an agent then I definitely had to get street on their ass or else risk everything!

What was weird is that the cocaine that I had snorted began to kick in and it definitely helped to medicate some of the damaged feelings that I had running through my system. I couldn't believe that I had just been raped by two dykes. Not in my wildest and most fearful dreams did I ever think that I would have experienced anything like that during my career.

I reached for some more of the cocaine and as I prepared to snort it my cell phone rang. I immediately recognized that it was Angela.

"Hello," I said as I tried to appear like everything was okay with me.

"Jessica are you okay?" Angela asked. I was surprised that she was actually showing some concern for me.

"Hold on, hold on a minute," I said as I put the phone down and snorted some more of the cocaine up my right nostril. Closing my eyes and quickly jerking my head I ran the palm of my hand from my forehead all the way down to my chin and then I wiped my nose with the back of the same hand.

"Angie, I'm sorry I took so long...I'll explain things to you later. Look, just have Joey drive the car and you guys head back to Queens. I'll catch up with you as soon as I'm done." I spoke as normally as I could for a person who was feeling both high and humiliated at the same time.

"Take your car? How much longer are you gonna be?"

At that point I snapped because I just wanted to be left alone. "Angela, just take the fucking car and go! I'll catch up with you later!"

"Jessica, watch your fucking mouth! Are you with Horse? What did G-Baby tell him? Do you think they'll sign White Lines?" Angela's questions were normal questions but I just couldn't explain to her anything that had transpired because I didn't want to blow the investigation.

"Angela," I said in a new calm and relaxed tone. "I'm sorry

for cursing at you. I just had an issue over some money that Gun Clap owes me for some previous work my company did with them. They're getting my money ready so it might take a while. Nothing was said about White Lines but I think everything looks good."

"You think so? Okay, that's good. I hope this G-Baby is not just some half-ass flunky that can't green light anything . . . Well look, how the hell are you getting home?"

"Angie, I'll be okay. I gotta go . . . I'll catch up with you later."

I didn't make it back to the house I was renting until about 3:15 that afternoon. I had decided to take a cab all the way home from Manhattan. Thankfully I had come down from the mini high that the cocaine had produced but unfortunately I was feeling like a sack of shit.

No sooner had I made it inside my house but my cell phone was ringing. Checking the caller ID I immediately recognized that the call was coming from Gun Clap Records. I started not to answer it but I realized that that would have been a mistake. Obviously somehow my cover had been blown and I needed to send a clear message that I wasn't a cop or an FBI agent and I had to send that message very quickly.

"Hello?" I said as I answered my cell phone.

"Hi, can I speak to Jessica?" the female on the other end asked.

"This is Jessica. Who the fuck is this?" I barked, sounding genuinely pissed off and out of character.

"Jessica, this is Horse's assistant. He just wanted me to

check with you to make sure that you got your money," his assistant stated.

"Put Horse on the phone!" I yelled.

"Horse isn't here, he just asked me—"

I cut Horse's assistant off and began ranting very convincingly.

"When you speak to Horse you make sure you tell that nigga that I didn't get my motherfucking money and I don't give a shit about the money! And make sure that you tell him to watch his back 'cause I'm gonna have his ass fucked up for that shit he pulled today!" And when I said that I hung up the phone.

No more than two minutes had passed and my cell phone was ringing again, and again it was Gun Clap's phone number that appeared on the caller ID, only this time I didn't answer it.

I felt like shit, like I had been raped by a man. I wanted to jump in the shower and scrub my body and wash away the humiliating experience that I had been through with the two dykes. But regardless of how I felt I knew that I had to respond in the most niggerish way that I could.

I had a male friend named Rahim who worked undercover for the DEA and I knew that I could call on him to help me out. I had met Rahim at a party that was given by a mutual law enforcement friend of ours, and we had exchanged numbers. And although Rahim was married, the two of us had managed to hit it off, and somehow he and I had found ourselves holed up in an Atlantic City hotel one weekend getting very sexually familiar with one another. So the two of us had some brief history and although I was supposed to keep the details of my investigation strictly confidential, I had kept Rahim up to speed on the ongoing status of the investigation into Gun Clap Records, so he was familiar with what I was doing. I reached out to him and explained to him what had happened and asked him if he would be willing to help me out.

"Paula, you know I gotchu," Rahim, the DEA agent stated.

"But Rahim, my name is Jessica, remember that, don't slip up and call me Paula," I warned. "I gotta send a message to these bastards that I'm not an agent."

Rahim assured me that he had my back and he knew exactly how to handle the situation. He agreed to meet me in Times Square in front of the Marriott Marquis hotel by 5 P.M.

"Okay, I'll be there," I said as I hung up the phone.

I went to my room and looked for some jeans that I could throw on. I thought about putting on some sneakers as well but I didn't want to be too much out of character so along with my jeans I kept on my high-heel shoes and changed into a regular top.

My nerves were still on edge from everything that had transpired so I poured myself a glass of Hennessy and Coke to help calm me down somewhat. While I put the drink to my mouth I simultaneously lifted my cell phone and looked at all of my missed calls from when my phone was constantly ringing while I was in the Sbarro's bathroom. I had thought that it had been Angela calling me and rushing me so that she didn't have to wait for me. But to my surprise what I realized is that my lead agent on the case—who is also my contact agent—was the one who had been calling my cell phone. He calls me from a prepaid cell phone that he discards every week and the number that was appearing in my missed call log was definitely from him. But for my protection he knows not to ever leave any messages on my voice mail.

I quickly called back my lead agent, who goes by the code name of Andrew Allen. He and I are very strict in that we always only use our code names when we talk on the phone and we rarely if ever meet in public out in the open. When we do meet face to face it would be disguised as a chance meeting at a crowded restaurant, bar, lounge, or something similar to that.

"Andrew, this is Jessica, sorry that I'm just getting back to you," I stated as I began pouring myself another Hennessy and Coke.

"Jessica, are you okay?" Andrew asked with some concern.

"Yes I'm fine . . . A rough day so far but I'll get through it," I said, not yet wanting to show any signs of weakness or failure.

"You had me scared as shit! You weren't picking up your phone and I called you like a million times!" Andrew barked.

"Yeah I know but I—"

Andrew cut me off and stated, "Look, Jessica, we gotta pull the plug on White Chocolate. And we're pulling it immediately! It's the end of the road for Jessica Jackson."

"What!" I yelled into the phone, not understanding Andrew's logic.

At that point my other line was ringing, and it was Horse, but I couldn't take his call just yet.

"Jessica, we got a CI sitting on both sides of the fence and he gave you up," Andrew explained.

At first I was in total disbelief at what I had just heard. CI meant confidential informant, and the only way a CI could have *given me up* is if the CI knew that I was an agent. That information was supposed to be top-secret info that should in no way, shape, or form have ever been leaked out.

"Who the fuck is the CI?" I asked.

"Mims," Andrew stated.

"Chris Mims?" I repeated.

"Yes. I was trying to call you as soon as I found out about the breach because I knew that we had to pull you. Now Jessica I know . . ."

I was so vexed that I thought I was gonna break a blood vessel in my brain, and the liquor I was drinking wasn't making my mood any better.

"Andrew, with all due respect to your position, this is fucking goddamn bullshit! And I'm not pulling out of this investigation simply because you fucked it up!"

"*I fucked it up?*" Andrew asked with contempt and disdain.

"How did the information about me get leaked, Andrew? This is bullshit! My life, the life of an agent is worth less that some gangster-rap-bodyguard motherfucker? Is that what you're telling me? You fucked it up because one of *your* men, my coworkers, snitched on me! How else could my cover have been blown?"

"Jessica look, I know that you're upset, but—"

"Upset!" I yelled through the phone. "Andrew, let me tell you something. Your fucking phone calls were about a half-hour too late! While you were calling me I had a goddamn forty-five rammed so far in my mouth that it was touching my tonsils, and I had two dykes fucking threatening to blow my head off! I'm past upset! Who the fuck gave me up and why?"

Andrew went on to explain that it was one of the agents from New York's Organized Crime Task Force that had blown my cover. And that the agent had immediately been suspended and pulled from the street and would be shipped out to a southwest office until full and authoritative disciplinary action could be taken.

As I continued to listen, I realized that my cover had been blown simply because the agents on the Organized Crime Task Force must have connected the dots and realized how I was gonna tie Paulie Calvino's daughter into my investigation in order to get at Paulie Calvino. Basically they were jealous of my success and jealous more so because I was a woman, a black woman at that. So rather than let me succeed in an area that they hadn't been able to make any leeway, their insecurities were so strong that they would rather have seen me lose my life on the job.

"Andrew, I'm not trying to disrespect your authority, but you don't have any idea as to how I was violated today! You have no idea! And I don't give a fuck, I'm not coming out. I can figure this out, just give me a few hours. And I'm not threatening you, but I will tell you this, if you pull me from this investigation I will scream to headquarters and I will scream to the media and whoever else I have to scream to in order to expose this sexist, racist discrimination bullshit that goes on in the Bureau, the same bullshit that almost got me killed!"

"*Sexist, racist discrimination?* Jessica, what the hell are you talking about?"

"Andrew, you know exactly what I'm talking about. You know that my cover was blown because the men on this job don't want women doing a better job. Hell, they don't even think that we can do the job or that we should even be on the job. Y'all brought me in to get close to the niggers. And as long as I was getting close to the niggers then y'all was cool with that, but because I was smart enough to tie in Calvino's daughter—that's where y'all fucking felt threatened!"

My boss sighed into the phone, and he knew that I was right. He tried to explain to me that my life was in danger and that was the only thing he was concerned with.

"Andrew, it's my life! If I wanna risk it that is my prerogative! I'm telling you I can work through this. Just give me some time and don't pull the plug just yet," I pleaded.

Thankfully my boss relented. And I know that he only did so because I had played the discrimination card. But I did what I had to to keep the investigation going. I could sense that I was almost where I needed to be in terms of getting close enough to Horse and his people. As soon as I got closer to them I was sure I'd be able to figure out a way to exploit them and get paid.

After my phone call had ended with my boss, I quickly placed a call to a cab service to come and take me to Manhattan. While I waited for the cab I sat at my kitchen table doing lines of coke and it was like a revelation hit me or something. That revelation was that *I didn't have to play by the rules anymore.* And why should I play by the rules?

Everybody has rules and every society has rules. Even the underworld has rules and that is why the people of the underworld hate snitches. They hate them because snitches break the code and mess things up for everybody else; snitches are basically selfish and look out only for their own interests.

Well, this had been my first experience in dealing with agent snitches in the FBI. I had heard of it before, but never in the life of my career did I think I would experience being snitched on by another FBI agent. That was a major violation of our written and unwritten code. Someone broke the rules and the code and it almost cost me my life.

I was now more determined than ever to complete this investigation—even if it meant that I had to break the rules of the FBI in order to do it. As they say on the street my attitude from now on would be . . . "What!"

When I reached the Marriott Marquis I walked into the lobby and waited for Rahim to show up. After about ten minutes of waiting, Rahim finally approached me.

"Hey baby," he said as he walked up to me and gave me a hug and a kiss on the cheek.

"Oh, what's up, hon?" I said as I was feeling nice from the coke and the drinks that I had had earlier.

"You met Mike before, right?" Rahim asked, referring to his partner.

"Yeah, yeah, I met him at the party. Hey, Mike. How you doing?" I asked.

Mike said hello and he gave me a hug.

It was so wild because if anyone on the outside was looking at the three of us, there is no way in the world that they would have expected that we were federal agents, me of course with the FBI and Mike and Rahim with the DEA. Rahim was about

six foot two and stocky. He reminded me a lot of the basketball player Stephon Marbury. He had the same complexion,
he had the tattoos like Stephon, and he had the same Coney
Island accent. And his partner, Mike, who was also black, reminded me a lot of the actor Omar Epps.

"So we better hurry up," I said as we made our way to Gun
Clap's office. We briskly navigated across the busy Manhattan
streets and as we walked I once again brought Rahim up to
speed on what had transpired with me about four hours earlier.

"A'ight cool. When we get to their office let me do the talking and if I'm off course you can jump in and back up my
words. Mike, just keep your eyes open to everybody and everything that's happening in the office while I'm doing the talking," Rahim commanded.

When the three of us made it to the security guard's desk
in the lobby, we walked right past the security guard and made
our way to the elevator. When the security guard questioned
us, I simply reminded him that we had been there earlier and
had just stepped out real quick to get something to eat.

Security was cool with that explanation and we proceeded
up to the Gun Clap offices. It was nearing the end of the
workday so I was hoping that everyone was still in the office
but mostly I was hoping that Horse was there.

When we stepped off the elevator we were greeted by the
same loud music that had greeted us earlier in the day. And
once again we were met by the same neck-twisting, eye-rolling
attitude coming from the receptionist.

I knew that we had agreed for Rahim to do all of the talking but I was far from being in the mood for the receptionist
and her ghetto-ass bullshit.

I marched right up to her and immediately snatched her up by her weave as I retrieved the small .22-caliber handgun from my bag.

"Look, bitch! I'm telling your ass right now, I am not in the mood for your bullshit. Is Horse here? Yes or fucking no?" I shouted as I held a fistful of the broad's weave in my left hand and my gun in my right, pointed at her head.

The receptionist violently tried to free herself from my grip but I was stronger and she wasn't having much success.

BOW!

I knocked the receptionist upside her head with the butt of my gun.

"You gonna answer me or what, bitch?" I yelled.

"Get the fuck off of me!" the ghetto receptionist yelled. "Horse ain't here! Now get off of me or I swear to God I'll kill you," she barked.

"Jessica, fuck that bitch! Come on," Rahim commanded as I violently pushed the receptionist to the ground. The three of us made our way into the main portion of Gun Clap's offices.

As soon as we entered, Mike drew his gun and held it on one of the thuggish-looking security guys that was standing near the entrance.

"You fuckin' flinch and I'll blow your fuckin' head off!" Mike threatened, sounding kind of convincing.

"Yo where is Horse at?" Rahim continually yelled as he went from private office to private office opening up doors to see who was inside.

At that point the ghetto receptionist had made her way inside the main portion of the office and as Rahim continued looking for Horse, she began to yell, "I told you he wasn't here!"

"Where the fuck is he?" Rahim screamed as he gripped his gun and continued to rummage through the office.

From the looks of things, it appeared as if most of the major players had broken out and gone home for the day. Mostly it was just support personnel left in the office. So as Mike held the security guard at bay, Rahim walked up to the receptionist and told her, "You see this lady right here? I want you to make sure that you tell Horse and whoever else you gotta tell, that nobody fucks wit' her! And if he ever pulls some shit like he pulled earlier today that I will personally kill his ass!" Rahim's voice echoed off of the walls in the office as all of the employees looked on in horror.

"You understand me, bitch?" Rahim questioned again, as he approached the receptionist in a very intimidating manner.

After saying that, Rahim proceeded to go from room to room and from desk to desk overturning papers and chairs and throwing computers on the floor, pulling platinum-record plaques off of the wall and basically trashing the entire Gun Clap office.

By the time Rahim had finished and we had left, the Gun Clap office looked like a tornado had hit it, and all of the employees that were in the office at the time looked like they were scared enough to shit on themselves. Needless to say, we had definitely made a very powerful statement. I was sure that when word got back to Horse about what had transpired in the office, there was no way in the world that he would still suspect me of being an FBI agent, simply because what I had just done as an agent—in terms of wrecking the Gun Clap office—was illegal. What real agent would engage in such illegal activity as trashing an office and threatening workers with guns? Most agents would not have had the balls and the guts to respond in that manner without also attempting to make some kind of an arrest in the process, and I was sure that Horse would think the same way. Nevertheless I was still curious to see what Horse's response would be and what the response of the FBI would be if they were to ever find out what I had done.

CHAPTER SEVEN

*a*fter we left Gun Clap's office, Mike went home, but Rahim and I had decided to spend the remainder of that night at the Marriott Marquis hotel. On one of the upper floors of the hotel there is a restaurant called The View, which has a floor that continually rotates 360 degrees and allows the patrons to see breathtaking views of the Manhattan skyline while they eat.

After eating, the two of us checked into a room at the hotel for another one of our secret sex rendezvous. As an agent, it was easy for Rahim to lie to his wife and get away from her presence. All he had to do was just call his wife and tell her that the case that he was working on had required him to do all-night surveillance or something to that effect and that he would not be able to make it home. And that is exactly what he did.

A part of me felt guilty when I phoned my fiancé Tony from the hotel room. He wanted to talk, and I wanted to talk to him about all that had gone down with me but it was kind of hard to do with Rahim literally going down on me while I was speaking on the phone to my fiancé.

I knew that I was being very scandalous by being with a married man, especially while I was engaged to Tony, but the thing was I really meant well and I really loved Tony, but I was only twenty-five and I was young and had to still do me. So I managed to block out my feelings as I usually do when I know that I'm doing wrong or being scandalous and I ended the call with Tony pretty quickly. I told him that I would get back to him at length the next day.

I hung up from Tony and continued to enjoy myself with Rahim for the rest of the night as the two of us got liquored up and literally had sex all night long.

The next morning I retrieved my BMW from White Lines and I contemplated marching, solo, right into the Gun Clap offices and raising more hell just to hammer home the point that I was still pissed off about what had happened and to further prove that I wasn't an agent. But after serious thought I knew that simply calling Horse and raising hell over the phone was the best option and that's exactly what I did.

Horse answered his cell phone on the first ring and he knew that it was me calling him.

"Yo, what's up ma'? I was calling you all day yesterday. Why you ain't pick up your phone?" Horse asked, trying to sound as if everything was normal. He caught me totally off guard because that was the last way that I had expected him to come at me.

I had to gather myself and make sure that I came across

totally in character and in a way in which Horse would respect me.

"Horse, you know what? You are so fucked up! I mean really. You got some major pair of balls on you. You ain't fucking stupid!"

Horse tried to interrupt me by asking what the hell I was talking about.

"You get on the phone with me today like everything is normal. And you have to know that you stood me and Angela up yesterday so your black ass wouldn't be around when those two man-looking women threatened to blow my head off!"

"What?" Horse asked, trying to sound surprised.

"Horse, I'm not some stupid bitch that you can play for a fucking fool!"

"Hol' up ma'!"

"No, you hold up a minute. And explain to me why you would think I was a cop. Horse, I've always been real with you from day one, and you know that! If you had a problem with me all you had to do was come to me and fucking ask me! And I'll tell you why what you did is so foul . . . Here you are thinking I'm a cop but meanwhile I got employees who don't wanna come to work no more because the feds keep harassing them at my office. And you know why they're getting harassed? They're getting harassed because I provided girls for your goddamn videos, Horse! So I guess they figure it's guilt by association!"

I paused and caught my breath because I was truly vexed, there was no acting or trying to be convincing involved.

I continued on, "And that's why your fuckin' office got trashed, Horse! You're lucky that nobody got killed and yo' ass is lucky that you wasn't there in the office yesterday!"

"Jessica, what the fuck are you talking about?" Horse asked.

"Oh my fuckin' God! I don't believe this nigga!" I shouted. "Horse, on the real, I gotta go. Word!"

Horse was quiet for a minute and so was I as I contemplated hanging up the phone. Then Horse finally spoke.

"Jessica, I'm gonna purposely slow my tone and say this shit to you one time and you make sure you listen to me . . . I don't know what the fuck you're talking about, that's number one. Number two, watch your muthafucking tone on this phone. Word up! Don't nobody talk to me with that kind of disrespect! Number three, if that was you that trashed my office like that I wouldn't be talking to you this calmly. I would have personally touched your ass for some shit like that! It was people from Frank Nitty's management company that did that shit!" Horse stated.

I couldn't believe what I was hearing. *Is this motherfucker for real,* I remember thinking to myself.

"Horse, I ain't fuckin' stupid!" I yelled into the phone.

"Jessica, watch your tone!" Horse shot back.

Then there was a brief moment of silence on the phone.

Horse then proceeded to talk. "Now, for the reason that I called you . . ." Horse tried to just calmly brush the whole situation off and that proved to me even more that he was guilty out of the mere fact that he wouldn't truly acknowledge what I was saying.

"Horse, I'm not trying to disrespect you, believe me I'm not, but all I'm saying is that I like working with you and I don't want nothing interfering with our relationship. And when you get some time we gotta talk because if you don't know what I'm talking about then that means that what I was told is probably true."

"What are you talking about?" Horse asked.

"Horse, all I'm saying is that when two dykes lock me in Sbarro's bathroom, which just happens to be downstairs from your office, and they put a gun in my mouth and finger-pop me in the ass, I get scared! I'm only human and I don't take that shit lightly. And if they do it because they think I'm a cop, well you know what? The cops would be the last people that I'd tell what happened to me in that bathroom. So I can't go to the cops, and I couldn't even go to sleep last night. I was a nervous wreck all day yesterday, snorting coke like I was a goddamn addict, just so I could calm my nerves down. But I needed answers and I started calling and checking around and when I told everybody how the two dykes was saying they had twenty-five grand in cash for me that *you* owe me, everybody told me that *you*, Horse, had to be the one behind it all, the one that set me up. Now you're denying it and telling me you don't even know what I'm talking about. And if that's what you're telling me then why should I doubt that? But this one guy that I know from Jersey, he has a lot of pull with politicians and different people, he checked into this shit for me and within three hours he got back to me and told me that *your* security person, Chris Mims, is fucking working with the feds. So when I heard that I was like even if he is working with the feds, why would this Chris Mims say that I'm a cop? Especially considering that I never even met him before. Or at least I don't remember meeting him . . . Horse, I'll leave it alone, but put yourself in my shoes. I'm sorry if I disrespected you, or if I disrespected your office or any of your employees, but if it wasn't you then it had to be somebody from your camp that set me up and I still don't have a clue as to why."

I knew that I had perfectly spun the situation in a way that would have Horse thinking and wondering if what I was saying was true. Even if he continued to deny what I was saying, as soon as I brought up Chris Mims as possibly being a rat, he had to take that seriously. And that was just my plan. Chris was the one that implicated me as being a fed and now I was the one implicating him as being a snitch. I had to divert the attention off of me and put it on someone else. My advantage was this: I knew that if it ever came down to it that I would easily be able to get an agent that I trusted to back up my story about Chris.

If it came down to it I would have to implicate Chris by using a trusted agent that I knew because, quite frankly, it was a total violation of FBI rules for us to reveal our informants' identities to other criminals. But hey, Chris had no problem giving my black ass up, which could have gotten me killed, so why should I give a shit if I gave him up, even though it might potentially cause his life to end with a bullet to the temple?

Horse spoke up.

"Jessica, slow down a minute . . . You're talking about like twenty different things at the same time and you're talking greasy slick shit at that . . . Now let me just tell you what I had to tell you and then you can explain to me just what the hell you're speaking on. 'Cause I don't know what the fuck you are ranting about."

"Okay," I calmly replied, knowing that I had gotten Horse's attention with the Chris Mims statement.

"I wanted to apologize for missing the meeting yesterday,

but my son had something at school and I make it my business to put him first, no matter what, and I didn't have my cell on me with your number in it to call you and let you know what was what. That was why I called the office and had G-Baby hear your boy spit. And I had your check on me, the twenty-five G's, I got it now and I can get it to you whenever . . ." Horse sounded so believable that it had me wondering if he was telling the truth.

"Oh, okay, that's understandable . . . You have to put your family first in whatever you do," I replied while trying to calm my nerves down.

"But O! Jessica, do you want a finder's fee for your boy?" Horse asked in a suddenly real animated manner.

"Huh?" I asked as I still wasn't sure if Horse was serious or not about why he missed our meeting.

"For White Lines? We wanna sign that nigga . . . I mean that white boy . . . G-Baby didn't wanna show it when y'all were in his office yesterday but he called me on some real shit saying that he was really feeling the dude. Ya' kna'imean? So I was just hollering at you first yesterday, out of respect, 'cause you told me about the cat and I wanted to see what was what with you before I hollered at the kid myself."

"Horse, listen, I told you from the beginning that I didn't want anything. Just do right by him and my girl that is managing him and look out for me for the print ads and videos and all of that."

Horse told me that he couldn't speak much longer because he had to go to a meeting but that he wanted to hear more about what I was saying in reference to Chris.

"Yo, tomorrow night I'll have you, your girl, and the white

kid picked up in the stretch Hummer and y'all can come with me to the *Underworld* magazine anniversary party in New Jersey . . . A'ight?"

I told Horse that that would be perfect and that he could have the limo pick us up from my office. There was no way in hell that I was going to let him know where I lived and rested at, not just yet anyway.

As the conversation ended I realized that Horse was one really smart person. See, most black criminals or blacks in general who are being investigated run their mouths nonstop, especially on the phone. Whereas with the Italians in organized crime, they know how to keep their mouths shut. Horse had to have set me up in that bathroom, but the way he spoke on the phone, you never would have thought that. Nor did he get rattled when I spoke to him about Chris. I was sure that he had spoken the way he had and not gotten rattled simply because he had to assume that his phones and his conversations were constantly being monitored.

Yeah he was good. But I knew what I was doing. And I knew that I had the pieces falling into place like I wanted them to. It would only be a matter of time before I could meet Supreme and rope him in and somehow get Angela to rope her father into the mix. I would figure it out, but in the meantime, I still had to be careful. If Horse hadn't bought my story about Chris or if he questioned Chris and Chris didn't fold up, then I would be under serious suspicion and probably get rubbed out for sure. I was ready. I would be ready for anything and everything by any means necessary.

CHAPTER EIGHT

*a*s I mentioned before, one of the good things about being on this investigation is that I am sort of like my own boss. I make my own hours in that I start working when I want to and end my day when I want. But the drawback is that I can't always end my day when I want to. Where the investigation takes me often dictates if and when I'll be able to start and finish my day or even do normal things like call home and speak to my family and my fiancé.

Speaking to my fiancé was becoming increasingly difficult and I guess that was because mentally I was getting more obsessed with my work, so much so that I was building this wedge between me and Tony. Subconsciously I think that I was building that wedge because of what I was contemplating doing if *it* became necessary.

Saturday, July 10, 2004 marked the fifth anniversary of *Underworld* magazine and as Horse had promised, he picked up Angela, White Lines, and me from my office which was located in the SoHo section of Manhattan. We were picked up in a huge yellow stretch Hummer limo. And apparently we were the last ones to be picked up to be escorted to the extravaganza. As the limo driver held open the door for us, I could tell that the twenty-two-passenger limo was just about filled to capacity.

Everyone inside the limo got deathly quiet as the three of us piled in the weed-smoke-filled limo. As we climbed over people to get inside to comfortable seats I saw a good mixture of guys and girls. And of course, most of the girls were scantily clad. Horse and another guy were both sitting next to two very attractive Asian-looking girls. I didn't know who they were but I wanted to do something to break the tension that the three of us had created. So as I passed Horse, I stopped and leaned over and gave him a kiss that wasn't exactly on his lips but it was right in between the corner of his lips and the start of his cheek. I was wearing a pair of tight jeans and when I bent over to kiss Horse, my red thong was fully exposed, as was the tattoo that was on my lower back.

"Hi sweetie," I said so that everyone could hear me, which was easy because the music had been lowered. "You're not gonna introduce us to everybody?" I asked as the Asian girl looked at me and cut her eyes out of disrespect.

"Never mind," I said as I reached my seat. "Hello everybody. I'm Jessica, for those of you who don't know me, I run White Chocolate Models, and this is my girl Angela and she manages White Lines."

Angela and White Lines both said hello to everyone in the car and White Lines proceeded to give all of the guys a pound.

Everyone said what's up and before long the driver took off and maneuvered us to the party.

"Turn that music up!" someone yelled.

In a matter of seconds I heard the voice of the Notorious B.I.G. and Jay Z blaring through the car's speaker system. I was determined to fit in with Horse and his crew so I immediately lit a cigarette and began reciting the hook to the song. *"I love the dough, more than you know . . . Gotta let it show, I love the dough . . ."*

As I nodded my head, I noticed that Chris Mims was in the limo and he was looking at me with a deathly ice-grille but I didn't pay him any attention and there was no way he was gonna rattle me. I also noticed that Supreme was in the limo sitting right across from Horse.

"Y'all want some Henny?" Horse asked, referring to the big bottle of cognac that was in the bar.

We all wanted some. And in a matter of seconds the three of us had our own glasses of Henny on the rocks. The tension in the limo was broken and before I knew what was up, a blunt was being passed around. White Lines took a hit and so did I. But Angela didn't want any part of it.

As I drank the Hennessy, I had to remind myself that I was working, and I knew that there stood a good chance that I would get high that night, so I wanted to make all of my observations as to who was in the limo before I got drunk or high.

Horse held the blunt out to me in a manner that asked if I wanted some more. Without saying anything, I simply reached out and took the blunt and sucked on it for dear life.

I passed it back to him and then began to drink from my glass. In no time, the combination of weed and Hennessy had me feeling very good and all of my inhibitions were starting to leave.

"Jessica, let me introduce you to my man . . .'Preme, this is Jessica, Jessica, this is 'Preme."

I stuck out my hand and told Supreme that it was nice to meet him.

"Yeah, you too," he replied as he gently shook my hand. And I remember thinking to myself, *so this is the almighty powerful Supreme? Him?* He didn't look like no big time notorious gangsta.

At that point, Ja Rule's hit song "Clap Back" came blasting through the speakers and even though Ja Rule was an artist on the Murder Inc. label, you would have thought that he was on the Gun Clap label with the enthusiasm that all of the guys in the limo began to show when the song came on. They all began to recite in thug unison.

"Clap back, we gonna clap back, we gonna clap back, we gonna clap back, let's take it war!" All of the guys shouted and exclaimed how that song was *"their shit!"*

I noticed that Chris was still looking at me like he had a serious problem with me, but again I had to dismiss it and not let it rattle me. I would be lying though if I said I wasn't worried about what had possibly transpired as a result of me telling Horse what I had told him about Chris.

I took a swig from my glass, finishing off the liquor that was inside of it and then I reached over and got the bottle and poured some more Hennessy into the glass. I knew that I was taking a big chance by drinking and smoking weed because it could impair my judgment and also later on down the road if I had to testify in court about my investigation, my credibility would be in serious question. But the truth of the matter was I was allowed to drink, but getting drunk, well that was not allowable, neither was the weed smoking or cocaine sniffing, but hey, after I had been crossed by the FBI I didn't give a shit anymore.

The weed and Hennessy was definitely making me feel real good. So good that it had given me the confidence to look at Supreme and pucker up my lips and throw a puckered-lip kiss his way. He smiled and I smiled back at him. Although he was a convicted criminal that once ran one of the most dangerous drug gangs in New York, he was still attractive, or at least that's what the liquor was telling me. I mean Horse was cool and he looked good too but he was too damn big and he had this lighter shade of brown skin, and I don't know what it was but it was just something about Supreme's dark skin complexion and dark skin guys in general that I liked.

I knew there was no way in the world that with me smoking weed and drinking Henny and flirting with Supreme, Horse or anybody from his camp would think that I was a *Federalee*.

DMX's old song came blasting through the speaker, the hook went, *"I-don't-give-a-fuck-about-ya'll-niggas-'cause-ya'll-ain't-killing-nothing!"*

I rocked my body in rhythm with the music and I continued to flirt with Supreme. Angela was also having a good time. She wasn't a weed smoker nor did she do any other kind of drugs, but she enjoyed drinking and having fun. Needless to say that by the time we arrived at the party—which was being held at a hotel near Newark Airport—both Angela and myself had had way too much to drink. But we were also primed and ready to enjoy ourselves that night.

Angela had invited all of her people from Howard Beach and they were supposed to meet us at the hotel, and just as we were arriving at the hotel her cell phone began to ring.

"Yeah, we just got here. We're getting out of a yellow stretch Hummer. Yeah . . . Okay, yeah, just meet us at the front of the hotel." Angela spoke in a strong New York–Italian accent.

By the time we all arrived at the entrance of the hotel it was about one in the morning and there were people everywhere. Normally there would have been some type of VIP entrance but being that it was at a hotel the only way into the party was through the front entrance.

As we congregated in front of the building I remember feeling drunk as hell and I didn't know how I would hold up throughout the night. There were people and expensive cars everywhere, and there was also a strong police presence. As I stood in front of the hotel and waited for everyone to enter, I remember being kissed on my cheek by someone.

"Hey, Jessie, how you doin'? You look good tonight," the voice said.

I realized that it was one of Angela's friends from the neighborhood. He was one of about twenty Italians who had showed up at Angela's request. He had the typical Italian *wannabe* gangster look, minus the three-thousand-dollar Armani suit. He, like all of his cronies, was dressed in expensive and stylish Sean John and Rocawear sweatsuits. I had forgotten his name, and the alcohol wasn't helping me remember it.

As I saw all else who had arrived from Angela's neighborhood I quickly realized that not everybody was a *wannabe* gangster. Angela's older brother was there, he was a captain in the Calvino crime family, a *made* man, and he was accompanied by about ten *made* soldiers from his crew.

They immediately checked on Angela and White Lines and made sure that they were okay, and in the process they were all introduced to Horse, Supreme, G-Baby, Chris, and a whole host of others from the Gun Clap entourage.

We were all let into the party for free. And as soon as we walked inside I noticed that there were wall-to-wall celebrities and it was packed with people. Funkmaster Flex was deejaying and he had the crowd going crazy.

Horse handed me a check and over the music he yelled into my ear and told me that it was the full amount that he'd owed me and for me to be careful with it and to put it away. I looked at it and saw that it was a little over twenty-seven thousand dollars and I couldn't have been more ecstatic as I folded the check and did my best to stuff it into the front pocket of my tight jeans. Before I knew what was what, Angela and White Lines were whisked off to the VIP section to drink champagne with Horse and both of their entourages.

Although I knew that I would have a lot of fun partying and drinking, I had to remember that I was still a special agent conducting an investigation. In fact, Supreme, one of the main targets of my investigation, had to become my priority. I knew that I had to get close to him if I wanted to make some progress with the investigation. So instead of following behind Horse and Angela and their entourages I walked up to Supreme. I didn't really know what to say or how to approach him, and I was so glad that my high hadn't worn off. As LL Cool J's song "Doin' It" was being played I grabbed Supreme by the hand and began dancing with him. I turned my back to him and moved in rhythm as he started grinding on my butt.

"I see you know how to dance like a video girl," he stated. I didn't respond to him and kept on dancing with him.

I then turned and faced him and continued to dance with him. I placed my hand on his crotch and whispered into his ear, "I ain't 'Superhead' but there's a lot of things that I can do like a video girl." Supreme smiled his sexy smile at me and I kept my hand on his crotch and I could feel him starting to get hard.

"Don't start something you can't finish." Supreme spoke into my ear as he began kissing on my neck.

Having Supreme's tongue touch my neck was really starting to turn me on and I couldn't believe that I was actually compromising the investigation like I was. But hey, it was the alcohol and the weed that were to blame.

Prior to going undercover with this investigation, all of my preliminary research had told me that Supreme, like most men, was a womanizer and had a genuine *thing* for attractive women. He had been known to consistently be seen around town with snowflake, Puerto Rican women, Asian women, and black chicks, so being an attractive woman gave me an *in* so to speak, but I knew that I had to be careful as to how far I took things with him.

The music was blasting out of the speakers as the lyrics went, *"It's our first time together and I'm feeling kind of horny, conventional methods of making love kind of bore me . . ."*

I loved LL Cool J and I especially loved that song. I began

to recite the lyrics. I was really feeling inebriated as I continued to groove with Supreme.

"I always finish what I start," I stated to Supreme in response to his earlier statement. I then grabbed his crotch one more time as I prepared to walk off to another part of the dance floor.

"Ma', you frontin' on me ma'... Where you walking off to?" Supreme asked as he followed behind me.

I took him by the hand and told him that we could *play* but that it was gonna cost him.

An embarrassed-looking smile came across Supreme's face as if to indicate that his ego had been bruised. "I ain't paying for no ass!" Supreme shot back.

I looked at him crossways and stated, "I'm not talking about money... Just introduce me to some of your friends from *Underworld* and some of the different industry people."

Supreme's confidence came back and although he wasn't a big imposing figure like Horse, he still walked around with this swagger and confidence that gave the impression that he would become threatening if he were not shown proper respect. His demeanor somewhat bordered on the line of arrogance, but that didn't matter to me because I wasn't looking to marry the guy, I was just doing my job, investigating him and trying to get closer to him and his circle of cronies.

"Oh no doubt ma'... I know everybody up in here, come on, let me introduce you to some of my mans-an-'em."

As the music continued to thump, I followed Supreme and the two of us couldn't step more than three feet without someone saying what's up to him, embracing him, or whispering something into his ear. Eventually Supreme introduced me to a guy named Mario who is one of the editors at *Underworld* magazine.

After embracing and showing each other some love, Supreme stated, "Mario, I wanted to introduce you to Jessica . . . She runs a modeling company and I'm just trying to put her on to some people that I know."

"A'ight, a'ight, that's what's up," Mario stated as he nodded his head and looked at my body.

I handed Mario a business card and then I went on to tell him about some of the music videos and clothing lines that my company had done work for.

"True story . . ." Mario said as he went on to give me his number and told me to contact him.

I had actually read *Underworld* magazine on a number of occasions and I was familiar with a section of the magazine called Sticky Pages where they have a lot of nice-looking models dressed in swimwear and thongs and things of that nature.

"Yeah, my girls could really take your Sticky Pages section to the next level. I don't think that there is any company or photographer out there that can even touch us!" I boasted.

Mario nodded his head and then adjusted his diamond-encrusted dog tag as he sipped from his drink.

"Yo, she might be right, I mean I ain't never seen no model chicks with no ass like this!" Supreme said as he pointed to my butt. He then gave Mario a pound as the two of them laughed. I playfully mushed Supreme and told Mario that it was nice meeting him and then Supreme and I walked off.

He continued to introduce me to numerous people and I gave out my business card to everyone. Although I was intoxicated I tried my best to remember names and faces and take mental notes that I would probably need to refer to again later. We eventually reached the lobby of the hotel and it was jam-packed with people.

"Come wit' me upstairs, we got a suite on fifteen," Supreme instructed.

I knew that if I backed out and didn't accompany Supreme to the suite that I would probably forever be blacklisted by him and I could forget any future chances of getting close to him. But I also knew that he didn't wanna just go upstairs to talk. So I had to think fast about how I could ward off his advances if he tried anything once we got to the suite. The elevator opened up and we got on. What was ironic is that as crowded as the lobby was no one else got into the elevator except for the two of us.

"So you think I got a nice butt?" I asked. I wanted to kick myself for asking that question because I knew where a question like that would lead to. But the liquor was still talking for me.

"Hell yeah! You got ass like a sista, but a face like one of those runway models," Supreme said as he came close to me and palmed my butt. He tried to kiss me but I stopped him.

"What's up?" he asked.

"I can't do nothing with you, Supreme. I mean it's nothing against you or anything like that. It's just that I'm engaged . . ."

Supreme laughed. "Engaged?" he said as the elevator reached its destination and the doors opened up. We walked off the elevator and Supreme wasn't sure which way the suite was. He explained to me that his man had booked everything and had just given him the access key when he was in the limo.

As we reached the room and Supreme opened the door, he

stated, "You didn't seem like you was engaged when you had my muthafuckin' dick hard enough to cut diamonds out there on the dance floor."

The music was already on inside the suite and I wasn't sure if we were the only two people there in the room. "I know but—"

Supreme cut me off and pushed me against the wall and started kissing on me and feeling on my chest. And part of it felt good but part of me didn't want to go there with him because of the investigation and because of how guilty I would feel since I was engaged and all.

But before I could blink, Supreme had unzipped his fly and pulled his pants and his boxers down to his knees. Without saying anything he just kind of gently pushed me down and guided me to my knees and just that quick I was face to face with Supreme's uncircumcised black dick.

"Hold on, hold on," I said as I stood up. "I wanna do this but I need some liquor or weed or something to loosen me up. It brings another side out of me."

Supreme proceeded to completely take off his pants and boxers and his shirt and he was fully naked. Looking at his big dick instantly turned me on but I tried to keep myself in check. He then reached for his Nextel and spoke to somebody.

"Yo, I'm in the suite. Where the weed stashed at?"

The person spoke back on the walkie-talkie feature and told Supreme where he could find it. I walked behind Supreme's hard naked ex-convict body as we entered the bathroom and inside the shower was a hug ziplock bag that looked like it had enough drugs in it to supply a small village in Colombia.

"Oh my fucking God," I said, trying to sound as gullible as ever.

Supreme opened up the bag and reached in and handed me a green pill that sort of smelled like NoDoz. And the pill had a picture of the carton character Snoopy imprinted on it.

"You ever take E's before?" Supreme asked as my heart pounded.

I shook my head no, but the temptation to try it was eating at me. Supreme sparked a blunt that had apparently already been rolled by someone. I asked him for a drink as I continued contemplating taking the ecstasy pill. We both made our way back to the plush living room that had a fully stocked bar and I poured myself some Jack Daniels-green label on the rocks. As I drank the whiskey I decided to just try the E pill and I swallowed it.

Supreme took some pulls on the weed and asked me if I wanted some, but I declined because I didn't wanna have so many drugs going through my system all at one time.

After about ten minutes or so, I noticed that I was feeling a whole lot happier than I had been feeling ten minutes prior. I remember smiling and just staring at Supreme real lustfully. Supreme took a pull from his blunt and then went and turned up the radio. He was still walking around with no clothes on but now his body was beginning to look a whole helluva lot better to me.

A full twenty minutes had passed since I took the E pill and I remember my body feeling real good like I had just had the most refreshing workout, combined with the euphoria-like feelings as if I had won a multimillion-dollar lottery or something.

The Bravehearts rap song "Oochie Wally" was playing on the radio and the system sounded as if Supreme had turned the sound up as loud as it would go. It seemed as if the loud music helped to intensify how good I was feeling. All the inhibitions that I had were now far removed from my mind as I began taking off my blouse and walking in Supreme's direction.

It seemed as soon as Supreme saw my fully exposed breasts that he instantly got hard.

"I told you I start what I finish," I said as I knelt down and began giving Supreme a blowjob as he leaned against the back of the plush sofa. It seemed as if his dick would not stop growing as I tried to put it deeper and deeper in my mouth. At that point I was beyond turned on and I felt like I was gonna cum just from giving him some head. With the way that Supreme was responding to my tongue action I could tell that he was enjoying my skills but I didn't want him to cum just yet.

"You gonna let me cum in your mouth?" he asked. While I continued sucking I looked up at him and smiled back and shook my head no.

I stood up and while unbuttoning my pants I said, "Oh, I see that you're a selfish lover . . . I wanna feel you inside of me."

I still had my heels on and my pants were not even fully off, they were around my knees. And like an animal Supreme pulled my jeans down to my ankles and he bent me over the couch and he slid my thong to the side and entered me from the back. The music was still thumping and I don't even remember the song that was on because I was too busy enjoying the dick that was being given to me.

"Damn your shit is so wet!" Supreme stated as he began stroking.

"That's what you do to me baby . . ." I said in a very erotic-sounding way.

"You ever been with a thug before?"

"Nohhh! Oh God yes!!! You feel so gooood! You're the first thug that I've been with baby. Show me how thugs do it!" I was thoroughly enjoying the condom-less sex that we were having. I was lying but I wanted to boost Supreme's ego and plus I just liked hearing myself talk all kinds of stupid shit whenever I have sex.

I attempted to stand up straight and change positions, but Supreme grabbed the back of my head. Gripping my hair, he forced my face back down and held me bent over the couch. The rough way that he handled me really turned me on and he kept pumping his dick inside of me. As he hollered at me he told me, "Yeah bitch, this is how thugs do it!"

Although he had not been inside of me for more than a minute or so, I was already having an orgasm. I let out a yell because my body had never felt so good and I had never cum that hard in my entire life.

While I was cuming, the walkie-talkie on Supreme's Nextel began chirping. Supreme ignored it and he kept handling his business.

"Yo 'Preme! Pick the fuck up!" the voice yelled.

Supreme continued to ignore it and I was cuming a second time.

" 'Preme we got a situation! Niggas is bussing at us!"

Supreme continued to ignore the Nextel and I could tell that he was determined to finish sexing me. As the voice on the Nextel came through one more time, I heard what sounded like rapid gunfire.

"Maybe you should answer him," I stated while I suddenly got hit with a dose of reality. Here I was bent over a couch fucking the guy I was supposed to be investigating and it sounded like a shootout or something horrible was taking place somewhere.

At that point my cell phone began ringing and I knew that it was probably Angela. I just hoped like hell that everything was all right and that the gunshots were not coming from the party downstairs.

"Don't worry about your phone! I'm almost there!" Supreme commanded. He continued talking and told me that he *already knew what was up and what was going down* and that I didn't have to worry about nothing.

The next thing I knew, while I was still bent over the couch taking it from behind, the door to the hotel suite burst open and about four guys came storming in.

"Yo 'Preme, niggas just wet Chris!"

Supreme finally pulled out of me and I tried to hustle and hurry up and pull up my pants.

"What?" Supreme asked.

"Yo we was in front of the hotel just chillin' an kickin' it with some bitches and this jealous-ass muthafucka comes up to Horse and blows weed smoke in money's grille. So Chris stepped to the nigga and was ready to choke the nigga up and the dude's man comes from out of nowhere wit' a gat and just lit Chris up! He let off like fifteen, sixteen shots and Chris dropped to the ground and niggas just started scattering. All of our heat was up in the room so we couldn't do nothing. But yo, the niggas ran off and jumped in a Benz and was out. Then niggas just started bussing off guns from everywhere. Yo, I don't know but that shit seemed like niggas did a professional hit on Chris! Word!"

"Where is Horse? Is he a'ight?" Supreme asked.

"Yeah, he cool. It's cops everywhere downstairs and they got the nigga hemmed up and questioning him."

"A'ight yo, if y'all came up here to get the heat, take the burners and stash them joints somewhere. Don't go outside with them shits. And look in the bathroom and handle that bag for me. I know Five-O will be up in here in a minute trying to find shit! I'ma be down there in a minute."

Supreme's cronies followed his orders though one of them couldn't help but acknowledge the obvious. "Yo, and um, . . . Pardon me, we ain't mean to just interrupt y'all like that."

Normally I would have been beyond embarrassed but the liquor, the E pill, and the weed from earlier all had me on cloud nine and I didn't even feel that much shame at all. As soon as the guys were out of the suite, Supreme took off his boxers again, and I got undressed, and like rabbits we were going at it again.

Part of me felt bad about Chris, but another part didn't care that he had been shot. And yet there was still a part of me that didn't even care about the investigation anymore, I was more concerned about keeping this high that I was feeling.

Supreme began stroking real deep and fast and I could tell that he was close to cuming. And although I was feeling real good, I wasn't dumb enough not to remind Supreme to pull out.

"Make sure you pull out . . . okay, baby?"

I guess that I said that too late because all I heard was Supreme let out a long moan and he gripped me real tight around my waist.

"Wheeew!" he said as he began laughing.

"Supreme! Why didn't you pull out?" I questioned as he laid his full weight on me.

"I'm sorry but it just felt too good to pull outta that."

I pushed Supreme off of me and told him that he was gonna get me in so much trouble. At that point my phone began ringing again. It was Angela wanting to know where I was at, where I had disappeared to, and if I was okay. I answered her questions without going into too much detail and assured her that I was fine.

"Jessica, we got a deal! We signed it about fifteen minutes before the shooting broke out."

"Angela, that is so good! Just don't forget about the little people like me," I joked.

Angela told me that she would catch up to me the following day because she was going to go home with White Lines, her brother, and his friends.

"Horse signed White Lines," I excitedly told Supreme as I made my way to the bathroom to freshen up. Thankfully, after I'd hung up from Angela I was smart enough to turn my expensive cell phone to the video-camera function. I needed to get something concrete out of the whole ordeal and hopefully I would be able to get Supreme to run his mouth and say something incriminating before the night was over.

"Yeah I know, he gave homey a million-dollar advance and I had to okay that shit," Supreme replied.

I was so glad that Supreme had gone there with his words. I was going to try to get some more information out of him, but I had to be careful not to appear too eager.

I yelled from the bathroom, "You know, either you are really horrible or you are a fiend. Isn't Chris your boy? You was so into *trying to get with me* that you didn't even want to go check on your boy?" I said, making sure to put emphasis on the words "trying to get with me," so that if it ever came up I could deny that Supreme and I had actually had sex and just state that he had tried to fuck me but I had warded off his advances.

I could hear Supreme laughing from the other room. Then he appeared at the entrance to the bathroom and he said, "I'm cool with homey but I ain't move that quick for duke 'cause he be on some shit."

I purposely kept quiet and didn't say anything. And Supreme laughed again and paused for a moment before he said, "Yo, I had been hearing about you. Matter fact that nigga Chris was riling niggas up saying that you was a fucking federal agent and all kinds of bullshit! That's just how stupid the nigga is. The nigga is a stupid muthafucka that don't know how to play his position and keep his mouth shut."

"Yeah, I couldn't believe that! All I do is work on my company twenty-four-seven. And I couldn't believe that my name would even be associated with something like that," I replied as I began slipping back into special agent mode.

"So I have to tell Angela that you are the one to be thanked for White Line's deal? What exactly do you do? Are you like an A&R?" I asked, trying to sound really innocent.

"A&R? Nah ma'. Gun Clap is my company. Fuck what you heard and what you see in the videos and all that," Supreme exclaimed.

That was what I needed to hear. Supreme had admitted to me that the record company was really his. To keep from raising suspicions, I didn't mention anything else. I wanted desperately to ask him what he meant while we were having sex when he said that he *already knew what was up*. My gut told me that he had probably ordered a hit on Chris. In fact he had to know what was going to go down and how it was going to go down. Through my drugged-up state I had to make a mental bookmark to remind myself of Supreme's exact words which were, that he *already knew what was up*. I knew that I would need to relay those exact words to my supervisor.

As the two of us prepared to leave the suite and join the confusion and mayhem in the lobby I remembered thinking to myself how I could actually get used to this undercover life that I was living. The good sex and the partying was a major perk, but I still had to get my hands on some of that dough that Supreme and Horse were holding.

CHAPTER NINE

by the time I made it back to Howard Beach I was more than ready to just hit the bed and sleep off the sledgehammerlike headache that I had. After the combination of weed, liquor, and ecstasy had worn off I had one of the worst hangovers of my life! I actually think that death would have been a better option as opposed to experiencing the nausea.

At 7:30 in the morning following the *Underworld* anniversary party, I found myself on my white-tiled bathroom floor literally hugging the toilet bowl, or as they say in the 'hood, worshiping the porcelain god. I had already vomited once and it did help me feel a bit better but my body was not done rejecting the poisons that I had put inside of it the previous night. I was sweating like I was inside of a sauna and the last thing I wanted to do was speak to anyone. But as I was throwing up for the second time that morning, my cell phone began to ring off the hook.

Ahh shit, I thought to myself as I realized that the blocked number might be my supervisor, Andrew. Quickly trying to wipe the spit and chunks of regurgitation from my mouth, I sat up against the bathtub and answered the call.

"Hello," I mustered up in the most groggy-sounding voice.

Never forgetting to refer to me by my undercover name, my supervisor's voice seemed to fill up the entire phone as he spoke uncharacteristically loud. "Jackson, what the fuck are you doing to me?"

"What?" I asked through my splitting headache.

"Didn't you tell me that you would be at that magazine party last night?"

"Yes I was there but—" I said as my supervisor cut me off in the middle of my sentence. I could sense a stern tone in his voice and I couldn't figure out why.

"And where the fuck are you now?"

"I just got home."

"Jackson, are you alone?"

"Yes and I was—" Again I was cut off by my supervisor.

"Jessica, this is what we have to get straight. When you're conducting an investigation and you're at an event where one of our informants gets his fucking head blown off, your first thought needs to be to contact me! I don't need my god-damn boss hearing about it on the news and then calling me on it with me having no idea what the hell he's talking about!"

At that point, in spite of the way I felt and in spite of my headache I had to come back strong and get my supervisor to respect me.

"Andrew, once again, with all due respect I need you to hear me out. First of all, I am fully capable of conducting this investigation and I'm making progress. Did it ever occur to you that I might have a plausible explanation as to why I didn't immediately contact you? Of course not! You and every other sexist, racist-ass male agent doesn't want to see me succeed and you're all looking for the first reason to pull the plug on this whole thing—"

"Jessica—"

"Wait, please, I listened to you, now you hear me out . . . I am risking my life for this government and this investigation and you have the balls to come at me? You are more concerned with this piece-of-shit informant than you are about your fellow agent! Did you ask if I was okay? Did you ask if I almost got my head blown off? Did you think that maybe I couldn't call you because I was busy warding off sexual advances from Supreme?"

My supervisor was quiet because he knew that he was in the wrong. And I sarcastically spoke up again. "Andrew, this is the explanation that you can give to your boss: while your *beloved* and *dear* criminal informant was getting his head blown off, your unrespected, unqualified female agent had to endure hours of exposure to marijuana smoke being blown in her face and she was practically raped by Supreme, yes the same Supreme that this Bureau so desperately wants to take down. And let him know that she not only witnessed firsthand Supreme in the possession of enough narcotics to send him away for thirty years but she also managed to videotape Supreme telling her from his mouth that he is the one that really pulls the strings at Gun Clap Records and that it is his company! And in reference to your beloved informant, tell your boss that Supreme, in his own words, let me know that the Chris Mims murder was a planned hit . . ."

"Jackson, you're shitting me," Andrew said with a totally changed attitude.

"I'm not shitting you! I'm telling you the facts. I will get you the evidence that you need on Supreme and Horse—that is not a problem. And I'm close to getting you Paulie Calvino but you and everyone else in this testosterone-driven FBI better support me and not undermine me if you want this to work!"

My boss had heard enough and I knew that I had gained his respect. He felt good about what I had told him simply because now he could look good in front of his boss since the investigation was making progress. He also told me that even with my video-camera evidence, which was in his words "phenomenal," that he didn't want to rest on just that. We would have to step things up in terms of getting Supreme to incriminate himself on a tapped phone or on a wire of some sort. We would also have to step up the video surveillance so we could make sure that we had more than enough evidence to bury Supreme and Horse underneath the jail.

See, I was hungover but I was not stupid. I had purposely planted seeds in my boss's head that would later help me out if needed. Seeds like telling him that the FBI cared more about their criminal informant than they did me. Seeds like saying I'd practically been raped by Supreme and that I had had marijuana smoke blown in my face all night long. I did that because I had to have outs. I knew that the surveillance would be stepped up and the last thing I wanted was Supreme on tape talking about how he had fucked me after giving me an ecstasy pill.

But if something ever came up I could always revert back

to the conversation that I had with my supervisor and let him know that I had not actually had sex with Supreme. If Supreme boasted about such a thing it would be him trying to talk and look good in front of his crew.

CHAPTER TEN

*t*ell Snoopy that I said hello."

"Snoopy?" Supreme asked with a huge question mark in his voice.

"Yeah, wasn't that a picture of Snoopy on that E pill from the other night?" I asked as Supreme started to laugh through the phone.

"Yeah, yeah, it was. Yo, you a wild chick, you know that, right?"

"I'm just being me that's all. But I do wanna see you later tonight or sometime this week," I said.

"You wanna see me so we can hang out or are you just hooked on that E that quick?" he questioned.

"Supreme?" I asked with a babyish puppy-dog question mark to my voice. "If I'm hooked on anything it's that dick," I said as we both started laughing. "I think your dick is possessed!"

"Yo, you crazy," Supreme replied.

I knew that if there was any way that a woman could quickly get to a man's heart it was by boosting his ego in the sexual performance area. If you let a man know or think that he is a king in the bedroom then he will genuinely be pulled to you and more than likely trust you because all men think with the head between their legs and not with the one on their shoulders.

"I don't know why I am telling you this but it's true. I never came harder than I came the other night when I was with you," I said as Supreme again started laughing.

"What the fuck is so funny? You don't believe me but it's true! The next time we do it I want you to do me the same way, but I want you to choke me while you're doing it to me. Act like you're raping me! Okay?"

"Whoa! Whoa! What did you just say?" Supreme asked.

"You heard what I said. I want you to just rip my jeans off and rip my panties off and just rape me! Make sure you do it real hard and rough and choke me while you're taking it."

"Wowww! Jessica you a wild girl! But I ain't into that kinky shit like that."

I assured Supreme that I wasn't some crazy whore and that I was deathly serious about what I was saying. I had to be careful though. Based on what I had witnessed in the hotel, in terms of the drugs, it was enough to get a judge to grant us permission to tap Supreme's phones. I couldn't be incriminating myself the way I was. What was funny was that I had just indirectly let Supreme into a past that I had rarely, if ever, let anyone into, and that being my incestuous past.

See, one of the demons that had repeatedly plagued me all of my life was an incest demon. The fact was that I had been a victim of incest since I was seven years old up until my junior year in high school. My father had consistently and repeatedly forced himself on me for a period of ten years. And during that time, my self-esteem became rock-bottom low and my sexuality and view of sex became totally warped. In fact, having a form of power and catching serial rapists and child molesters were not my number-one reasons for wanting to join the FBI but those certainly were motivating forces.

So when I became of age when I could engage in sexual activities with another consenting adult it was hard for me to separate the rough and forceful actions of my father with the actions that my sexual partner would be performing on me. And although I hated what my father did to me, in a sick way, now years later as an adult what he had done to me years ago sort of became my only normal view of sex.

I would also have to say that my incestuous past kind of prepped me for my undercover work as an FBI agent simply because I got so used to being *two people* when I was growing up. On one hand I knew how to hide pain and show my friends and the public that manufactured *good* side, so that they would think that my siblings and I were part of this picture-perfect all-American family, but on the other hand while I was hurting inside I knew how to hide that hurt and be this person that did everything right in order to please and protect my father. It was like I sort of learned how to be my father's *wife* when I had to and how to turn that switch off and be his daughter when I had to.

That incestuous past and the emotional pain involved with it is what led me to alcohol at an early age. It was like I could ease the pain when I drank alcohol and later on when I tried stronger drugs like marijuana it helped even more to ease the pain. It was like alcohol and marijuana and cocaine became my ways of escaping the unfortunate realities that my father had put me through. I had never become an addict, but I had become more than just a recreational user of drugs. Drugs became the thing that helped me feel normal and feel good about myself.

CHAPTER ELEVEN

*F*ollowing the death of Chris Mims, the media had a field day with the fact that here it was, another incident of violence surrounding the record label whose name seemed to endorse violence. Horse was still under pressure because the murder weapon of rival rapper Frank Nitty had been found in his home along with illegal narcotics, so needless to say the Chris Mims murder was the last thing that Horse needed.

Although Horse and Supreme were delinquents at heart and Supreme had a lengthy rap sheet, they were smart businessmen and master promoters. Horse especially knew how to take the worst incidents and turn them into promotional genius.

Horse had a dynamite Manhattan publicist by the name of Nina Terry and I was certain that some of his promotional genius could easily be attributed to her. She more than likely was the one that called the press conference to discuss the recent Gun Clap Records shooting incident. This time, I was actually present at the packed media event, as a guest of

Supreme and Horse, and I laughed on the inside as I listened to Horse spin the whole Chris Mims incident.

Draped again by his son, Horse spoke and denied that he or his company had had anything to do with the unfortunate and untimely death of one of his closest and most trusted bodyguards. Also present at the press conference were Angela Calvino and White Lines.

"But Horse, what about the allegations that Chris Mims was killed because he might have been providing information to the police? Was his murder really a professional hit by you and your organization?" a reporter asked.

Horse charismatically replied, "You know, the old me would have flipped on you and screamed at you for asking a question like that. But this is the reason that I wanted to hold this press conference—specifically for questions such as that and to set the record straight and let the public know once again that Gun Clap Records did not sanction a hit on anyone. Chris was loved and respected by everyone at Gun Clap and if he wasn't I don't think he would have put his life on the line for me and everyone else at Gun Clap the way he did. I've already sent my condolences to his family. And I assured them—and I also give everyone that can hear my voice this assurance and my word—that his immediate family members will be taken care of financially and all of his children will have scholarship funds set up immediately. And you asked me about my *organization*, well I am not part of any *organization*, I'm part of a family. Gun Clap Records is a family and only a family would look out for their loved ones when they're gone and that is exactly what we'll do in the case of Chris Mims."

As another reporter was going to ask a question, Horse cut

him off and got to the *real* reason that he had called the press conference.

"And speaking of family," Horse proudly said. "I want to introduce everyone to the newest member of the Gun Clap family. He's not gonna be the next big thing in rap music, but he's gonna be the next big thing in all of music! Period! He's standing right next to me and he hails from Howard Beach, Queens... Everybody... The newest edition to Gun Clap Records... My man, White Lines!"

At that point, White Lines and Horse embraced as Angela—who looked as beautiful as a movie star—beamed in the background. Horse then made reference to the fact that he was a uniter and not a divider and he spoke about this racist incident that had happened in Howard Beach more than fifteen years ago when a black man had been beaten and chased to his death by a mob of bat-wielding white men.

"Who would have thought that I would be able to walk through the streets of Howard Beach and get the kind of love that I got yesterday when I spent the day with White Lines in his 'hood. I think after that awful incident some fifteen years ago, yesterday marked a day where the city of New York had come full circle and we could finally put that ugly incident behind us, unite, make hit records together, and just have fun and enjoy life. That's why I love all of ya'll. I love this country in spite of the accusations and all the negativity that goes with this rap game... This is what it's all about," Horse said as he pointed to White Lines. "It's about taking music that was created in the ghetto, and using that to bridge a gap in communities and unite people in ways in which we couldn't have dreamed of in the past."

I smiled as I listened to Horse speak. I couldn't believe how he could just twist things that easily and come across so convincingly. The press conference totally shifted from Chris Mims and focused on White Lines. Horse bragged about how on a half-hour's notice White Lines went into the studio and laid down a rhyme that was so hot that it would soon be released on a song that he would do with Ashante who was on the Murder Inc. record label. He also stated that White Lines would have his own single out within the next six months and that his album would be completed within nine months.

After Horse introduced Angela Calvino as the person who had brought White Lines to his attention, the reporters were in absolute shock. They had thought that she looked similar to the Mafia don's daughter and now it had been confirmed. As the press conference ended, the media swarmed Angela and asked her a million and one questions. Like her flamboyant Mafia don father, she seemed as if she was born for the spotlight and she relished the moment.

CHAPTER TWELVE

Iike just about everyone else, I had heard of Sylvia's Restaurant but I had never eaten there. But here I was on a warm summer night sitting down and preparing to eat at the world-famous Harlem restaurant.

Angela was really trying to engross herself in everything that was *black* and everything that was hip-hop and we had come to the restaurant based on her urging. When I say we, I am referring to she and I, along with two black models from my agency, Trina and Melissa.

As we sat in the packed restaurant I was certain that Angela didn't feel too self-conscious because there were other white people that seemed to be relaxed and enjoying themselves. But apparently Angela didn't feel as secure as I thought she did as she stated, "You know, I have to say that I feel so white right now . . ."

Everyone laughed and made light of the situation.

"Girl don't trip about being white. This is Harlem, and just about anything goes in Harlem. I mean Harlem definitely ain't trippin' over white people 'cause white people are moving to

Harlem by the droves. Matter of fact Bill Clinton has his office here!" Trina stated in an effort to make Angela feel more relaxed. "Plus you're Italian, which is as close to black as they come."

Everyone at the table laughed.

"Okay so what should I order?" Angela asked. Melissa quickly suggested that Angela get smothered chicken, collard greens, cornbread, and black-eyed peas.

After the waiter took everyone's order the four of us began to talk and Angela asked Trina and Melissa if they knew of anybody who was looking to get signed to a record deal.

"Do I know anybody?" Melissa sarcastically asked. "Angela, everyday I get a million and one guys coming up to me because they recognize me from the music videos and after hitting on me and undressing me with their eyes, they're always asking me how can they get *put on* and telling me about their demo tape and can I pass it along to this person or that person."

"Really?" Angela asked.

"She ain't lying, we both get it," Trina added for good measure.

Before long our food had arrived at the table and after we got ourselves situated we continued talking and eating our food at the same time. Angela commented on how good the food tasted and she admitted that she had never eaten black-eyed peas before but that they tasted so good.

"Ummmhhh, this is so good!" Angela exclaimed. "This is what cornbread taste like? It tastes more like cake! I never knew it was so good. I always thought it was dry and hard, similar to stale bread or something."

We all laughed.

In addition to the food we had also all ordered apple martinis. As I sipped from my martini, Melissa spoke up. What she said hit me in a way in which a lightbulb goes off in your head and you just want to kiss and thank a person for bringing up what they brought up. Her words were the missing link to my hustle, she provided the information that I was looking for but didn't know exactly where I was gonna find it or how I was gonna find it.

Melissa spoke and said, "Angela, I know that you're really feeling good about this rapper that you helped get signed but—"

Cutting her off Angela stated, "Feeling good is putting it lightly. It feels better than the best sex you could ever have! I mean he got a million-dollar advance and I made ten percent of that. One hundred thousand dollars and I barely did shit! It's fucking unreal!"

"But Angela, I'll tell you this like I tell all of the people that are asking me to pass along their demos. The key to this music game is *ownership*. As a manager you can make good money and I can get you a thousand demo tapes and introduce you to a thousand people that wanna be rappers, but I'll be honest with you, what you should do is get your own record label so that you start owning the music that your artists are making," Melissa stated as we all continued to eat.

Apparently Melissa and Trina had discussed this before because Trina chimed right in, "Yeah, when people see us in these music videos they stereotype us as being chicken-heads, whores, and sluts but the reality is we have brains and we speak to the people behind the scenes, the real shot callers. And what Melissa is saying is that yeah, they gave your artist a million dollars and if the album goes platinum guess how much the record company will be making off those sales in comparison to the artist? Angela, what you need to do is get your weight up and renegotiate that deal, try to get your artist back and then start your label and let them sign your company to a distribution deal. That way you'll have control and ownership of your own label and then you can call the shots instead of controlling the crumbs."

Angela thought about what was being said and then she stated that she really didn't know nothing about running a record company.

"Well did you ever meet Supreme?" Melissa asked rhetorically. "That nigga don't know shit about owning a record company but he owns Gun Clap Records!"

I tried to act surprised as Angela didn't yet know or understand what Melissa was talking about. "I thought that was Horse's company," Angela stated with a curious look on her face as she put some black-eyed peas into her mouth.

"No. See that's just a front. Have you ever seen a store in the 'hood where it looks like a candy store or a grocery store because it has products in the window of the store but when you go inside you realize that all of the potato chips are stale and the milk is sour and the shelves haven't been restocked in weeks? That's because the store is just a front for selling drugs. It works the same in the music business. Supreme came home from after doing like ten years in the joint, and the new hustle was the record business and Supreme wanted in on it but he didn't have the money. But what he did have was a connection to these mob soldiers who were supplying him with drugs and they had a bunch of dirty money that they wanted to wash, so Supreme came up with a way that he could wash the money for them. His plan, which he carried out, was to create a record company and pass the mob money through that record company and he got his record industry boy, Horse, to run the show and make true hit records so that everything would really look legit on the surface. He felt that if they made enough hit records and kept a low profile that nobody would even question where the start-up money for the record label came from. So behind the scenes it is and has always been Supreme who is really calling the shots." After Melissa had finished breaking things down, she licked the barbecue sauce from her French manicured fingers.

Angela caught on quickly, and I'm sure that she did simply because of her family's criminal background, but I wanted to make sure that I fully understood where Melissa was coming from.

"Melissa, the only place that you're losing me is with the dirty money thing. What I mean is that if Angela would be basically negotiating her own label deal, are you saying that Supreme or somebody would front her some of their drug money so that they could launder it?" I asked.

Melissa sucked the meat off of one of the ribs and after sucking on the bone she spoke up. "No that's not what I'm saying. What I mean is this: Angela, if you can come up with like two to three million dollars then you could easily get your own label going and get a distribution deal. But the problem is most people don't have that kind of money. Supreme didn't even have that kind of money when he first came home from the joint. He was just getting back into the drug game and trying to build his empire back to that multimillion-dollar point, so he kind of got lucky that the mob trusted him to let him launder their money. He was also lucky that he had Horse who had the music smarts and talents to make hit records. So what he and Horse were able to do was, they approached some execs at Def Jam, who shall remain nameless, and they had the execs legally put up the money to launch Gun Clap Records. So money flowed out of Def Jam's bank account and into Gun Clap Records' bank account and on paper it all looks good and legit especially with Def Jam being partners with Gun Clap, it was like one partner gave money to the other partner. But under the table Supreme simply slid the three million dollars of mob cash back to the Def Jam execs and the Def Jam execs simply funneled the cash back into their accounts little by little. You follow?" Melissa asked.

We all nodded our heads and I could tell that Angela's wheels were turning big time. And after Angela confirmed that she was gonna bring the whole record label thing to Horse to see what he had to say about it, I could tell that *this was it*. I knew that now I had the information to rope Paulie Calvino into the mix. And the reason that I was so certain about it was because when the Mafia finds out about a dollar that can be made they react to it in the manner in which sharks react to blood. The Mafia and hip-hop would soon be married and I would be the one officiating at the wedding ceremony.

CHAPTER THIRTEEN

*M*y fiancé Tony had been threatening to fly into New York and see me. I was adamant and persistent in telling him that he would be putting me in a dangerous situation if I were to see him. Fortunately for me I had the built-in excuse of being able to tell him that because of the sensitivity of the investigation I could not fully divulge all of the details of what I had been doing and been through.

"I don't even know what the hell your goddamn name is anymore!" my fiancé blurted out.

That was just the type of talk that I didn't need and I knew exactly where this phone conversation was going.

"Jessica, Jessie, Jeshua, Jay, J-Lo, whatever you fucking call yourself. Jesus Christ! I need for you to explain to me what in the hell kind of engagement is this that we're supposed to be having? You don't call me, you don't call your parents, and when I do speak to you everything is about the investigation! Well what about the wedding plans that we have? See, I knew it from the beginning that this whole undercover operation was gonna be no good for us. I knew it but you wouldn't listen to me!"

"Are you done?" I sarcastically asked before proceeding. "Look, I have enough pressure on me as it is, I got people who would blow my brains out in two seconds if they knew who I really was and all you can do is call me and rant and rave on the phone. You are so fucking selfish! You'd think that maybe once I could get some support from you. Just once!"

My fiancé went on and on about how he thought that maybe we should just break off the engagement. And I knew that he had said that as sort of like a scare tactic. But the truth of the matter was I really could have cared less. The fact was I wasn't yet married and there was no reason for me to act like I was. After he'd tried to use the scare tactic on me I should have ripped into him and told him that if his dick wasn't so small and if he was handing out multiple orgasms like Supreme was then maybe I would have some real reason to wanna rush back home and get married.

I didn't dare say that because I knew that it would've crushed him. I really did think he was being way too selfish and childish about the whole thing though. What was weird is that he thought that trying to run a guilt trip on me for not staying in steady contact with my family was a good move on his part. But that just showed how much he didn't know about me. I had never told him about the incest and sexual abuse that my father put me through and which my mother turned a blind eye to. Had he known that he would have known that even my immediate family was not the biggest of my concerns. I had no problem detaching myself from family, friends, and situations and becoming a new person. Had he known that, he would have known that is why I was able to be so effective as Special Agent Jessica Jackson.

CHAPTER FOURTEEN

*a*bout a week had passed since Angela and I had eaten at Sylvia's Restaurant and I hadn't spoken to her since that time. But I made it a point to call her and tell her to meet me at the day spa and that after getting our massages and nails done that I would treat her to lunch. My supervisor was really pressing me to get some more solid information so that he could continue to justify keeping the investigation going. I knew that I had to start being direct with Angela but I also knew that I had to gain her trust.

After we left the hair salon, we found ourselves headed out to the Cheesecake Factory in Long Island which was located near Roosevelt Field Shopping Center. The whole ride there we basically spoke about nothing as I tried to seek the right opportunity to get information out of her. After we reached the parking lot of the Cheesecake Factory and got out I asked Angela a question.

"Angela, don't take this the wrong way and I hope that I'm

not overstepping my bounds by asking you this but have you ever been with a black guy?"

There was silence. Angela looked both ways as she walked to make sure that she didn't get hit by any of the passing cars. I didn't know how to read her facial expressions. But thank God that as she tried to look like a fabulous blond-haired diva she did crack a bit of a smile.

"Why do you ask?" she nonchalantly replied.

"I was just curious."

There was silence as we entered the restaurant and told the hostess that we needed a table for two. After we were seated I spoke again, "Okay, let me be straight with you. The thing is this, I run this company and I'm constantly busy and all of that and I'm always around people and going out to parties but the truth is that I really don't have anybody that I'm really close with, someone who I can just call and talk to about anything. And really that's because I feel like I can't trust anybody, especially not women. I always think women want to get close to me so that they can accomplish their own agenda. But with you it's different. You're real, you're your own person and you're not trying to advance no agenda. You—"

Angela cut me off and she started laughing. "Jessica please! Cut the bullshit! What is your point?"

I laughed because I guess that I was overdoing it with the praises.

"So why did you ask me if I'd ever been with a black guy?" Angela inquired for a second time.

"Okay, this is just between me and you but I gave Supreme some," I said as I looked around like I didn't want anyone to hear.

"Some what?" Angela asked as she sipped from her glass of water.

I just looked at her as if to say, *come on now, you know what I'm talking about.*

"Well, how was it?" Angela asked. I went on to explain that it was the best sex that I'd ever had and that I wanted some more. Then out of nowhere Angela almost spit out her water as she started laughing.

"What the hell is so funny?" I asked.

"Well, Horse had called me and was asking me what was up with you and I thought that he was just playing with me. But he was like, you wanted Supreme to act like he was raping you and you wanted him to choke you while he fucked you or something sick like that! What was that about?" Angela asked.

At that point I wanted to melt in my seat because I had no idea that Supreme had kissed and told.

"Can we order now?" I playfully said, blatantly trying to change the subject.

"Yeah, let's look at this menu," Angela replied with a smile.

"Well, Angela if you need me to speak to Supreme about the whole label deal situation, just let me know. I guess the whole world knows now but I am kinda close to him."

As Angela looked at the menu she didn't look in my face as she spoke. "To answer your question, yes I have been with a black guy before."

I looked at Angela and a big smile came across her face. "What?" I asked.

"I let Horse hit it a few days ago," Angela uncharacteristically said as she smiled and continued to look at the menu.

This was the first time that I had seen her let her guard down. She was finally acting like a soft woman and not this hard-as-nails dominant-dictator figure.

"Get outta here!" I said as I raised my voice.

Angela went on to say how it was good but that having sex with Horse would have to take some getting used to because he was so large. She then shocked me and told me that it wasn't just some one-night-stand type of thing and that she could really see herself developing real feelings for Horse.

"Shuuuut uppp!" I said in shocked response.

"No really, I could," Angela replied.

The waitress came and we ordered our food. "Now about this raping and choking thing," Angela said as she again started laughing.

"New subject please," I blurted out. "I am gonna kill Supreme when I see him!" I yelled out with laughter mixed with embarrassment.

Against Angela's wishes I insisted that we switch subjects.

"So what do you think you'll do about setting up your own label? Do you think you can get up the money?" I asked.

"Well first of all, Horse is real hot for the idea. So that is not an issue," Angela stated.

I nodded my head.

"LaCostra Nostra Records. That's what I'm gonna call it," Angela continued on.

"That's hot!" I replied. LaCostra Nostra meant "this thing of ours," and that was the term that all made members of the Mafia used to refer to the mob.

"So where the hell are you gonna get the money to start it?" I asked, knowing that I was really pushing the envelope.

Angela looked at me and she had suddenly reverted back into the silence that she must have been trained to exhibit growing up in a Mafia household. I thought quick on my feet.

"Angela, don't tell me that you got kryptonite in your pussy or something! You got Horse to front you that kind of money?"

Angela laughed, and I could tell that she again felt comfortable. As our food arrived we adjusted our place settings and Angela said, "Jessica, there are some things that simply go unsaid, but let's just say I got connections, and we can leave it at that."

I knew that I should leave it at that but I needed something more and I had to press my luck. As I put food in my mouth, I nodded my head and whispered, "So this probably works out good, your father can wash some of his money and not have to worry about it since you'll be overseeing everything, right?"

Angela didn't respond, at first she didn't even look at me. But after putting a fork full of food in her mouth she looked at me and nodded her head up and down in agreement but she cut her eyes at me in a fierce way.

What Angela didn't know was that I had a small but powerful miniature tape recorder strapped to my inner thigh really close to my vagina. The miniskirt that I had on gave me easy access to the recorder and so that I wouldn't incriminate myself I had started recording at the moment I brought up the subject of Angela setting up her record label.

The thing was, the recorder couldn't record Angela's head movement. I needed her to open her mouth and verbally say something in agreement to the money laundering scheme that could implicate both her and her father and Gun Clap records.

"Angela, I might be talking out of turn but I know your father can trust you to wash his money. But do you think you're doing the right thing by taking his money and mixing it in with Gun Clap? The feds will be all over that."

Angela looked at me and I know she was getting suspicious if she hadn't been already. She suddenly asked me to escort her to the bathroom. At that point my heart began to beat much faster because I knew that she must have been thinking that the table we were sitting at was possibly bugged or something. I just hoped that she didn't ask me to strip or anything like that. As we walked to the bathroom Angela placed her hands on my right hip and ran them all the way around my back and over to my other hip.

"You can walk ahead of me," she stated, as she pretended to be polite.

I had on a backless top so if I had on a wire she definitely would have seen the slightest bulge from it. As we reached the bathroom Angela felt my chest, she didn't bother to go about it nonchalantly as she cupped both of my titties she stated, "I don't know how you wear a shirt like this, I couldn't do it, my tata's need some support. And you don't even have on a strapless bra."

"This is just my style. I like to feel free so every now and again I let the twins hang free," I quickly replied as the two of us started laughing.

Angela proceeded to wash her hands and said that was the reason for her coming to the bathroom. She claimed that she hated to eat without first washing her hands. I knew that was a lie because if she were that anal about it she would have excused herself and gone to the bathroom long before any of the food had arrived at the table.

As she dried her hands I was still washing mine. We were the only ones in the swank little bathroom but Angela seemed to be nervous and looking around, sort of making sure that no one else was present.

"You know, Jessica, I wanna tell you this and this better be the last time I have to mention this. I don't understand, what is with you and the million and one fucking questions? You sound like somebody's informant or something," Angela said in a serious tone. Her face had become hard like cinder blocks.

I began to dry my hands and played dumb. "What are you talking about? What did I say? Is it because I asked if you had been with a black guy?"

Angela put a disgusted smirk on her face. "Jessica, don't fucking play stupid! You can ask me about who I'm screwing, you can ask me about my clothes, my cars, and you can even ask me about my business, but don't mention my family unless I bring it up. Okay?"

I didn't respond. I just continued to dry my hands.

"Jessica, do you understand what I'm saying?" Angela asked a bit more sternly.

Again, I didn't respond as I purposely tried to disrespect Angela by walking out of the bathroom. Angela grabbed me by the shoulder and prevented me from walking out. I reached in my bag and grabbed a fifty-dollar bill and told Angela to pay for the food and that if she wanted me to drive her back home that we would have to leave right then and there.

"Oh, Jessica! Would you stop acting like a sensitive little bitch? Jesus Christ!" Angela exclaimed.

I had to do the best acting job possible because I felt that if Angela began to question my credibility then I would probably be written off by Horse and everyone else involved in Angela's camp and the whole Gun Clap Records camp.

"Angela, no disrespect but you just don't understand. I just try to stay low key, mind my business and not cause any waves but it seems like I always find myself in somebody's goddamn bathroom getting accosted and accused of being an FBI agent or an informant and I just don't get it! You and Horse and everybody else are just a bunch of paranoid assholes who are suspicious of everybody that moves!" I stated in Academy Award–winning fashion.

"FBI agent? Who the hell accused you of being a fed?" Angela asked.

"Angela, Horse never admitted it to me, but between me and you he had two dyke-looking females threatening to blow my head off that day that we'd gone to his office and you and White Lines had waited out in the car for me. They had me locked in the bathroom and things just got ugly, the bitches were practically raping me. And all of that was because Chris Mims, who was really a snitching-ass rat told Horse and his peoples that I was a fucking agent! So now you know why it had really taken me so long to come back outside that day. But I never said anything because I knew that you would probably believe the lies. And then after Chris got hit—which by the way, Supreme practically told me he ordered the hit—everything seemed to be cool. Or at least up until right now with you, and I'm like here we fucking go again! Now instead of being an agent, you think I'm an informant! I really don't need this!" As I said this I gave a look as if I was going to cry from the anger.

"Jessica, I could kill you for not saying anything about that! Why didn't you tell me?" Angela asked with genuine concern.

"I didn't say anything because I didn't want to screw up the deal with White Lines."

"Jessica, you brought me to Horse, all you would have had to do was say the word that you even thought someone tried to cross you and I would have pulled out of that shit! If there is one thing that I am it's loyal. You understand me?" Angela asked.

I didn't respond as I tried to make my way out of the bathroom. Angela put her hands on the door and she said, "Okay, Jessica here is the deal. My father told me he would get me the three million in cash. He didn't tell me where it was coming from but I know it's coming from gambling and drug operations around the city."

I nonchalantly nodded my head, acting as if I wasn't making a big deal over what I was being told. But inside I was screaming and jumping for joy. I was also hoping like hell that the tape recorder had not stopped or malfunctioned in any way.

Angela immediately interjected, "Now this is the thing, I make my own way, I don't want any handouts from anybody because then they feel like they can tell you what to do and how to do it. I'll pay my father back every dime of his money because I don't want nothing hanging over my head. You understand where I'm coming from?"

As Angela and I made our way back to our table to finish our lunch I explained to her that I knew exactly where she was coming from and why she would want to pay her father back. After her stern warning that I had better keep my mouth shut about her father and the money I assured Angela that she didn't have to worry about that.

What was weird was that as we finished our food, I remember feeling sort of as if I had just bonded with Angela. It was like she had opened herself up to me and trusted me enough to tell me a hugely secretive thing about her world and that sort of made me connect with her.

So as I sat at the table I reached under my skirt and stopped the tape. I did that because I felt like I could trust Angela with one of my secrets. For my entire life I had never let anyone in on my incestuous past. There are a number of reasons that I'd kept something so dark, so secret, for so long. And never in my wildest dreams did I think that the first time that I would divulge parts of my past that it would be while I was in the middle of an FBI investigation and speaking to someone that I was investigating.

But something came across me and I just wanted to reveal to Angela something that would definitely help her trust me more but at the same time it would help me fight off demons that had plagued me for years. I figured that the best way for me to bring up the topic was for me to tie everything in to the sexual request that I had put in with Supreme. This way Angela would be able to see how I had come at my sick thoughts.

"Angela, when I told Supreme that I wanted him to choke me and rape me while we had sex, I had said that because my mind is all screwed up when it comes to sex and relationships."

Angela looked intently at me.

"Basically my whole sexuality is screwed up, and the reason is because when I was young my father . . . Well, how should I put this? Basically my father used to . . ."

CHAPTER FIFTEEN

*a*fter I was able to verify from Angela that her father was game to put up the cash to jump-start her record label, we were able to obtain a court order that gave us permission to step up our surveillance on Angela as well as on her father.

Angela knew how to follow the rules of the Mafia society when she was out in public. She knew what to say and what not to say. She was always aware that a rat might be lurking in the wings. But one thing about Angela is that she lived on her cell phone. And when it came to the Mafia's unwritten rule of not running your mouth on the phone, well she held no regard for that rule.

I had begun to spend more and more time with Angela, and in doing so we had also begun to develop a certain bond and trust. Or at least I thought.

See, Angela had never let on to me that her father had started to have reservations about handing over the three million. I had to learn that through the wiretap that we had on Angela's phone.

Angela had a bunch of friends, some who were closer to her than others. But it seemed as if all of her friends dared not to ever disagree with her. They were all *yes* people. It was sort of like Angela was some sort of goddess or princess in their eyes. And it was through a recorded conversation with her chief *yes* friend, Pamela, that we learned that Paulie Calvino was having doubts about going through with the whole record label thing.

"Pamela, do I look like some fucking degenerate or something?" Angela asked.

"Angela, listen, you are the smartest girl that I know. Of course you're not a degenerate," Pamela stated as we continued to listen in on the wire.

"Well then Pamela, if I'm not a degenerate, you tell me why my father would drag his feet on giving me the money?"

"Angela, like I said, you are a smart girl and—"

"Pamela, cut the shit! I know that I'm smart and beautiful and all of that. But I asked you a specific question and I need a specific answer from you. Why is my father dragging his feet with the money for my record label?" Angela asked as if Pamela held some kind of special answer.

You could tell that Pamela was fearful of saying the wrong thing to Angela as she sort of stuttered in her speech. "See, Angela you just said it. You cut me off from what I was gonna tell you, but that's just it. You are a beautiful girl. You're still daddy's little girl in his eyes, and I think that he's just worried about his daughter being mixed up in a world with a bunch of gangster rappers."

Angela was quiet for a moment before screaming into the phone.

"Jesus fucking Christ! Pamela, why doesn't he just give me the money? I'm a grown woman!"

"Angela, listen. You just have to get your father to build some confidence in the people that you'll be in business with. That might help," Pamela said.

Angela didn't respond to Pamela's last statement. She simply sighed into the phone and said, "I need this like I need a hole in my head. Pamela, I gotta go," she added as she abruptly hung up the phone without the silent mention of a *good-bye,* or *I'll speak to you later.*

As I sat with my supervisor and his supervisor and the head of the New York Organized Crime Task Force, we all wondered if something had spooked Paulie Calvino. We also wondered if there was some type of information from the inside that had been leaked, which Paulie had become aware of. We just didn't know why all of a sudden he was not warm to the idea of potentially making real big money in the record business.

"Look, we're probably just jumping the gun," my supervisor stated. "Let's just give things some time to play themselves out. In the meantime, Jessica, see what you can come up with."

I knew that there wasn't much to be worried about. I was siding with Angela's friend Pamela in that Paulie Calvino was probably wondering how much he could trust a bunch of gangster rappers around his daughter. Not to mention that three million dollars is a lot of money, it doesn't matter who you are.

After about a week or so Angela had finally confided in me the reservations that her father was having. She also told me that her father was leaning toward more than likely going through with the arrangement to put up the money for her but that he needed to have his people meet with Horse and Supreme and his people, so that all of the details could be discussed and worked out.

Angela had spoken to Horse and in a matter of days she was able to set up a meeting. The meeting was to be held at a little nondescript social club in Queens that Paulie Calvino and his crew frequented daily. The club wasn't located too far from Angela's Howard Beach neighborhood.

Unfortunately I wasn't able to go to the meeting. But with the Mafia, if you had no business or involvement in something then your presence at inappropriate times would only raise the level of suspicion.

The FBI had long known about the Queens social club that Paulie frequented. We were never able to bug it but we were able to rent out a nearby apartment that gave us a direct view of the social club so that we could get photo and video surveillance when we needed it.

So on the day of the meeting I found myself holed up in the surveillance room watching and waiting for all of the participants to show up to the meeting. And at around 7 P.M. all of the players began to arrive. Angela and her brother, Paul Jr., arrived first in a black Lincoln Navigator. Ten minutes later, Horse, Supreme, and G-Baby showed up in a white Yukon Denali. Soon thereafter a white Lexus pulled up and two known Mafia captains exited the car and went inside.

We watched and waited for more than an hour and there was no sign of Paulie Calvino, Sr. and it didn't appear that he was gonna show. We didn't know what to make of his absence but we felt confident that something productive was going on since the meeting was lasting for so long.

I would just have to wait to speak to Supreme or Angela to find out exactly what had transpired.

CHAPTER SIXTEEN

*J*essica, on the real, I wanna see that muthafucka put a bullet in my head!" Supreme yelled through the phone as we spoke.

"'Preme, what exactly happened?" I asked as I tried to get a handle on things.

"What do you mean, what happened? I told you, the muthafucka Paul left a message on my goddamn phone talking mad reckless! The dude said that he ain't have a problem doing business with us but that if me or my man Horse or anyone else for that matter so much as looks at his sister the wrong way that he would personally put a bullet in all of our heads," Supreme explained.

"'Preme, don't worry about that. He's just looking out for his sister," I said while trying to diffuse the situation.

"Fuck that! Can't nobody threaten me like that and live! I don't care who it is or who his father is!" Supreme yelled.

I remained quiet for fear of saying the wrong thing.

"Yo and I bent over for the nigga, I wasn't on no sheisty shit but fuck that! Fuck him and fuck his three million dollars!

His dumb ass should know that you don't give a man three million dollars and then threaten him!" Supreme reasoned.

"Supreme, I'm sure that this can all be squashed and forgotten about. We can all move on and make money and just forget about it before things get ugly for no reason," I explained.

"Nah, I ain't squashing shit! Yo, I sat down with those cats and gave them my word that we would do right by them. Horse is gonna hold Angela by the hand and teach her the music business. They even asked us if they could have White Lines as their premier artist and we already got the dude signed but I still was wit' it. Now, nah, fuck that, I ain't releasing that nigga White Lines to them, let them find their own goddamn artists. They wanna play hard, this is my mutha-fucking game! I run this rap shit. And my nigga Horse is gonna keep hittin' his hoe-ass sister!" Supreme vented.

"Supreme, come on, you know what this whole thing is about. It's about Horse, a black guy, messing with Angela, who's white," I explained as I tried to make sense of everything for 'Preme.

Supreme wasn't trying to hear anything.

I was supposed to be meeting him at the Gun Clap offices in Manhattan so that he and I could hang out later on that night. He was already there and I wasn't too far away. So after finding a place to park I made my way up to the office.

This time there was no drama from the receptionist or anyone else, as I was easily let into Horse's office. Supreme wasn't on any of the Gun Clap paperwork but he did have an office of his own which was adjacent to Horse's office. Supreme claimed to be the manager of many of Gun Clap's biggest artists, such as S&S. He really just held the title because he never actually did any of the work that a manager does. He would also give himself executive producer credits on most of the albums that Gun Clap recorded. Yet he never did any of the work of an executive producer. But because he held those titles, his having an office at Gun Clap's head-quarters could be justified.

I walked into Supreme's office and Horse and G-Baby were both sitting down. Supreme continued to rant and rave about how he had been disrespected.

"Hey baby," I said to Supreme as I gave him a kiss on his cheek. Supreme barely acknowledged me as I took it upon myself to take a seat next to G-Baby.

"Yo, word is bond! We need to call the team and tell them niggas to strap up. I'm ready to go see that punk-ass Paul to-night!" Supreme added.

G-Baby tried to be somewhat of a mediator as he spoke up and said, "What I say is we call the nigga man-to-man, get him on the phone and see if he switches up his tone and shows us some respect, and if not, if he's still talking greasy, then we bring it to his ass! I mean yeah, them cats is Mafia, but big damn deal, they still bleed red!"

"My nigga!" Supreme stated as he slapped G-Baby five. Horse was uncharacteristically quiet.

As a law enforcement official, I really couldn't just straight out condone violent acts, and if I had knowledge of a poten-tial act of violence I would have to notify my superiors and at-tempt to thwart it. I was just hoping that things wouldn't go that far.

"I hope I'm not talking out of turn or anything like that, but did anybody reach out to Angela because I think she might be able to shed some light on the whole situation," I said.

"Angela wasn't the one that disrespected me, her brother was!" Supreme stated. "Get his ass on the phone right now."

G-Baby spun the desk phone in his direction and put it on speaker as he looked up Paul's number in his cell phone. Once he found it he began dialing.

Everyone was silent as the phone rang about four times.

"Bitch-ass nigga, pick up the phone!" Supreme yelled into the room.

Almost on cue Paul picked up.

"Yeah," he said.

"Is this Paulie?" Supreme asked.

"Yeah this is Paulie, what's up?" Paul said in a cocky Italian street accent.

"Yo, my man, this is 'Preme. I had to get at you and let you know that I ain't appreciate you and that real bitch shit, calling my phone and talking reckless with that message you left."

"Listen, first off, I'm not your man. All right? That's first. And—"

"Whoa! Money, that's what I'm sayin', you a real disrespectful muthafucka! Let me let you know straight up, I don't care who your father is, and I don't care who y'all roll wit', you disrespected me, spittin' out threats so now I gotta bring it to you," Supreme stated.

"Supreme, you don't wanna fuck wit' me! You and your moolie friends might get respect in Harlem, or the South Bronx, or South Jamaica, Queens or whatever slum you come from with that rap shit. But that don't mean nothing to this white boy! You don't wanna fuck wit' me 'cause you will not win!" Paulie stated rather convincingly.

"Oh word? I tell you what. Your boy, White Lines, won't ever release a record on anybody's label. And that million dollars that I gave him, I'm not eatin' that as a loss, not when I got three million of your father's money to make up for the shit!" Supreme stated. "And my man is gonna keep breaking your sister off. What!"

"Okay, those are the rules that you wanna play by? No problem. But I promise you this, you fighting a war that you can't win. Dumb fucking nigger!" Paul said as he hung up his phone and ended the conversation.

Supreme then instructed Horse to call Gun Clap's lawyer and have him get the three million dollars of front money that they had put up wired back into their account. He also went on to say that after being disrespected the way he had been, there was no way that he was giving up the three million in cash that he had received from the Calvino crime family, money which was originally supposed to replace the three million that Gun Clap had put up to make everything look legit.

I sat and thought to myself how the marriage between the hip-hop world and the Mafia world that I had orchestrated, had to have been one of the shortest-lived marriages in history. And like most divorced couples I was sure that the breakup was definitely gonna be a bitter one.

"G-Baby, get everybody on the horn and tell them to stay strapped up and to keep on their Teflon 'cause we at war with the Calvinos!" 'Preme commanded.

CHAPTER SEVENTEEN

i'll never be able to understand how grown men can act and behave like such kids. The mob, Supreme, Horse, and all of those involved in this newly started war were sounding like grown bullies. A little more than a week had passed since the confrontational conversation between Supreme and the mob's Paul Jr. And during that time it was like the mob had let their guard down.

It was like Angela was the queen bee and all of the members of the mob were out to protect her honor or to show her father that they would guarantee the honor of the family name. We picked up so much conversation on our wiretaps about how Horse was gonna get his dick chopped off and stuffed in his mouth. We heard threats that the building that housed the Gun Clap headquarters should be blown up. We heard all kinds of things from these grown men who all sounded like seventh-grade bullies.

Out of all of the chatter that we heard on our wiretaps, there were two common themes that ran throughout all of the conversations. And that was the fact that Paulie Calvino

Sr. was pissed off that his daughter had been sexually soiled by a porch-monkey gangsta-rap nigger that went by the name of Horse. Horse had to die, there was just no question about that. The other theme was that they had to get back that three million dollars that they had anted up for Angela's record label. Supreme would have to die for his blatant disrespect of the Mafia and their money. But it was implied that Supreme shouldn't be killed until they got the money back.

On the other side, Gun Clap's side, there was the same type of talk. Everyone had loose lips and was talking about how much they didn't fear the mob and how they would bring it to the mob with no problem. In the eighties Supreme had run a Queens drug empire known as the Supreme Team. By late 2004 most of the Supreme Team was either dead or in jail, but there were still about fifty Supreme Team members in New York City who yielded a lot of power and still got a whole lot of money through many illegal methods. Money which the FBI believed but could never prove was constantly being laundered through Gun Clap Records.

Supreme and Horse made sure that they told everyone on the Supreme Team what was going down. And like the mob, the Supreme Team also had two constant themes that ran through the chatter that we had recorded. One of those themes was that the mob was not getting that three million dollars back. It was reimbursement money as well as money to pay for the blatant disrespect that had been shown by the mob. The other theme was that Gun Clap and the Supreme Team would wait and see what happened. They knew that the mob was gonna come at them but they were gonna wait for the mob to strike first before they made any moves.

The best thing for the FBI was that both sides were giving us all kinds of powerful information that would be devastating at a trial. Throughout everything, Supreme had been trying his best to get with me so that he could *hit it* again. But although being around him would provide the FBI with possibly more inside information than we would ever get on a wire, I had to start keeping my distance just a bit.

For one, my superiors didn't want me alone with Supreme out of fear that if the mob came after him I might get caught out there and lose my life if and when his killers came gunning for him. The other reason that I began to keep my distance was because I just couldn't put my life and my career at risk over some good sex. My fiancé was also in the back of my mind, but honestly, things between he and I were just about on the outs. The job that I had was a twenty-four/seven type of job, which left practically no time for family or friends or a fiancé.

So I began drawing away from Supreme and Horse in instances where I felt that I would be in a one-on-one situation with them. Instead I began trying to stay in contact with them strictly by phone. If, let's say, there was to be a record industry party or event, then I would have definitely been there. But my boss had made it perfectly clear that no matter what event, from now on I would have to be tailed by other agents just in case something erupted.

The whole setup was okay with me because I didn't want to be directly in harm's way either. My plan was to try and spend more time with Angela, if I could, and work the investigation from that end.

CHAPTER EIGHTEEN

*a*t like three in the morning my phone began ringing nonstop. I was so tired that it took me a
minute to gather my senses. When I finally
reached over and got ahold of the phone, I saw that it was my
supervisor, Andrew.

"Jessica, turn on your radio to 1010 WINS, the AM news
station. You won't believe this," he said.

As I scrambled to get up and turn on the light I kept asking
Andrew to tell me what was wrong.

"Andrew I can't get this station to come in clear, what's up?
What happened?"

"S&S, Tech-9, and their whole entourage of like seven
other people, including their bodyguards all just got killed
out in Los Angeles!" Andrew said with a raised voice.

That definitely woke me up and erased all of the groggi-
ness that I was feeling.

"Are you shitting me?" I asked.

"No, it's all over the news, but we got a call from the Los

Angeles office because of the way everything went down," Andrew explained.

"What do you think?"

"It's definitely the Calvinos' first strike. No doubt about that in my mind. But the media is saying that it has to do with an East Coast/West Coast rap rivalry. For our investigation's sake, it's good that the media is portraying it that way," Andrew stated.

"But what if it was retaliation by someone from Cell Block Records? I mean, Frank Nitty was killed and we caught Horse with the murder weapon. Even with him denying his involvement I gotta think that the people at Cell Block Records, a West Coast label, had to be waiting for one of Gun Clap's artists to come that way so they could retaliate," I reasoned.

"But Jessica, all of the witness accounts say that S&S and Tech-9 were leaving the club when a black Hummer pulled up and two gunmen with masks got out and sprayed their whole entourage. Now that sounds like it could be Cell Block behind that, but what happened next was that after the gunmen drove off, Tech-9 and S&S were hustled to their limo which wasn't parked too far off and when they got inside, the driver started the ignition ready to rush them to the hospital, and BOOM! The limo exploded!"

"Holy shit! That is a mob hit," I said.

"Exactly! These rap guys are not doing anything that sophisticated," Andrew explained.

"Listen, I'm gonna get on the horn right now and see what I can find out," I said to Andrew as I hung up.

See, S&S and Tech-9 were two major artists on Gun Clap's label. S&S was the more established artist with two multiplatinum albums under his belt and Tech-9 was the new artist who was just getting ready to release his new album, but many people were saying that his album sales would probably top those of S&S. But in any event, losing those two artists would definitely be a major blow to Gun Clap.

I immediately called Horse but I got no answer. I also called Supreme and I got no answer. I didn't leave a message for either one of them. I decided to just wait and call them back later. In the interim, I placed a call to Angela just to feel her out.

When she picked up the phone I could tell that she had been sound asleep.

"Angie, I know you were sleeping but I just wanted to see if you had heard about what happened," I stated.

Sounding as if she was adjusting herself in the bed, she asked in a sleepy voice, "Did I hear about what?"

"S&S and Tech-9 and their entourage just got killed out in LA," I said.

At that point I heard more moving around on Angela's end as she sounded more alive. "Oh my God. Jessica, is Horse okay?" Angela asked, sounding as if she had genuine concern.

"As far as I know he's okay, but I haven't been able to get in touch with him," I said.

"Yeah, me either, he hasn't been returning my calls. Jessica, this whole record label thing has gotten so blown out of proportion it's not even real! I'm sick over the whole thing. My father is sick about his money. My brother is sick about Supreme disrespecting him. White Lines is sick about his whole deal falling apart. It's just crazy," Angela said as she began to wake up a bit.

"So what exactly happened?" Angela asked as she sort of switched subjects.

"I don't know. One of the models called me and told me about it. She said that it was all over the radio," I said, stretching the truth just a bit for obvious reasons.

"Jessica, I just hope that Horse is okay. Oh gosh, this is so crazy," Angela said, sounding stressed.

"Listen, Angie, I just wanted to tell you. I mean sorry to be waking you up with that kind of news but . . ."

"No, thank you for telling me. Look, I gotta go. I'll catch up with you later," Angela said as we hung up the phone and departed ways.

I immediately tried Supreme's cell phone to see if I could get him. His phone rang three times and this time he answered.

"What?" 'Preme asked in a tone that said he was way past pissed off.

I knew that I had to play things off to ease the tension. "'Preme, thank God you're all right. I heard what happened and I didn't know if you was hurt or what. Is Horse okay?" I asked.

"Yeah, yeah, Horse is good."

"What about G-Baby? Is he okay?" I asked, trying to come across as genuine as possible.

"Yeah, all my niggas is good, they here wit' me right now," 'Preme said. As he was talking I could hear somebody ranting and raving in the background. It sounded like Horse but I wasn't sure.

"Yo, who dat? Is that Jessica?" the person in the background asked.

The next thing I knew the phone was taken from Supreme and I was now talking to Horse. And he was as vexed as I'd ever heard him.

"This Jessica?" he screamed.

"Horse, I'm so sorry about what happened out there in LA. Thank God you and 'Preme and everybody is all right. I called as soon as I heard," I explained.

"Jessica, you don't know. This ain't a fucking game! They killed my mans and 'em!" Horse vented as he paused for a minute to breathe real hard into the phone. He then continued. "Yo, where you at right now?" he asked.

"I'm in my house. I—"

Horse cut me off. "You calling from your house phone or your cell phone?" Horse asked.

"My cell. Why?"

"A'ight listen. Stay with me on this phone and I need you to grab your house phone and dial my cell phone right now," Horse instructed.

"Huh?" I asked as I was trying my hardest to figure out where Horse was going with his instructions.

"Jessica, you heard what I said! Do the shit right now!"

"Okay, okay," I said as I retrieved my home phone and dialed Horse's cell phone.

"Yo, pick that up and make sure she don't hang up," Horse instructed someone.

"Horse, what is this all about?" I asked.

"Jessica," Horse said in a low, calm, but serious tone. "I'm gonna ask you something right now, and I don't need you to play games wit' me. 'Cause if you play games wit' me I'm gonna know that you had something to do with this and I swear on my son's life that I will murder you before the sun comes up!"

My heart began to race because I didn't know what Horse was gonna ask me.

"What?" I said in a nervous tone.

"When I ask you this, Jessica, if you do anything other than give me a straight-up answer or if you hang up either one of your phones, I'm not playing, you will not live to see the light of day! You hear me!" Horse roared.

"Yes, I hear you. Horse, you are really scaring me. What's up?"

"What's up is that my people is laying dead and shot the fuck up and blown the fuck up out in LA and I know them Italian cats is behind this shit. And guess what? Since yo' ass introduced me to them I'm holding you the fuck responsible unless you give me Angela's address right now!" Horse commanded.

"Horse—" I said as I was cut off immediately.

"Ain't no need to say my name! Just give me the goddamn address right now and don't hang up these phones!"

Horse had really backed me into a corner and I didn't know what to do or what to say.

"Jessica, you are taking way too long with this shit!" Horse yelled. I sat and wanted to kick myself for having even called Supreme and Horse to check on them. *Why didn't I just wait until the next day to follow up with them?* I thought to myself.

"Give me the goddamn address!" Horse screamed like he was insane.

"One-five-one-dash-four-nine Eighty-third Street," I regretfully said, hoping that would get me off of the phone.

"Yo, kid, one-five-one-dash-four-nine Eighty-third Street," Horse yelled out. After which I heard all kinds of moving and rumbling going on the background.

"Jessica, don't hang up the phone, don't hang up none of the phones. You gotta stay on this phone with me until my people go verify this address you just gave me."

There was a pause on the phone. And I didn't know if Horse was serious or not but I was just thankful that I had not given a fake address.

"Horse come on!" I said.

"What the fuck you mean, *come on?*" Horse asked.

I sighed and didn't say a thing.

"My people are coming from southside, it ain't gonna take no time for them to get there. Just hold on the phone and talk to me," Horse instructed.

"Horse, why don't you just give everything time to play itself out? I mean I know the whole label thing fell apart, but what happened to S&S and Tech-9, that could have been anybody who did that," I said in a desperate attempt to prevent things from getting totally out of control.

"Fuck that! Them cats had something to do wit' this," Horse screamed. "You ain't gotta say nothing, just don't hang up and you'll be a'ight. And that address better be good. Word is bond!"

I held on both lines and neither one of us said a word to each other for about ten minutes. During that time I could hear Horse talking to Supreme. I also heard him taking a piss in the bathroom and at steady intervals I heard him inhaling and exhaling as if he was smoking weed or a cigarette.

"A'ight, let me ask her," Horse yelled to someone.

"Yo, Angela's crib, is it a white brick crib with a Denali that be parked in the driveway?" Horse asked me.

"Yes that's it. But Horse, please listen to—" Horse cut me off.

"Yeah, she saying that's the crib. Tell them niggas to light that shit up!" Horse barked as he abruptly hung up both phones.

CHAPTER NINETEEN

hen the morning television news shows came on there were two main stories that were being reported. One was the deaths of the two Gun Clap recording artists and their entourages, and the other lead story, which seemed as if it was getting bigger attention than the hip-hop deaths, was the story which centered around the early morning drive-by shooting of the home of reputed mob boss Paulie Calvino.

Apparently Horse had dispatched his team of thugs to shoot up the home of Paulie Calvino. And according to the early news reports it appeared that whoever conducted the shooting meant business. It was estimated that close to two hundred rounds of ammunition had been unleashed on the home that Paulie Calvino shared with his family.

I listened intently as one reporter spoke with a high-ranking police official.

"It appears that whoever conducted this shooting meant to do harm to the occupants inside and at the very least they wanted to send a message. With the high-powered guns that were used such as M-16s and Calicos, it's clear that the message that they were trying to send was a message of power," the police official said.

This is way out of control, I thought to myself.

My supervisor thought the exact same thing. He called me and had me on a conference call with his boss, the head of the organized crime unit, as well as the head of the New York FBI.

"Jessica, we have to pull the plug on this whole thing. It's gotten way out of control," my supervisor's boss told me.

I didn't want the investigation to end but I also didn't want to come across as confrontational.

"Well, we got enough to connect Paulie Calvino to the money laundering scheme. We can connect Supreme and Horse to that as well. And my direct testimony can link Horse to this drive-by shooting. I understand the need to want to end the investigation but I really think that if we wait we can get Paulie Calvino on a wire conspiring to commit murder, especially now after his home was violated," I said.

All of the bosses felt that I had done my job in an exceptional manner. I had managed to link two worlds together like no one would have ever dreamed up. We had gathered enough evidence on both Supreme and Horse that we felt would stand up in a courtroom. So for me to stay on in an undercover role would only jeopardize my safety as well as prolong the feud between the Gun Clap participants and the Calvino participants.

Fortunately for me, the New York head of the FBI was more of a risk taker and a realist. He spoke up and stated, "If we completely pull Jessica right now, that might set off all kinds of red flags and it could actually blow the investigation.

She has to stay on, for at least another month. She needs to be somewhat visible because after all, she was the common denominator to both sides. And if Jessica thinks we can get Paulie Calvino Senior on conspiring to commit murder, if we can get him in his own words, then that is what will stick in court. We've been down this legal road with this guy before, and nothing was ever able to stick, so I say it's worth a try."

As we prepared to end the conversation, I thought of just the right thing to do in order to send Paulie Calvino Sr. right over the edge. And I was sure that if I proposed my idea to Supreme that they would love it and jump at it. It would also go a long way in helping to keep me in good graces with them.

CHAPTER TWENTY

a few days had passed since the drive-by shooting had occurred. I spoke to Angela and she told me that her father was sending her to Miami for a few weeks so that she would be out of harm's way *while the family handled things.*

So with Angela out of town I felt that it was the perfect time to strike and try to sell my plan to Supreme. I hadn't spoken to Supreme or Horse since the night of the shooting so I wasn't certain how receptive they would be to interacting with me.

I called Supreme from my home phone and after he picked up I asked him if it would be okay if I put him on hold and three-wayed Horse.

"Yeah, what's up ma'? Everything good?" 'Preme asked.

"Yeah, everything is good I just wanted to bring up something while I had both of y'all on the phone, that's all. Hold on a minute," I instructed.

I dialed Horse's cell phone and while the phone was ringing I conferenced the call so that all three of us were able to hear each other.

"What's up, Horse? This is Jessica. I got 'Preme on the other line," I stated.

"A'ight. What's good?" Horse asked. "'Preme, what up, baby pa?"

"What up, nigga? What's the deal?" Supreme replied.

"Listen, I just wanted to let both of y'all know that I realize that I'm the one that introduced Angela to Gun Clap. And I feel real bad about that. I mean it's like I'm blaming myself for what happened to S&S and Tech-9. I don't really know all of the ins and outs of everything as far as what exactly is behind the drama and beef. But I just want to go on record with both of y'all right here, right now, and let y'all know that if it's a matter of choosing sides, then for me there really ain't no choice, I'm definitely siding with y'all and I'm definitely riding with y'all," I said, as I was trying my best to come across as convincingly as possible.

"That's what's up," Supreme commented.

"Word, that's peace right there," Horse stated as he added, "I knew how you was riding when you gave me Angela's address and it wasn't a phony address."

"Okay, I'm just putting it out there because I know how easily signals can get crossed when there's beef," I added.

"But Jessica, I thought Angela was your girl, why you not riding wit' her?" Supreme asked.

I had come prepared for that question as I said, "Well, I'm just keeping it real. Angela told me how she was sick over the whole thing and she told me how her brother was sick about the fact that y'all disrespected him and—"

Supreme cut me off, "Yo, ain't nobody disrespect that nigga! That nigga is the one that called my phone talking reckless! Fuck that nigga! Punk ass!"

"'Preme, I know. I know. And that's what I told Angela. I told her that her brother was the one talking out of turn and talking out of his face and that if anything he needed to be a man and step up and apologize and everyone could just move on from there." I lied with a straight face that they could not see through the phone.

"Exactly!" Horse added.

I wanted to play up my position even more, so I continued on. "Yeah and when I was telling her that, her arrogant ass had the nerve to tell me to shut the hell up and that I was so stupid and that I didn't know nothing."

I paused and then I added, "It's like she thinks her and her family are some kind of gods or something that can't be wrong. She acts like they can't be touched. And after her house got shot up I told her that she really needed to end the whole thing because she and her family obviously weren't untouchable. And man, when I said that she cursed me out and called me a nigger lover and all kind of twisted talk."

"Nigger lover?" Horse asked. "She acting like you ain't black or something."

I sidestepped his question and to cover myself I added, "But with Angela, she is such a loose cannon, I bet you she'll be calling me later and talking to me like everything is cool between me and her."

"Nigger lover! Yo, 'Preme, you see how these white chicks do? I know Angela was really feeling me. It wasn't just about no music business. She was really feeling me, but look how quick she's switching up sides on a nigga," Horse stated.

"What y'all really need to do to get at the Calvinos is do what y'all do best. Just make good music and put out a dis record. And what I was thinking is I could get one of the girls from the agency that looks like Angela and we could get the best makeup artist to make her look even more like Angela and put her in the video just being totally disrespected. I think a single like that would sell off the shelves, especially if the video was hot," I instigated.

Supreme and Horse both agreed with me and were enthusiastic about the suggestion. Horse promised to put his all into lacing the track with one of the best beats he'd ever created and they figured that they would get their up-and-coming star, a rapper who went by the name of Black Chris to rhyme on the record. They hadn't thought about it until I brought the idea to them but it would be the perfect way to promote their artist and recharge life into Gun Clap Records, especially after the death of their two biggest acts.

I just loved being the instigator that I was. Being that double person helped to keep my juices flowing.

CHAPTER TWENTY-ONE

a little less than a month had passed since I had suggested the idea to Horse and Supreme about making the dis record. During that time the investigation had sort of hit a lull. From the FBI's standpoint we couldn't understand why there had been no retaliation from the Calvinos toward Gun Clap after the home of Paulie Calvino Sr. had been totally violated. And in addition to that, the three million dollars had not been returned to the Calvinos and that was more than enough reason for vengeance.

We knew that an act of revenge would follow but we just did not know when. So during that lull time, my interactions with Horse and Supreme had been somewhat limited. Instead of interacting directly with Horse and Supreme on a daily basis, I had filled most of my days conducting surveillance with a team of agents. We followed Paulie Calvino Senior and Junior, along with many of the Calvino captains and soldiers. We also followed Horse, Supreme, and many of the Gun Clap and Supreme Team associates.

Our thinking was that if any acts of violence or revenge were to break out we wanted to be right there to squash it and to have a *caught red-handed* excuse to arrest somebody. But unfortunately for us there was nothing but uncharacteristic silence from both sides. It was sort of like a truce or something had been declared. So we just waited patiently for something to happen. Because as they say in the streets, we knew that it was just a matter of time before something *jumped off*.

The only exciting part of that month-long stretch was the night that I'd spent at the Gun Clap Records Manhattan recording studio, which was nicknamed, of all things, *The Crack House*.

I had been invited to the studio in order to hear the live recording of the dis record which hadn't yet been released to any of the radio stations. The video for the song was gonna be shot two days later so I had wanted to hear the song just to get a feel for it so that I would know which girls from the modeling agency would be the best to use in the video.

I arrived at the recording studio at two in the morning and after being buzzed in, I made my way to the tenth floor where I entered a studio that was literally packed wall-to-wall with thugs. The air was thick with weed smoke as guys stood arm-to-arm bobbing their heads to the sounds of the loud hip-hop music and drinking all types of brown liquors.

There were about six guys that looked like professional wrestlers clad in Teflon bulletproof vests who were posted in different parts of the studio. As I attempted to walk near Horse who was seated at the mixing board and Supreme who was standing a few feet away from him, I was violently stopped by one of the bald-headed, Zeus-looking, bulletproof-wearing bodyguards.

"Yo, it's cool! Shorty's a'ight! She here to see me," Supreme stated to the bodyguard.

The bodyguard eased his monster-tight grip of my arm and let me walk pass.

"Mmm Wa," I said as I reached up on my tippy toes and gave Supreme a kiss on the cheek.

"What's up, Horse?" I said as I looked for a place to sit among the thugs.

"What up, baby? We making history up in here tonight!" Horse shouted as he gestured for me to come have a seat next to him on one of the stools.

"Is this the track?" I asked.

Horse nodded his head as he turned up the volume so that I could get a better listen. "That shit is hot as hell right?" Horse asked.

"Horse, that beat is off the hook!" I genuinely replied. "You are gonna kill them with this one."

"Jessica, you want some E and J or some Cask and Cream?" one of the thugs asked. I didn't remember having ever seen him before so I was surprised that he knew my name.

Liquor was one of my weaknesses so I immediately gave in to the request.

"Oh hell yeah! Pour me some of that Cask and Cream," I responded. Before I knew it a large red plastic cup had been handed to me and Cask and Cream was quickly poured to the rim.

I quickly began to drink down the smooth drink and I noticed that I was not the only chick in the studio. There were about five well-developed sisters walking around who looked like they had just came from an underground strip club or something. They too were dancing and moving their bodies to the music, only they were doing it as if they were looking for someone to tip them.

"Let me get some of that E and J, baby," I said as I held out my cup for a refill.

"Goddamn ma ma! I ain't know you drink like that," the same thug said to me. He suddenly appeared cuter to me than he had before I had gulped down my first cup of Cask and Cream. "You better be careful mixing drinks like that," he warned.

"I'll be fine. I'm a big girl," I stated as the cute thug chuckled to himself.

"Horse, can you let me hear the lyrics?" I asked.

"No doubt. Matter of fact you gonna hear Black spit this shit live," Horse stated as he instructed Black Chris to go inside the booth.

As Black Chris made his way inside the booth, I tried my best to guzzle the E&J as that demon had once again crept inside of me and was enticing me to *hurry up and get drunk.*

The name of the dis song was "The Hit." And some of the lyrics went something to the effect of: *"you ain't a real don / all that Mafia shit is a con / you a fake a faggot a phony a pussy! / Horse ran up in your daughter—left her moist and mushy / You ain't a real don / all that Mafia shit is a con / Horse be that don / that new Godfather—Yeah he hard / got Angie on tape screaming oh God / yes daddy yes / potnah, you ain't a real don / all that Mafia shit is a con / my man hit your daughter so you put a hit out on my man / it's a'ight though / 'cause that hit cost you some dough / three mil' to be exact /*

we might give you some to get your house intact from when them shells
went blaadat blaadat / next time you and your crew will get your wigs
push back / you ain't a real don / All that mafia shit is a con!"

"I'm feeling that! I like that!" I said as I continued to down my E&J. "They are gonna be so vexed when they hear this song," I stated as Black Chris continued to rhyme.

I was definitely beginning to feel nice from the liquor. I began to talk real hyped and excited.

"Do you remember that video that Biggie did back in the days when he dissed Faith Evans? He had that chick that looked like Faith and he was throwing her out of the house and throwing her clothes out in the street! You remember that, right?" I asked in a real loud voice.

All of the thugs that were within earshot of my voice nodded their heads up and down and chuckled and smiled as they puffed on their blunts.

" 'Preme you remember that, right?"

"No doubt!" Supreme responded.

"What would be crazy is if in the video y'all do a scene at a club or somewhere that Horse is performing or Black Chris is performing and we could have the only white chick in the crowd who looks just like Angela . . . Right . . . And she would be looking like a real groupie, and have Horse scope her out in the crowd and he could tell his man to go find out who she is and invite her backstage. And when she's backstage we could have a scene where Horse and all of the Gun Clap cats is running a train on her and when it's over y'all could throw her out in the street with no clothes on. And just throw her a T-shirt or something for her to barely cover herself up with!

Tell me that wouldn't be hot!" I shouted as I stood up and held up my hand so that Horse could give me a high-five.

I wasn't a video director or anything like that, but I must have struck a chord because everybody was feeling my idea.

"Yeah, hell yeah, I'm feeling that shit. Do you got the chicks to pull it off?" Horse asked.

"Where's that E and J?" I asked as I disregarded Horse's question. My only concern was refilling my now-empty cup of liquor.

"Of course I do! But I definitely got the perfect girl to play Angela's role. Don't worry. I got y'all, I'm gonna hold y'all down!" I stated in an attempt to sound as down as ever.

"Keep spitti,' Black Chris! I'm feeling you!" I yelled as I held my drink up in the air and moved my body to the sound of the music.

As I danced I could tell that the other black girls must have been wondering to themselves who in the hell I was. But all of my inhibitions were gone due to the liquor and I continued to draw attention to myself. I knew that there was no way in the world that Horse or Supreme or anyone for that matter could have any questions or doubts in their minds now as far as me being a cop or a fed.

The beat continued to blast in the background and everyone was having a good ole time and Supreme came up to me and whispered in my ear.

"I got that Snoop for you," he said.

At first I wasn't sure what he was talking about. I thought that he might have been talking about a Snoop Dogg record or something. But when I looked at him and noticed that he was holding his hand open and down around his upper thigh, that's when I noticed the ecstasy pills that had the engraving of the Snoopy cartoon character.

I didn't want to show an immediate reaction so I just kept dancing with my drink still hoisted up in the air. I looked at 'Preme and slowly rocked my head up and down to let him know that I knew what he was talking about. I was more than tempted, especially considering that I'd never seen an opportunity to get high for free which I'd easily passed up. But I knew that I had to be extremely careful because there were a number of agents staked out outside of the studio as part of the surveillance.

With Supreme being the opportunist that he was, he took it upon himself to pass me one of the E pills as he pulled on his blunt. So with the liquor talking to me and with the influence of the entire atmosphere of weed and loud music, I once again readily gave in to my weakness and quickly popped the E pill into my mouth.

I'll be okay, I convinced myself. *I'll be able to maintain and none of the other agents will even know that I've been drinking.*

"So when is this gonna hit the radio?" I asked in my intoxicated state.

Horse looked at me and held up four fingers. "In about four days I'm personally dropping it off to Funkmaster Flex."

I nodded my head and then resumed dancing to the music. The E pill was starting to take effect as that feeling of euphoria was overtaking my body. I felt like opening up my wallet and just throwing money at people because that was how happy and carefree I was starting to feel.

"I'm sorry, I don't even remember your name," I said to the

cute guy that had poured me the liquor when I first arrived at the studio.

"O-Water," he replied.

I couldn't help but laugh. Although there was nothing funny, the liquor and the E pill just made me feel all giggly and happy.

"What the fuck is so funny?" O-Water asked.

"Nothing. I'm sorry. I didn't mean to laugh like that. But O-Water, do you see how foul your man is? I came in and you was real polite and asked me if I wanted a drink and all that. But 'Preme been over there pulling on that blunt the whole time I been here and he still ain't offer me none. You see how he treats me like shit?" I said in a joking manner as I began hugging on O-Water.

Supreme looked over at the two of us and he didn't say anything. He just gave O-Water a quick head nod and a smirk.

"I gotchu, love," O-Water stated as he took me by the hand and led me to another room that was in a secluded part of the studio.

When we arrived at the other room I noticed two of the stripper-looking girls that had been parading around were in the room giving a blowjob to one of the thugs that I didn't know. O-Water quickly spread out some coke on a small table and he prepared some lines for me to snort.

"Don't ever say that I ain't take care of you," O-Water said as he sat at the small square table. "Sit down," he urged as the guy moaned in ecstasy in the background.

I sat down and although I was feeling extremely good, I only snorted one line of coke.

"You don't want no more?" O-Water asked.

I didn't respond verbally. I just stared at him and smiled with my right elbow on the table and the palm of my right hand cupped underneath my chin.

"What's up?" he asked.

I still didn't respond. I just stared into O-Water's eyes as the two girls continued to give the blowjob on the other side of the room.

At that point O-Water stood up and began massaging my shoulders. That instantly got me wet. And before long his hands were down my shirt and cupping my breasts. Before I knew what was what, I had my pants down around my ankles and I was bent over the table and O-Water was sexing me from behind.

The sex felt good, but it wasn't as good as it had been with Supreme. I enjoyed every stroke though. I also remember thinking to myself, *Jessica, this is an investigation, what the hell are you doing?*

CHAPTER TWENTY-TWO

a week had passed since my sexual encounter with O-Water at the recording studio. And while my superiors didn't have any idea of what I had done with O-Water, Supreme, or about my drug use, I didn't need the stress and worry that I had to lug around in the days following my little drug and sex escapade.

I had to constantly cover my tracks because I never knew what an agent was likely to hear on one of the wiretaps. I mean, suppose O-Water and Supreme were on tape talking about how they both banged my back out or something? Or what if they were caught talking about the coke that I'd snorted? How would I explain that?

The truth of the matter was that there wouldn't really be any way to explain my actions, but I began walking around with fake grams of cocaine and fake ecstasy pills. If my superiors ever brought me in for surprise questioning I would attempt to cover my tracks by showing it and explaining that in certain circumstances I would act like I was snorting coke or popping E pills in order to boost my credibility among those that I was investigating but that I was only ingesting harmless look-alike drugs. I figured that doing that would be better than just denying the drug use. But regardless of my schemes to cover up my actions, I knew that a simple drug test would easily have busted me, so I vowed to myself, like I had done a million times before, to never have another drink and to never touch a drug of any kind. And I especially vowed to myself not to sex any more of the people that I was supposed to be trying to lock up!

The music video had been successfully shot and it was scheduled to be aired on MTV and BET within the next couple of days. But in the interim, Horse had delivered the single to all of the radio stations in the New York, New Jersey, and Connecticut tri-state area. Needless to say, "The Hit" was a smash hit. It was getting heavy airplay on all of the radio stations and it had instantly created a buzz that spread like wildfire.

All of the local newspapers began running stories about the Mafia being hip-hop's newest enemy. Many reporters also began writing stories that questioned if there had ever really been an East Coast/West Coast war in hip-hop or if the Mafia had been the one warring with hip-hop all along. And of course came the swirling allegations that drug money wasn't what had funded Gun Clap records, rather it was Mafia money that had funded the label.

So now all eyes were on hip-hop and from the FBI's standpoint, we wondered if that would cause a delay in the Calvinos inevitable act of retaliation. We didn't know for sure so we just had to sit and wait.

But our wait was short lived.

Gun Clap Records, like all of the major hip-hop labels, had sponsored a team to play in the famed Entertainers Basketball Classic at Rucker Park which was held every year on the Polo Grounds up in Harlem.

Seventy-two hours after the dis song had hit the radio, Gun Clap Records' team, which included NBA stars Stephon Marbury and Vince Carter was scheduled to play in the EBC championship game against Fat Joe's Terror Squad which included NBA star Rafer "Skip-To-My-Lou" Alston and megastar Lebron James.

The stands surrounding the basketball court were full to capacity. The entire park was rammed with people. It was so packed that there were people who had climbed into trees just to get a glimpse of the action that was taking place on the court. The streets were also packed with cars and people. Many of the big names in hip-hop were present. But without a doubt everyone had come to see the two teams get it on.

I was excited and happy to be personally invited to escort Supreme to the game. I sat on the bench along on the sidelines and I watched as Supreme and Horse barked orders to the players on the court as Fat Joe's smash hit song "Lean Back" rang out throughout the speakers that were placed near and around the court.

"Yo turn that shit off! No disrespect, Joe, but everybody

wants to hear that new joint 'The Hit.' Am I right?" Supreme asked the crowd as he spoke into the microphone that was reserved for the commentator.

The crowd's thunderous and enthusiastic response showed that they did indeed wanna hear the new hit song.

The DJ immediately switched up the song. And as soon as the beat dropped, it was like every person in the park had lost their minds as everyone went into a frenzy. The song had just hit the radio but yet it was like everyone knew the lyrics. Horse and Supreme smiled and bopped their heads up and down as Supreme turned up his bottle of Kristal and began guzzling it like a true baller.

All the while the game was still taking place. People had stopped paying attention to the game for a moment as they danced and partied to the new hit record. And just as people were really beginning to enjoy themselves and the close game that was being played, rapid gunfire erupted from what sounded like every direction.

"Get down, get down!" Supreme yelled to me as he, Horse, and I ducked for cover.

"Who the fuck is shooting?" Horse asked.

I didn't catch any reply from Supreme, as all I could hear was the loud sound of people yelling and screaming and running.

"We gotta get outta here!" Horse nervously yelled to Supreme.

"Oh shit!" Supreme yelled back. "Nah, stay right here, just stay down. Niggas is shooting from off the rooftops of the projects!" Supreme informed.

It didn't take much of a brain to figure out that Supreme

and Horse had to have been the target of what appeared to be an unprovoked shooting. And I knew that if they were the targets then I had to quickly get my black ass up off of that park cement.

I got up and quickly bolted without saying a word to Supreme or Horse. At that point I could hear police sirens coming from every direction and I quickly got lost in the sea of running people. I was just hoping not to fall and get trampled to death and I was hoping that I didn't get shot.

The gunfire seemed like it would never stop so I kept running until I reached 145th Street and Amsterdam Avenue. There I ducked into a store and quickly called Andrew, my supervisor.

"Jessica, are you okay?" he asked.

"Yes, I'm okay," I replied as I breathed real heavy into the phone.

"What the hell happened out there?" he asked.

"I don't know. They turned on that new song, and all hell just broke loose after that! But listen, I lost contact with everybody and just bolted out of there. I need you to come pick me up. I'm on the corner of Amsterdam and One hundred forty-fifth Street," I stated.

My supervisor told me that he was only five minutes away. He had been nearby on surveillance, hoping to get a glimpse of one of the Calvinos or their associates.

When Andrew arrived I quickly scanned my surroundings, hoping that no one would see me entering the black Jeep Cherokee with dark tinted windows.

Once in the backseat, I didn't even acknowledge the other male agent in the front passenger seat—he looked like he was from that school of male agents that didn't respect female agents.

"You think that was the Calvinos?" I asked Andrew.

The other agent butted in. "That was definitely niggers with a capital N who were responsible for that. It had nigger written all over it!" The agent said as he chuckled.

Andrew chimed in, "I agree, I mean it seemed planned but it was sort of random, like anyone could have been a target. I think that if anything, the Calvinos were behind it and they probably just paid someone to do the shooting for them. It would be a cold day in hell before they would troop to the projects in Harlem during broad daylight to engage in a shooting."

I figured that Andrew was probably right. But as the evening quickly approached and things relating to the shooting began to unravel, everyone could see that the shooting had definitely been Calvino influenced.

Three people had been wounded during the shootout, and all three were Gun Clap and Supreme Team associates. Horse and Supreme had managed to escape injury but G-Baby was not as fortunate. Or at least that was the rumor that had quickly begun to swirl. Apparently, during the melee, G-Baby, who had been standing on the sidelines of the basketball court with everyone else watching the game, had been kidnapped by someone and was being held in an undisclosed location.

Kidnapping was definitely a Mafia practice.

The Calvinos had struck back. Now it was time to see how Gun Clap would respond.

CHAPTER TWENTY-THREE

*a*ndrew and I and a team of four other special agents listened in intently as Supreme, Horse, and what seemed like the entire Supreme Team and Gun Clap camps spoke back and forth on their cell phones.

From what we could make out, no one had heard from G-Baby nor had anyone seen him since the shots rang out a few hours ago in the park. But one thing was certain, and that was that at least four people had given both Supreme and Horse their word that they'd seen someone hit G-Baby over the head with a champagne bottle which knocked him out cold before snatching him up and carrying him off to an all-black 600 Mercedez-Benz that had dark tinted windows.

"Word is bond, player! Shonnie with the big ass told me that G-Baby was running for cover with the whole crowd and some cat stepped up from out of nowhere and just snuffed him with a champagne bottle and dropped him!" Supreme repeated through his cell phone for what had to have been his tenth time telling the story.

"She said it looked like some Brooklyn niggas who did it. And after they dropped him, two cats scooped him up and threw him in the Benz and sped off toward the FDR Drive," Supreme continued on.

"Brooklyn niggas?" the unidentified male asked Supreme.

"Yeah, but I know them fucking Italian cats is behind this shit!" 'Preme stated.

"So what's deal, what y'all niggas wanna do? I'm ready for whatever. Just give me the word," the unidentified male assured Supreme.

"Well yo, we at the office right now. It's like fifty niggas deep up in this joint. Come meet us 'cause we ain't decided on nothing yet but if shit jumps off you'll be right here wit' us," Supreme stated.

The guy gave Supreme his word that he would meet them at the Gun Clap headquarters within the hour and their conversation ended. The end of the phone conversation meant that we, the FBI, were now in the dark. See, without me physically present around Supreme and Horse to get information, we had to rely strictly on the different wires that we had. So when no one was on the phones we were in the dark.

I quickly came up with an idea to try and get close to Supreme. I didn't wanna run the idea by my boss because I knew that he might object, but I just had to get physically closer to the action. I went with my gut and right there on the spot I began dialing Supreme's telephone number.

"Quiet everybody, we got something," my boss yelled to all of us in the room, not yet knowing that it was me who was dialing 'Preme.

"Yo!" Supreme stated in his usual manner of answering the phone. "Who dis?" he asked.

At that point I held up my index finger to my mouth and indicated for everyone in the room to be quiet.

" 'Preme, thank God I got you on the phone!" I stated, trying my best to come across like I was stressed.

"Jessica?" 'Preme asked with his deep voice.

"Yeah it's me. Oh my God! Listen, I wanted to call you but the cops had scooped me up in all of the craziness that happened after the shooting. And then they had to take me to the emergency room to check out my leg," I lied.

"What the fuck? Don't tell me you got hurt! I had seen you next to me and the next thing I know you was gone!" 'Preme recounted.

I blew air into the phone for dramatic effect before adding, "Yeah I was just so nervous with the gunshots and I saw G-Baby start to run and my instincts just told me to run with him. So he was running ahead of me and he didn't know I was following behind him 'cause he was about twenty feet ahead of me. And while I'm running it was like from left field or something this guy just whacked G-Baby in the head with a bottle and—"

"Wait! Hold up! You saw that shit too?" 'Preme asked me.

"Yes! I was right there!" I emphasized.

"Yo, this is Jessica on the phone. She saying she saw G-Baby get dropped," Supreme yelled, informing the people around him.

"Jessica, we can't get in touch with the nigga. He ain't picking up his phone. You sure it was him who got hit?"

" 'Preme, I'm telling you it was him!" I stressed. I was pretty confident that the G-Baby rumors were true so I ran with it to my advantage. And for my sake, those rumors had better been true.

"So who was it that did it?" 'Preme asked.

"That's the thing. I would be lying if I said I know for sure. But it was definitely three guys. One guy hit him and two other guys picked him up and ran off with him. I was trying to keep up with them after they picked him up but with all of the shots ringing out I couldn't. Then I tripped and when I got up my knee gave out on me. And I guess because I was one of the only girls out there at the time or something, I was able to flag down a cop in all of the madness and I told them what happened and I got in their car and we sped off looking for the guys that had run off with G-Baby. But to be honest I wasn't even sure what their car looked like, I just knew that it was a black car so we went speeding off looking for a black car but we didn't find one," I said in one long breath, hoping that I was coming across believably.

Supreme was about to say something else but I cut him off and asked him where exactly he was at.

"We in the office trying to sort this whole shit out," he stated.

"Listen, I'm not that far. I'll come by in like twenty minutes and I'll finish telling you what the cops were saying and I'll tell you what happened with my knee," I said.

"A'ight no doubt. We here. One!"

With that I hung up the phone and faced a roomful of shocked-looking overworked agents.

"What?" I asked.

"Jessica, are you out of your fucking mind?" Andrew screamed at me. "What if G-Baby wasn't kidnapped, what if none of those other stories that were relayed back to Horse and Supreme turn out to be true? Do you know what kind of position that'll put you in?"

I didn't have time to sit and listen to that. My job as an undercover agent was risky as hell and I knew that. But I also knew that at times I just had to go with my gut instincts and trust that. And my gut was telling me that the G-Baby rumors were true so I ran with it.

"I'll be okay. Trust me on this," I said as I grabbed the keys to Andrew's Cherokee and proceeded to exit the office.

"I need to borrow your car. I'll be back as soon as I can."

"I swear to Christ that you must be a goddamn man 'cause you have some pair of balls!" Andrew yelled as I walked out of the office.

CHAPTER TWENTY-FOUR

*t*o help play things off, I had called Trina, who was one of the models that worked with my White Chocolate modeling agency and asked her if she would ride with me over to the record company and she agreed. On the way there I had filled her in on all of the events that had transpired at Rucker Park and I also made sure to tell her my fake story about how I'd seen G-Baby get smashed in the head with the bottle.

Trina told me that aside from hearing on the news about what had happened at the park, that her cell phone had been blowing up all evening long with different industry people gossiping about what had gone down and about how G-Baby had apparently been kidnapped.

Trina lived in the Lower East Side, so picking her up didn't delay our arrival to the record company by that much. But by the time we had arrived at the Gun Clap headquarters there had apparently been a major development which had oc-curred in the hour or so that it had taken me to get there. It was quickly evident that no one would even care about what the cops had supposedly said to me or what had supposedly happened to my injured knee.

As Trina and I walked into the large conference room, I noticed that the room was packed with guys standing around while some sat in the plush high-backed leather chairs that encircled the long mahogany table. A few of the guys spoke to me and Trina, but regardless of how attractive the two of us might have looked, pussy was the furthest thing from the minds of the guys in the room.

"Yo, I don't give a fuck, we paying the goddamn money!" Supreme shouted at Horse as I tried to decipher just what the hell was going on.

There was a lot of rumbling and talking going on in the room and Horse looked as pissed off as I had ever seen him. He paused and looked at everybody in the room before cursing and demanding that everyone shut up and show him, as he so eloquently put it, "some muthafuckin' respect!"

There was quickly dead silence in the room.

Horse deliberately said nothing until he finally broke his silence and said, "Nah, fuck that! I ain't budging. Them niggas is bluffing, they ain't gonna kill 'im. And 'Preme, I thought you was straight gangsta so whatchu mean we should give them the money?"

"First of all nigga, don't ever question my gangsta! A'ight? I'm just saying that that's my man that they holding and if they want the dough, then we give them the dough and we lose this battle but that's our man they holding! If it was you we would give up ten, twenty, thirty million!" Supreme preached.

"But it ain't me!" Horse fired back.

"Horse, all they asking for is the three million. We ain't losing on this!" 'Preme tried to explain.

"Yo, are you crazy? You was the main one in this same office barking about how them Calvino cats had disrespected you and all that, and now you saying it's their money? That's our money!" Horse argued as I was able to piece together what was going on. I had figured that it would be a good time to wear a wire because I guessed that no one's suspicions would be raised. And man was I right. I had the recorder near my upper thigh and the tape was rolling, recording every word that was being shouted across the room.

"Horse, they said they gonna start torturing the nigga! Come on man!" 'Preme urged.

"Yo, if you roll wit' Gun Clap then you know how we get down! We gangsta to the core! I don't gotta tell you that, 'Preme. And G-Baby knows that. He was riding wit' you and the whole Supreme Team since he was damn near twelve years old. He seen you torture niggas personally! He knows how the game gets down. And he gotta know that he got caught out there so now he gotta take one for us! That's it!" Horse hollered as he walked out of the conference room.

Out of respect everybody remained quiet. Trina and I both used that silence as a cue to shuffle ourselves into two open seats that were available near the middle of the table.

G-Baby was being held for ransom somewhere by the Calvinos and apparently they had threatened to torture him if the three million dollars was not returned. From the looks of the faces in the room you would have thought that a funeral was taking place—that was how somber the mood was.

As we sat and looked at each other the black telephone

that was located near the front of the table began to ring. Horse quickly made his way back into the room and pressed the speakerphone button.

"Holla!" Horse stated into the air.

"Holla!" the person said on the other end, in what sounded like a very Italian voice. The caller was definitely trying to mock Horse.

"I love the way you rap guys do that . . . Holla!" the Italian guy stated as he started laughing. "Did I sound too white when I said that?" he asked. I hoped liked hell that the Bureau was able to trace the origin of the call.

There was silence.

"Okay. Horse, let's be serious here. We gave you guys half an hour. What's the story? Where is my money?" he asked.

"Yo, listen, you wasting your muthafucking time calling here with that bullshit!" Horse arrogantly said.

There was silence.

The silence was then broken by the sound of a thud, followed by the loud sounds of someone screaming.

"Horse, you hear that? We just broke your boy's right kneecap! Give me my fucking money or this ugly scumbag is dead! Horse, you don't wanna test me! You don't wanna test me on this! You guys need to stick to making music and let us stick to being gangstas! That's your fucking problem," the Italian guy said over what I assumed was G-Baby still howling in pain in the background.

"Hang up the phone!" Horse ordered. But when no one listened to him he walked over to the phone and snatched the handset before violently slamming the phone down and ending the call.

Supreme shook his head before speaking up. "Horse, it's the wrong move, kid!" he stated.

"'Preme, all due respect but I don't wanna hear it. He told me to test him so I'm gonna test his ass!" Horse replied.

At that point my cell phone began vibrating. It was a blocked number and I knew that it was probably Andrew. So I quickly excused myself from the table and went out into the lobby area.

"Hello?" I said as I spoke into my phone.

"Jessica, can you talk?" Andrew asked.

"Yes but make it quick."

"Are you at Gun Clap?" he asked.

"Yes, I'm here, why?"

"So then you know what's going on. Listen, whoever is holding G-Baby must be calling from a prepaid cell phone or something because we can't trace that number. Is there anything you can do to step in that situation? Otherwise we're gonna have a murder on our hands," Andrew stated.

I was already feeling stressed out, because in a way I kind of viewed this whole situation as my fault. After all, it was I who had helped to instigate things by encouraging the dis record. But I couldn't stress myself too bad because a dis record wasn't the Mafia's main concern. Getting back that three million dollars was.

"I'll see what I can do. But there is not much that I can really input. I'll explain later. I gotta go," I said as I quickly ended the call and made it back into the conference room. I took my seat among the many long faces.

Finally someone other than Horse or Supreme spoke up.

"Horse, on the real, I'm sayin', 'Preme is right. You can't let them just torture G-Baby like that. Gun Clap did a hundred million last year. So three million and ain't no money. Especially if it was money that we was just gonna wash for those cats anyway," the slim thug said.

Horse looked at him and didn't respond.

The slim thug continued on, "Horse, look at it like this. What if that was your son they was holding? Wouldn't you—"

Horse quickly cut him off. "Hold up, money! Leave my son the fuck outta this! 'Cause it ain't my son that they holding! They holding G-Baby and he knows the rules to this street shit! He knows the codes of the street. I guess the next thing is y'all gonna be bitchin' up and saying we should start snitching and call the police, right?"

No one said anything. There was silence in the room for about a minute or so until the phone rang again. Horse just looked at it as it rang three times. Supreme then reached over and answered the call, again putting the phone on speaker.

"Get at me," 'Preme said. He spoke with his head sloped downward toward the phone.

The Italian guy's voice quickly filled the entire room. "Horse, you had to test me. You got some pair of balls. I'll tell you that. But I'll be fair and give you and your crew this one last bit of advice. Stick to making music and no matter how much of a gangsta you and your crew think you are, and no matter how many drugs you sold, or how much time you did in the pen, that don't matter, and we gonna keep coming at you and coming at you and coming at you. Now listen to this and ask yourself is this really what you want?"

The next thing I heard was the sound of a loud gunshot echoing through the speakerphone. Everyone in the room jumped. I placed my hand around my mouth as I was somewhat in disbelief. That single gunshot was followed by at least twenty other gunshots and two seconds after the gunshots ended, the loud sound of a dial tone filled the room.

Supreme turned and rammed his fist through one of the platinum album plaques that was hanging on the wall. The force of his blow was so strong that it put a huge hole in the wall. He then ran his hand down his face before cursing and storming out of the room.

"'Preme, them cats is fronting, 'Preme! They ain't kill him!" Horse shouted. Horse didn't want to let on to it, but with the way the muscles around his eyes appeared to be a little tighter, I could tell that he didn't believe what he was saying. He knew that G-Baby had become a casualty of this hip-hop versus the Mafia war. And it would have to eat at him, knowing that he practically sanctioned G-Baby's death by not giving in to the Calvinos demand that they return the three million dollars.

The room slowly started to empty out, and for the first time since I had been investigating Gun Clap and the Supreme Team, I can honestly say that it was the first appearance of humbleness that I'd seen displayed by any of the Gun Clap and Supreme Team crew members. Surprisingly there was no gangsta talk about strapping up and going back at the Calvinos. And I think that was because instinctively they knew that they were fighting a war that they were losing, and they were also fighting a war that it seemed like they wouldn't win.

Horse had to keep up the image of the tough leader. He didn't wanna relent for one second. But after Trina and I had sat with Horse and a few other Gun Clap employees for forty-five minutes waiting for the Calvinos to call back and prove to Horse that they had indeed just been bluffing, we decided to leave.

I got up and walked over to Horse and rubbed his back with my right hand while giving him a kiss on the cheek. I made sure that I didn't say a word, because nothing that I could say at that point would have been appropriate.

Trina and I walked out and made our way to the elevator, as I wondered to myself just how long Horse would sit there and wait for a phone call from the Calvinos. A phone call that he would never receive.

CHAPTER TWENTY-FIVE

*t*wo days after G-Baby had been kidnapped, Horse was still in denial about his death. His denial lasted until G-Baby's naked bullet-hole-riddled body was found dumped in the street right near Rucker Park.

G-Baby's hands had both been chopped off. And while he himself had not personally stolen the Calvinos three million dollars, everyone knew that his hands being chopped off were the Calvinos way of indicating that his death had occurred as the result of thievery.

The network news stations and newspapers were having an absolute field day with all that had been going on. They chronicled the events that had led up to the death of rival rapper Frank Nitty. They reported and recapped the violent deaths of Gun Clap rappers S&S and Tech-9. They showed all of the different memorial services that had been held for the recent fallen soldiers in hip-hop, as well as commenting on what they labeled *Horse's crocodile tears*.

But with the recent shooting of Paulie Calvino's home, followed by Gun Clap's dis record of the Mafia, and the shootings at Rucker park and then G-Baby's kidnapping and death, the media seriously portrayed the *alleged* escalating war between the Calvinos and Gun Clap Records.

One reporter from Channel Four News in New York was actually the most accurate with his reasoning that a war was in fact in progress even though both warring sides continually dismissed such rumors.

In his ten-minute segment on the news, the reporter showed Angela Calvino and what was to be the next big thing in rap music, the rapper White Lines happily gloating at a press conference together with Horse. The reporter asked very sensible rhetorical questions such as: "If there wasn't a war, why was it that Gun Clap Records had dropped White Lines from their roster of artists after recently signing him to a million-dollar deal and not even releasing an album for him?" "Why had the socialite Angela Calvino suddenly disappeared off the face of the earth?" He went on to answer those questions, and for the most part he was right. For example, no one had been able to get in contact with Angela, and while we knew that she had been shipped off to Florida, the reporter stated that, "Clearly she must have been shipped to Florida and was being kept secluded from everyone so that she would not be a pawn in the war and suffer the same fate as G-Baby."

The reporter did, however, end his report by saying that in the midst of all that had been going on, Gun Clap was still smiling at the end of the day, no matter how many crocodile tears came from the company's employees. And that was because of the phenomenal amount of records that had been sold by Gun Clap since the war had started. He mentioned how in the week following the release of the dis record, the single had sold close to two million copies and was the most requested song throughout the country. All of Gun Clap's artists had seen a dramatic rise in record sales. But he ended his report by asking the question, "How many more people would become casualties of this war and what would it take to settle the war?" He answered his last question by saying his sources were telling him that it would take at least three million dollars to end the war and that on the 11 P.M. version of the news, he would explain just how the three-million-dollar figure had supposedly come about.

As the news report went off I couldn't help but think how this whole *hip-hop marrying the mob* idea that I had constructed was totally going in a direction than I could have never envisioned. I knew that more bodies would fall if I personally didn't step in and put an end to the whole thing. The Bureau and I just needed something else a bit more solid to nail Paulie Calvino Sr. to the wall. Because so far, Paulie Calvino Sr., being the smart mobster that he was, had totally kept himself clear of the radar in terms of being on tape saying incriminating things.

Fortunately for me—and I say that it had to be an act of God—I saw some light at the end of the tunnel. That light came from a phone call that I received with a 305 area code. The call was from Angela and although she had been missing in action she definitely had not lost her arrogant ways.

"Hello?" I said with a curious tone to my voice, as I did not recognize the number.

"Jessica, you fucking bitch!" the person on the other end said to me.

"*Okaaay*. And hello to you too," I sarcastically responded. "Who is this?" I asked.

"Jessica, you know exactly who this is. This is Angela! How could you let Horse use your girls in a video that is mocking me and making me look like some kind of slut?" Angela vented.

I thought quickly on my feet, as I knew that maintaining contact with Angela would be vital in closing out this investigation.

"Angie, I swear on my life, I had no idea that Horse would use my girls for a video like that! He called me and told me how many girls he needed and what kind of girls he was looking for and when he needed the girls for. Just like he does for any video shoot. And, trust me, when I saw that video, I practically ripped him a new asshole! I wanted to call you as soon as I found out about the video but you were nowhere to be found. You told me that you were going to Florida, and the next thing I know your cell phone number was no longer good. So what was I supposed to do, Angela?" I stated like a Hollywood A-list actress.

There was a pause on the phone and then Angela blew out some air into the phone before saying, "Jessica, I'm sorry. I shouldn't be taking anything out on you. I'm just so stressed out over this whole thing!"

I cut Angela off and told her that I would call her back in two minutes. "Angela, I have to take this call. But can I call you back at this number that's on my cell phone caller ID?" I asked.

"Okay, call me back but do not give out that number! You understand?" Angela warned.

"Yes, no problem. Okay, I gotta go," I hurried and said before hanging up.

I had no other call, but what I wanted to do was get Angela tied into a recorded line. So I quickly called Andrew and told him what was up. He instructed me to call into one of the Bureau's taped phone lines that was being manned by a special agent and then to three-way Angela back into the call.

I did as he told me and before long I called Angela back. I knew to call her from my cell phone so that I wouldn't raise any of her suspicions.

"Hello," Angela answered.

"Angela, it's me. Sorry about that. I just have so much going on with this business that it is crazy for me. My days are just so hectic," I stated.

"Well, like I was saying, this whole music shit has me so stressed out. I mean my father sent me down here because he didn't want me in New York until this whole money thing was settled," Angela said.

I played dumb.

"Wait a minute, Angela, are you telling me that Horse still hasn't given your father his three million dollars back?" I said with a tone of disgust and disbelief.

"No! And that's the whole thing that's pissing my father off. He don't want me calling Horse, Supreme, or anybody from their camp. And I wanna call Horse and tell him to stop acting so damn childish and just give back the money so this whole thing can just go away and everybody can move on. It's really making me sick as a dog. Not to mention how bad I feel for White Lines," Angela stated.

I knew that I had to try and take the conversation to a more incriminating level so I said, "Well, to be honest, I don't even want to speak to Horse after this little video thing that he pulled. Plus I've been keeping my distance. Too many people have been getting killed and shot and I know it's probably because Supreme and Horse have been doing dirty deals . . . Did you hear what happened to G-Baby? That is exactly what I mean. But speaking to you now, I can probably put two and two together and guess that your father ordered that hit on G-Baby."

The phone went silent and my heart rate increased. I prayed that I had not raised Angela's suspicions but I also hoped that she would say something incriminating. To help play things off, I yawned into the phone and reached to turn on the radio so that there could be some type of noise in the background.

"Jessica, why do you think I am so stressed and upset over this whole thing? Of course my father ordered that. And I can't say that I blame him. I mean, Horse shot up my house, Jessica, and they took my father's money. What else was he supposed to do?" Angela rambled on.

"Angela, this is crazy. It's like something from straight out of a movie or something. Is there anything that I can do?" I asked.

Angela sighed and then said, "Jessica, actually I am gonna need your help. If you can do this for me, I don't know, you let me know."

"Of course, Angela, what is it?" I asked.

Angela sighed again into the phone.

"Jessica, this does not leave your mouth, you understand?" Angela said.

"Yes, you know me Angie, I don't have a big mouth," I replied.

"Well, let me tell you what I need from you and then I'll fill you in on why I need it. Okay, I need you to spot me like fifty grand. I know it's a lot of money but I am good for it. I'll get it back to you, you got my word on that," Angela said, surprisingly sounding as humble as I had ever heard her.

Without thinking, I replied, "Yeah, umh, I think I should be able to do that for you, but what's going on?"

"Thank you, Jessica, you are a sweetheart. Okay, when this whole three million dollar thing became an issue, in terms of Horse and Supreme not wanting to give my father his money back, my father was so pissed off at me for having gotten involved with *a bunch of niggers*, as he put it. He claimed that niggers can't be trusted and he went on and on. But he was more pissed off about the arrogance that they had in stealing his money and disrespecting his house. So he shipped me down here to Florida until everything was worked out and settled. And other than me being isolated from my friends, I was cool. I mean Miami is a nice place to be at so it wasn't too bad. But then when that record came out, he wanted to know if I had ever *really been with* any of those niggers."

"You mean sexually?" I asked.

"Yes," Angela answered. I nodded my head up and down, even though she couldn't see me.

She continued on, "So I didn't lie about it because what if Horse really did have a videotape of me and him having sex? If that tape exists and it got into my father's hands, he would have killed me for lying. He always stressed to us growing up that lying to him was the one thing that he would not tolerate. So I told him the truth. And Jessica, he went crazy! *Ming! Madone!* He cursed me and called me every kind of whore. And he actually flew down here to Miami and beat my ass! I'm a grown woman and he actually beat my ass like I was a damn twelve-year-old kid."

"Wow! Oh my God, Angela. Are you okay?" I asked out of genuine concern.

"I'm okay, but he basically cut me off. He cut me off from money and from everything. And Jessica, I don't know if you know, but when Italian family members stop speaking to you, it's like you might as well be dead or something. And especially with the influence that my father has, he put the word out for no one to speak to me or to help me out, and none of my friends or family will want to cross him and go against his commands, forget about it," Angela explained.

"Angela, that sounds a bit drastic to me. I mean I understand that you sort of brought him into the whole money thing with Gun Clap, but he's not cutting you off because of that, he's cutting you off just because you had sex with Horse, who happens to be black?" I asked in disbelief. I felt guilty for having cooked up the dis record idea. I continued on, "And I guess he saw the music video and really lost it," I stated.

"Well, I don't know if he saw it or not, but I do know that it's definitely not gonna help the situation at all. That's why I was so pissed off. It's like as soon as I think this thing can die and go away; this fucking record comes out, and then the music video. It's too fucking much and it's making my father look bad! But to answer your question, it's not just a matter of me having had sex with a black guy that's pissing my father off. Even if he is at war with the guy that had sex with me, what it is, is that I'm pregnant by the guy, Jessica," Angela stated in bombshell fashion.

For a split second, I came out of my FBI agent role, and really wanted to be there for Angela in terms of a genuine friend, but I knew that I had a job to do.

"Oh my fucking God! Angela, you have got to be kidding!" I said with real genuine dramatic affect.

I made sure not to insult Angela by asking her if she was sure that Horse was the father of the baby. She had to know who she had been with sexually and I was certain that she knew what the deal was.

"Does Horse know?" I asked.

"No. How would he know? I haven't spoken to him. And Jessica, you better not open your mouth about it either," she warned.

"I won't say anything. I haven't really been speaking to Horse and Supreme that much anyway. I don't like how they do business, and then after that dis record that they put out and dragging me into the middle of it by using my girls in a video that they know I would never have had any part of—that made me realize that I really have to distance myself from them," I said as I played both sides of the fence beautifully.

"So are you're keeping the baby?" I asked.

"Of course I am! I'm not with that abortion shit!" Angela replied.

There was silence on the phone for a few seconds and then

I said, "Well, Angela, look, why don't you come back to New York, stay with me, I'll give you the money, and you can sort things out. If you want you can even come in and help me out at the modeling agency."

Angela didn't respond.

"Living with me isn't the best thing but it would have to be better than being cooped up down in Miami by yourself. Especially now with the baby on the way and all. But you let me know, the invitation is open, and anything that you need me to do just give me the word," I reiterated.

"Thank you, Jessica," Angela said. I could tell that she was smiling through the phone. Then she added. "Jessica, actually there is something you can do for me."

"What's that?" I asked.

Angela blew some air into the phone and she said, "Tell Horse to really be careful. Just tell him that you spoke to me and that you can't really elaborate, but tell him that my father is not gonna stop until he kills him. And tell him to just give back the money and things might cool down and my father might not come for him. But honestly, Jessica, at this point, it's past being just about the money as far as my father is concerned. I hate how Horse and Supreme are handling this whole thing, but they really have to watch their backs. It was so easy for my father to get someone from *their own* Gun Clap crew to get G-Baby, so just tell Horse to be careful even with the people that he thinks are his boys," Angela stated.

"Okay, I definitely will do that," I informed Angela.

"Jessica, I don't know what it is. I mean, I can't say I have real feelings for Horse, because it's not like that. But I mean, he is gonna be the father of this baby that I'm carrying. And I don't know. Bottom line is that I don't want to see anything happen to him, that's all," Angela stated.

As I ended the conversation, I told her that I understood. And for the first time I was actually starting to see the *human being* underneath Angela's brash tough-as-nails demeanor.

She agreed that she would come to New York very soon and stay with me and sort things out. Little did she know how her phone conversation with me had just made things real tough for her father.

I was certain that she would eventually find out though, because she had just given us that rock-solid evidence that we needed to get at Paulie Calvino, the so-called *Teflon Don.*

CHAPTER TWENTY-SIX

i had made plans to attend G-Baby's funeral with Trina from my modeling agency. The funeral was held at Christian Cultural Center, a five-thousand seat mega-church located in Brooklyn. Five thousand seats weren't enough to accommodate the massive number of mourners who turned out to pay their last respects to G-Baby. At least a thousand people were standing in the balcony, on the steps, and along the aisles.

Trina and I sat in about the fifth row, where we had a clear view of the open casket that held G-Baby's lifeless body while cleverly hiding his severed hands. Horse and Supreme and the entire Gun Clap family sat in the first three rows along with the family of G-Baby. It seemed as if the entire hip-hop community had come out to the funeral. P. Diddy was in attendance, as was Jay-Z, Russell Simmons, Rev Run, LL Cool J, 50 Cent, and the list goes on and on. And of course the place was littered with special agents, undercover NYPD officers, and uniformed officers.

I would have to say that, out of all of the wakes and funerals that I had been to, including the ones for S&S and Tech-9, that this was the saddest of them all. Without a doubt, I had never heard so much wailing and crying. I don't know what exactly it was, but I think that everyone in attendance was just drained mentally and emotionally. The sentiment from everyone was that enough was enough. All of the killings had to be put to an end.

From what a lot of the newspapers were reporting and from the overall buzz in the industry, it was clear that people were falling tired of Horse's act. Surprisingly, Russell Simmons was one of the most vocal. Even at the funeral he indirectly urged Horse to either be a music man or a gangsta.

"There used to be a fine line that was walked, but now you got music executives that are purposely blurring that line between gangsta and music. And that can't keep continuing on like that. And then there is this twisted notion that you gotta strike back at the people that struck at you! Man, come on! What is that? A lot of us in this church today are multimillionaires. We can't continue running around and responding to ignorance with ignorance!" Russell stated.

His words drew thunderous applause, and it was as if the applause was directly heralded at Horse, who many had learned through the grapevine was the one who had opposed paying the ransom money to G-Baby's kidnappers.

Throughout the funeral Horse remained stone-faced. He showed absolutely no emotion. If anything, he showed a face of defiance. And when the funeral was over and the thousands of mourners piled out of the church, Horse was at the center of the media's attention.

Cameras snapped pictures and reporters asked questions.

"Horse, is there any truth to the rumor that G-Baby was killed by the Calvino crime family?" one reporter asked.

Horse replied, "I make music, that's what I do for a living. You see those guys over there with the blue uniforms on? Go ask them that question. It's their job to find out who murdered G-Baby!"

"Is it true that you stole money from the Calvinos? Allegedly, it was money that was supposed to be laundered through your company," a female reporter asked.

Horse turned and laughed. "I have absolutely no idea what you're talking about."

As reporters continued to ask him questions, he excused himself by saying, "Look, my man just died. Can there be some respect shown to him and his family? I really can't answer any more questions."

"Horse, what is confusing—and many influential people in the hip-hop community seem confused by this—is why if G-Baby had such close ties to you did you not simply pay the alleged ransom money that his kidnappers were seeking?" a reporter managed to throw in.

Horse had resumed his defiant demeanor as he responded, "First of all, I'm a grown man who doesn't answer to anybody. I'm a multimillionaire! And that means that I come and go as I please without answering to anybody. I can do whatever the hell I wanna do! Russell Simmons, and everybody else for that matter, can kiss my ass!" Horse stated as he briskly walked off with his entourage to a fleet of waiting SUVs.

What Horse was too arrogant and stubborn to realize was that it was the abrasive way he spoke that was turning so many people against him. But he had an image and a reputation to maintain. At least in the public's eye anyway.

A week or so after the funeral, and a day before Angela was scheduled to arrive in New York and begin staying with me, I phoned Horse just to talk him up and to fill him in on some of what Angela had told me.

I called him on his cell phone and he picked up on the first ring.

"Hey Horse, it's me, Jessica."

"Jessie, what up? Yo, I know I gotta get you that dough, right?" Horse stated through the phone.

"Yeah, but that's not why I'm calling. Don't worry yourself about that," I assured.

Horse blew some air into the phone. "Jessie, you don't know. It's hard being me! Word is bond!"

"I can imagine. I never got a chance to really talk to you after G-Baby's funeral. I figured you probably wanted to be left alone and have some time with yourself," I stated.

"Yeah, actually I took a few days away from this music thing just so I could get my head straight. And you know what is wild, is that it was just me and my son, we flew to this private resort in St. Barts, and when I was down there, I was like he's the only thing in this world that matters to me. It was like no stress at all down there. And my son, he has like no cares in the world about anything. And I was just feeding off of that. We was playing video games and it just hit me like, 'what the fuck am I doing? Am I working too hard or something?' Jessica, between me and you, I'm thinking about just saying fuck this music shit. I mean I already got enough cake for three lifetimes. I don't gotta deal with this drama and this heat. You kna'imean? From now on I'm thinking about just making it be about me and my little homey? Ya' heard?" Horse stated after rambling on.

"Stop with all of that, Horse. You know you can't give up this music business!" I said in a gleeful way.

"Nah, Jessica, word is bond! I think I'm done with this shit. On the real," Horse replied.

"Whatever Horse. Listen, I don't mean to stress you out any more but I spoke with Angela the other—"

"What the fuck that bitch want?" Horse said, sounding very bitter.

"No, Horse don't sound like, I mean I hadn't spoken to her in I don't know how long, she said that she was staying somewhere in Florida—"

Horse cut me off again. "Good! Tell that bitch to stay her ass down there!"

"No, Horse, listen. She was calling with love. She wasn't talking slick or nothing like that. Actually she just wanted me to relay a message to you and to tell you to be real careful because—"

Horse's bitterness had cut me off yet again. "'Cause what? I don't care if she was calling on some love shit or not! Tell that bitch I'll fly down there and murder her ass!"

I paused and didn't say anything.

Horse was also quiet.

"See, all of that shit you were just telling me about leaving the music business so that you could just chill with your son, that's bullshit Horse, and you know it! You got too much of an ego to leave this business," I boldly said.

Horse didn't respond.

"Just hear me out though. The reason that I said she was calling on a love trip is because she told me to tell you to watch your back so that the same people who gave up G-Baby to her father wouldn't do the same to you," I relayed.

"What the fuck that bitch talking about?" Horse asked.

"Well she was saying something like it was some dudes who roll with you that gave G-Baby up. She told me to tell you not to trust the cats around you 'cause for the right price they would give you up too," I added.

"She think I'm stupid! Ain't nobody from my crew rolled over on G-Baby! Fuck outta here! She just tryin' to cause a split between me and my niggas!" Horse emphatically stated.

"Well I don't know," I said.

There was a brief pause in the conversation.

"What are you doing later?" I asked, breaking the silence as I did not want to get into a back-and-forth debate with Horse. "There were some more things she was telling me. It's on a totally different thing though," I said. In my mind I was thinking about her pregnancy, which she had told me to keep to myself.

"We just gonna go to Chelsea Piers to bowl. And after that I'm going home and tomorrow I'm just chillin' with my son," Horse informed.

"Oh, I love bowling! What time are y'all getting there?" I asked.

"Around ten or ten thirty," Horse responded.

"Okay, I'll call Trina and see if she wants to come with me. And when I see you later I'll tell you what else Angela was saying," I stated as I prepared to hang up the phone.

I managed to kill some time for the rest of the day before getting dressed and picking up Trina to head to the bowling alley. As it turned out, that night of bowling would forever change the course of the investigation and in some respects, forever change the course of my career.

CHAPTER TWENTY-SEVEN

*M*e and Trina have to be on the same team!"
I demanded. I hadn't bowled in a long
time, but bowling was one of my most fa-
vorite things to do.

"Jessica, what name you bowling under?" Trina asked as
she set up our lane's computer with all of our names.

"White Chocolate!" I shouted as Lloyd Banks's song "On
Fire" blasted in the background.

"We on fire up in here, it's burning hot . . . we on fire!" Supreme
recited along with the song.

Trina had entered my nickname into the computer, then
she entered hers, *Video Diva*.

"Video Diva?" Horse asked with a smirk on his face.

"Yeah, that's what's up," Trina stated as she looked for a
bowling ball that comfortably fit her fingers. Trina had a body
to die for and it seemed as if all of the guys in the bowling alley had their eyes on her. It was a Friday night so the bowling
alley was pretty packed.

There were a total of ten of us. We were split into two teams of five. Trina and I were the only girls but it didn't really matter because we knew that we could hold our own against the men.

Supreme and I were on opposing teams and we both were talking competitively against one another. We set it up so that he and I would be bowling last in the rotation of bowlers and would bowl right after each other. And since there were ten of us, we knew that we had some time to kill before our individual turns came up.

"Yo, anybody want any food or something from the bar?" Supreme asked. "Me and Jessica 'bout to walk over and get some food."

As everybody put in their respective orders, I remember thinking to myself how I was not gonna even let myself have a drink. And I knew that 'Preme was gonna offer me something, either weed, E, or something. I had to stand my ground. The bowling alley had a lot of FBI agents floating around so I had to be totally alert and on point. There was no way that I wanted to get caught out there slipping.

As we walked toward the grill, Supreme began brushing up real close to me.

"Your body's looking real good! You been hitting the Stair-Master or something?" Supreme asked as he grabbed my butt.

"'Preme!" I said as I quickly pulled his hand away from my butt. "Look at all these people in here. You making me look like a whore or something."

Supreme smiled and looked at me. I couldn't tell if he was high or what the deal was. As the summer anthem, "Lean

Back," came on, everyone in the bowling alley started cheering like they were at a concert or something.

"I think I'm just gonna get some chicken fingers," I stated, trying to take Supreme's focus off my backside.

"Oh word?" he said. He was looking at me like he wanted to take me and do me right there in the middle of the bowling alley.

"'Preme, would you stop looking at me like that?" I said as I slapped him on his rock-hard chest. "You're scaring me! Are you drunk?" I asked as I laughed.

Supreme didn't respond to my question. He just told me to order what I wanted and that he had to run to the bathroom real quick.

It couldn't have been more than thirty seconds from the time Supreme walked off until I heard screams coming from every direction. The screams were followed by rapid gunfire.

I quickly took cover behind the metal garbage can that was near the bar. In no time, there was absolute chaos in the bowling alley. There was no more gunfire but people were running every which way for their lives.

Since I no longer heard gunshots, my instincts told me to stand up and survey what was going on. Still, all I could see was chaos. I decided to run back to the lane in which we were in and I saw a huge crowd of people surrounding something or someone. My heart dropped as I wondered if Trina had gotten shot.

"Call an ambulance!" somebody kept frantically screaming.

"Horse got shot!" I heard someone else yelling. I still couldn't see what was going on.

Then the cops came from every angle.

"NYPD! NYPD! We need everybody to back up! Please,

people, we need some room here!" the police officers shouted. The majority of onlookers didn't heed to the officers' commands so the cops began forcefully pushing and shoving people out of the way.

Finally the space where I had been sitting only five minutes prior was now in my view. And what I saw was Horse laying on the floor writhing in pain as blood poured out of him. I know I was doing my job but I couldn't help but feel for horse. My hand instantly covered my mouth after my jaw had dropped in both shock and disbelief.

I couldn't believe that only Horse had been shot, but I was probably feeling the shock. I knew had I not walked off to get something to eat with Supreme, that I too might have taken a bullet.

I ran and grabbed Trina, who was hysterical. We embraced and she hugged on me so tight that I thought I was going to pass out.

"Jessie, oh my God! Oh my God! I can't believe they just came and shot him like that. I was right there talking with him, Jessie!" Trina screamed as she trembled with fear. "Jessica, look at this!" Trina instructed through her fear.

She showed me a bowling ball that was shattered.

"Jessica, I had that in my hand when they started shooting," she informed me. She told me she had dropped the bowling ball upon impact from the bullet.

Just then Supreme came running over. He could not believe what had happened. He disobeyed the orders from the police officers and ran right to Horse's side.

"Horse, get up! Sit up, man! You gonna be a'ight" Supreme stated as he attempted to help Horse sit up.

The cops commanded Supreme to let go of Horse and they told him that if he didn't step away immediately that he would be arrested.

"'Preme, I can't feel my legs! Ah shit! Ahh!" Horse screamed in pain. His entire midsection was soaked in blood.

"Yo, make sure my son is a'ight! Don't tell him what happened to me but make sure he's a'ight. We was supposed to chill together tomorrow," Horse said. The paramedics had finally arrived and quickly began working on his wounds.

Trina and I continued to embrace one another as the cops began roping off the inside of Chelsea Piers with yellow crime-scene tape. Horse was in pain and he looked very scared. He had that look that I had seen all too often on a man's face when he is staring death in the face.

"Ahh!" Horse screamed. I wasn't sure, but to me it looked as if I saw a tear run down the right side of Horse's face as he yelled out in pain. He asked the paramedic why he couldn't feel his legs.

"Just relax. Try to relax," the paramedic said. "We have to get you to the hospital! That's our main concern right now."

The paramedics worked on Horse for about ten minutes before lifting him onto a stretcher and quickly whisking him away to St. Vincent's Medical Center.

As Trina and I still held onto each other, I could feel her body trembling with fear. I have to be honest and say that at that point I could have cared less about the investigation. I mean, I knew that whether Horse lived or died we would certainly have to wrap up the investigation ASAP. But the human part of me couldn't help but think about Horse's son. I wondered if Horse had *really* been serious about wanting to just leave the industry and go off to some faraway place with his son and watch him grow up.

I don't know if he was for real about that. But I do know that he was facing his biggest enemy and possibly his last enemy, he was staring that enemy right in the face. That enemy went by the name of death. Only God held that victory over death, and we all prayed like hell that God would be with Horse on that night.

CHAPTER TWENTY-EIGHT

Clapped!"

That was the headline on the front page of the *New York Daily News* on the day that followed Horse being shot. The subtitle to that headline read: "Gun Clap Records CEO Gets Clapped in Chelsea Piers Bowling Alley."

"Horse Maimed"

That was the headline on the front page of the *New York Post.*

"Hip-Hop Hotshot Is Shot"

Read the front page of *New York Newsday.*

"Horse Is Hobbled"

Read the front page of *The New York Times.*

. . .

The news about Horse being shot had made the front page of just about every newspaper in the country. Fortunately for Horse he was still breathing, but the night at Chelsea Piers bowling alley had left him crippled.

At the numerous press conferences that were held with the medical staff at St. Vincent's Hospital, the doctors explained how one of the bullets that had entered Horse's body had pierced his spinal cord and that there was little that the doctors would be able to do to bring the feeling back to Horse's legs. Barring a miracle from the *man upstairs,* Horse would be confined to a wheelchair for the remainder of his natural life.

In the days following the assassination attempt on Horse, Angela had arrived in New York and she began living with me as we had arranged. I don't know what it was but there was just something so surreal about her actually being in my presence on a twenty-four-hour-a-day basis. I say it was surreal because although it was me who had suggested Angela come and live with me, I did not genuinely trust Angela, and I was starting to second-guess my decision to let her live with me.

Thoughts kept creeping into the back of my mind that would tell me that Angela knew that I was a federal agent and she was just setting me up to have me taken out. The first night that she arrived at my place, I was actually tossing and turning all night long in my sleep. I remember thinking back to how I had been given up by another agent when this investigation had first begun and how that had almost cost me my life.

What if another agent gave me up to the Calvinos? I constantly began thinking to myself as I lay in my queen-size water bed, while Angela slept on a futon that I had in the guest room down the hall.

I was becoming more and more paranoid and I knew that if I had to start second-guessing myself and looking over my shoulder that it was definitely time to come out of my under-cover role and put an end to the White Chocolate investigation.

From the minute that Angela had stepped off the plane, she began asking me about the fifty grand that I had promised her. While I knew that I would be able to get the money from my superiors, I didn't just want to waste government money if I didn't have to.

I gave Angela $2000 and kept promising her that I would have the entire $50,000 for her within a few days. My thinking was that if she and her family had made me out to be a fed, then they would more than likely keep me alive until I produced the $50,000. So I had to just keep dangling the idea that the $50,000 was soon coming in order to stay alive and to buy time so that the FBI / NYPD joint task force could properly make the arrests and close out the investigation with a bang.

The morning after tossing and turning in my bed all night long, I woke up to the smell of food coming from the kitchen. Surprisingly, Angela had woke up early and took it upon herself to make breakfast for the two of us.

"Angie, I didn't know you could cook," I said as I made my way to the kitchen in my white terry-cloth robe.

"Of course I can cook. I'm Italian, ain't I?" Angela replied with a smile. She looked like she had been up for a while. She looked showered and she had gotten dressed and it was only a little past 8 A.M.

"Well I'm black, and I can't even boil a pot of water," I said as the two of us began laughing.

"You look like you've been up and about for a few hours. What are you doing up so goddamn early?" I asked.

As Angela put sausages and eggs on my plate and poured us both some orange juice, she replied, "To be honest, Jessica, I can't sleep. I just don't feel good about a lot of things. I'm thinking about this baby that I'm carrying. I'm thinking about Horse being paralyzed. I'm thinking about my father disowning me. And Jessica, I know it's not going to stop."

"What do you mean?" I asked.

"This whole war shit! My father is going to keep on and keep on until he kills Horse and everyone on that side. I grew up with this, Jessica. And it was always like one of those things where you knew what was going on, in terms of the killings and the illegal money and all of that, but no one ever spoke about it," she explained. And I was happier than a pig in shit because I had my tape recorder in the pocket of my robe and it was recording every word that Angela said.

I took a fork full of eggs and put it into my mouth and acted as if I was surprised by what Angela had said. "No way! Angela, do you think that your father is the one that had Horse shot last night?"

"Jessica, I don't think so. *I know so.* And that is what is eating me up because in a lot of respects my father is like some spoiled-brat-fucking-bully! It's like enough already! He and my brothers are all the same way. But I can bet you that even though Horse can't walk, they will still keep coming after

him. And God forbid if my father finds out that I'm pregnant and that Horse is the father. Myyy God!" Angela said in
exasperation.

I didn't respond. I just kept on eating my food.

"So can you get the money for me today?" Angela asked.

"Oh, I forgot to tell you, it'll be a few more days before I
can pull all of that money out of the account because—"

Angela cut me off. "Why? I mean it is your money, right?
The bank can't tell you what to do with your own money."

"No, it's definitely my money but it's tied up in some projects that I got going on and I'm just waiting for some checks
to clear. But I got another two thousand for you. I'll give you
that today and that should hold you for a few days and by that
time the money should be clear," I explained.

Angela didn't say anything.

I finished my food and told Angela that I had to go take a
shower and asked her if she wanted to come with me to the office later that morning. She agreed and told me that she was
gonna clear the table and do the dishes and wait for me to get
ready.

"Angela, you are really shocking me! I didn't know that
you were this domesticated," I joked.

"Fuck you, Jessica," Angela jokingly said.

I quickly made my way to my room, picked out something
to wear. I disrobed and went to the bathroom to shower. As I
lathered up my body I knew that I would have to come up
with an excuse for Angela so that I would be able to get away
from her for a few hours. Andrew, the rest of the bigwigs at the
FBI, and I needed to coordinate the simultaneous arrests of

Angela, Horse, Supreme, Paulie Calvino Sr. and Jr. and a whole host of their associates.

I couldn't think of a good enough excuse so I didn't press myself. I knew that I would find an out somewhere along the path of the day.

After getting out of the shower and drying off, I brushed my teeth, lotioned my body, and wrapped a towel around myself. As I opened the bathroom door I was somewhat surprised by Angela's presence. She was standing in the hallway and appeared to have been coming out of my bedroom.

"Oh man! Angela, you scared the living shit out of me!" I said, jumping from being startled by her presence.

She didn't respond to me. She just looked at me in a piercing way as if her eyes were looking right through me.

I didn't know exactly what to make of her look, but I wanted to break the uncomfortable tension that seemed to have popped up from out of nowhere.

"Angela, I don't know how you'll feel about this, but I was just thinking when I was in the shower how I should go see Horse while he's in the hospital. I just—"

Angela cut me off. All of her warm domestic skills that she had been displaying, seemed as if they had vanished in the wind and the *old* Angela had returned.

"Yeah, I bet you wanna go see Horse so that you can bring your little fucking tape recorder and tape him the same way you were fucking taping me!" Angela barked.

My heart immediately fell to my feet. I smiled nervously and I immediately broke the rules I had been taught in the academy about lying.

"Taping you? What are you talking about?" I asked.

"Angela, do not play me for a fucking fool! You know exactly what I'm talking about! You better explain to me what the fuck is going on, Jessie," Angela demanded to know.

I didn't know what to say so I just brushed past Angela and made it into my room.

"Jessica, don't ignore me! What the hell is up with this fucking tape recorder?" Angela screamed, holding the tape recorder in her hands.

I knew I was busted and my heart was racing. I didn't know what to do. I simply continued to ignore Angela and proceeded to get dressed. I took off my towel and was butt naked as I rummaged through my closet for something to wear.

I then began mumbling so that Angela could hear me but also in a way where I tried to show that I was pissed off.

"Here we fucking go again!" I said under my breath as I threw on a pair of jeans with no underwear. I then reached for a shirt and put that on. I didn't have time to put on a bra as I had to quickly get dressed. There was only one way out of the jam that I was in and I realized that.

"Jessica, I am not playing with you! Stop getting dressed and turn your ass around and tell me what the fuck is going on!" Angela demanded.

I ignored her and slipped on a pair of sneakers. I reached down into my closet and reached for a box that was purposely hidden underneath a huge pile of clothes. I opened the box, reached in, and grabbed what was inside.

Before pulling my head out of the closet, I said, "Okay, you wanna know what the tape was about?" I stood up, turned around, and quickly faced Angela. I pointed my gun at her head and held my badge into the air.

"FBI! Angela, get your hands up in the air! I gotta place you under arrest!" I shouted.

That was my only out. I had to come clean at that point. Angela wasn't a dummy. She knew why I had the tape recorder. And had I left that house with her and given her some flimsy excuse, there was no doubt in my mind that the investigation would have been blown. And a lot of lives would have been seriously at risk, including my own. But by coming clean and arresting her, I would be preserving the life of the investigation. With Angela under arrest we would have to quickly arrest the rest of those involved before they were alerted to the fact that Angela had been arrested and try to flee.

"What the fuck are you doing with that gun and badge?" Angela asked as she sort of smirked at me. "You're not an agent!"

"Angela, I don't have time for games!" I said as I placed my badge in my pocket. I made sure to keep the gun aimed at Angela as I reached for my cell phone and pressed the speed-dial key for Andrew.

"Angela, if you move, I will blow your fucking head off! Don't test me on this!" I barked.

Andrew picked up.

"Yeah, this is Jessica. I'm at the house. Get someone here as soon as possible. I'm placing Angela under arrest . . ."

CHAPTER TWENTY-NINE

i held the gun on Angela for about ten minutes. Not once did I lower the gun. And for the entire ten minutes Angela called me every curse word in the English language, as well as every curse word in Italian.

She finally relented from the cursing as she stated, "So I guess this means that I'm not getting the fifty thousand."

I didn't respond.

The room was eerily silent.

"Jessica, you are so fucking dead! I swear on my uncle's grave! You are fucking dead!" she barked.

I didn't respond. Angela's eyes were locked on me. The doorbell rang and it sort of startled me. I was distracted for no more than two seconds. That two seconds was all that Angela needed as she charged me and caught me off guard.

Angela rammed into me as if she was playing linebacker for the New York Giants. "Ahhhhh!" she screamed as she knocked the wind out of me and simultaneously caused me to drop the gun that I had been holding. I knew that I had to get my hands on that gun or else I would surely lose my life.

"You fucking rat bastard bitch!' Angela screamed as she proceeded to throw a fury of punches at me. "I'll kill you!" she threatened as she continued to punch me.

I was not fighting back, as my only concern was getting my hands on the gun. Angela paused for a second as she must have realized that I was reaching for something. She turned and saw the gun on the floor and we both lunged for it at the same time like two basketball players diving for a loose ball.

I let out a loud karate type of scream as I realized that Angela had managed to reach the gun before me. I grabbed her wrist and tried to twist it so that she would drop the gun. I had never realized how strong Angela actually was as she held onto the gun with one hand and threw a series of elbows at me with her free arm. It definitely felt like she had broken a rib or two of mine.

At that point I heard a lot of commotion downstairs in the house.

"FBI! Is anyone in here?" someone yelled from downstairs.

"Upstairs!" I yelled back. With the wind knocked out of me that was all I could yell as Angela managed to get to her feet with my gun in hand.

"I told you that you was going to die! You bitch!" Angela screamed as she aimed the handgun at my forehead. I closed my eyes and hoped for the best as my heart pounded away in fear and anticipation of being shot.

"FBI, drop the gun!" one of the agents shouted at Angela.

Angela did not listen to the agent's command.

"I said drop the fucking gun!" he ordered once more.

I was frozen in fear but I wanted the agent to shoot Angela. I had been around criminals long enough to know when a criminal meant business or when they were just bluffing. I could sense that Angela, with that gun in her hands, meant business.

Shoot her! I urged on the inside.

"Jessica, you are such a fucking cunt!" Angela yelled.

At that point the agent must have heard my inner urgings as he wasted no more time and pulled the trigger. The one round from his 9mm handgun had managed to drop Angela to the floor and caused her to lose her grip on the gun.

I quickly grabbed my gun from the floor. I gasped and gulped in air almost as if I was hyperventilating.

"We need a bus!" one of the other agents yelled into his cell phone as the agent that had shot Angela continued to hold his gun on her.

"Jessica, are you okay?" The agent asked as Angela groaned in pain on the floor in a pool full of blood.

"Yeah I'm good," I replied.

"Okay, the ambulance is on its way," the agent informed as he went to attend to Angela's gunshot wound.

As I sat on the ground in shock, I hoped like hell that Angela would not die and I also hoped like hell that the media would not get wind of the shooting, at least not until we rounded up all of the players that needed to get arrested.

"Hughh!" Angela grunted in both pain and frustration.

CHAPTER THIRTY

*t*hirty-six hours had passed since Angela had been shot. Fortunately she had survived the single gunshot wound to her chest. Both she and the baby that she was carrying would be okay.

During those thirty-six hours I literally had not slept. The entire investigation had been riding on those thirty-six hours and it was crucial that no mistakes be made. I was involved in rushed and frantic meetings with the top brass of both the FBI and the NYPD as we coordinated major points of concern. Those points included successfully rounding up and arresting all of the major players from the Gun Clap camp as well as all of the major players from the Calvino crime family. In addition, we had to get the roundup done before the media got wind of Angela Calvinos FBI-inflicted gunshot wound.

While Supreme and the other Gun Clap cronies were about to be raided and arrested I had made it to the hospital to visit Horse with another agent. Horse was still recovering from his wounds and was not allowed to have more than one visitor at a time. The nurse at the desk told us that someone was already in the room visiting Horse. Normally she wasn't supposed to let us go up and see him but considering who we were she made an exception. This hospital visit was crucial and I had to make sure that I said all of the right things so that the Bureau and I could get out of Horse what we wanted without him becoming hostile toward us.

"Hey baby," I said as I walked into Horse's room and kissed him on the forehead. I looked around the room and I didn't see anyone else and I figured that either the nurse had been lying and playing the role of gatekeeper for Horse, or his visitor had left the room before we'd arrived.

Horse looked as if he had seen a ghost when he saw me. He also looked really hard at the black female agent who had accompanied me.

"I came by to see you. I know I should have called or something instead of just popping in but—"

Horse cut me off. "Jessica, what the fuck! I don't want nobody seeing me like this!" Horse barked. "And who the hell is this? Don't be bringing people up in here unannounced!"

Horse looked as if he was very weak. But his spirit was still vibrant enough to talk in his trademark cocky, arrogant, and abrasive tone.

"Horse, this is my friend, one of the models, Sherry. She just came with me real quick to check on you," I stated.

"Jessica, no disrespect but I'm really not trying to see nobody right now. I just need time to sort shit out and think. I mean goddamn! I can't even walk. Yo, you don't know what I'm dealing with right now!" Horse said.

"Sherry, can you give us a few minutes?" I asked.

Sherry took my cue and made her way out of the room.

"I'll be outside," she replied.

I was now all alone with Horse. Since we had actually come to the hospital with the intention of placing Horse under arrest, being alone with him wasn't what I had wanted but it would later prove for my sake to have been somewhat of a blessing in disguise.

"Horse, just give me five minutes. You know I'll love you regardless of how you look or if you can walk or not. You mean a lot to me, Horse," I said with real sincerity.

Horse didn't respond. He simply looked at the television that was suspended from the ceiling.

I reached for the remote control and promptly turned off the TV.

"Horse, I need you to look at me and just listen to me."

Horse reluctantly gave me his attention.

"Now first of all you are gonna snap out of this little funk that you're in! That's the first thing. Stop feeling sorry for yourself, you know that you are way too talented and bright to be thinking the worst of your situation," I said.

"Jessica, I don't need no pep talk and all of that bullshit. I know you—"

I cut Horse off. "This ain't no pep talk, Horse, this is serious what I'm about to tell you. I need you to listen to me and I need you to trust me. And if you do, when you get out of here you're gonna have that chance to spend that time with your son like you were talking about doing."

Horse looked at me and didn't say anything.

"Horse, it's time to end this whole war nonsense that Gun Clap has with the Mafia. And to be honest, it's time for you to just shut down the whole Gun Clap company."

Horse still just looked at me. We both were silent for a moment.

"So that's what you had to tell me?" Horse asked.

"No, Horse, here's the deal. I know the whole code-of-the-streets bullshit about not being a rat and not talking to the cops and the feds and all of that. But here's the deal. Horse, you've been talking to the feds for a while and you didn't even know it," I said.

The room was eerily quiet as Horse looked at me.

"What the fuck are you talking about, Jessica?" he asked.

At that point I reached into my pocket and pulled out my badge. I held it out for Horse to see.

"Horse, *I am* an FBI agent and I've been investigating you for some time now," I informed him.

The room was again silent. I moved closer to Horse so that he could get a real close look at my credentials. He reached out his hand and calmly took the badge from me along with my ID. He examined them closely.

An *oh shit I'm busted* smirk came across Horse's face as he said, "So your real name is Paula?"

I slowly nodded my head up and down.

"And y'all were able to get up in here to see me because y'all are fucking feds, right?" he asked.

Again I slowly nodded my head. Horse looked at me and the smirk of busted disbelief reappeared across his face as he shook his head two times from side to side.

"Horse, we came here to place you under arrest. And before I leave here today I will but there are some things I need to talk to you about first," I said.

Horse's mind was not focused on what I was saying as he

said, "So if you're a fed how was you fucking niggas and smoking weed and doing all of that shit?"

It was statements like that that made me glad Sherry had left the room. See, that was a major element of the investigation that I could not let out or else I would risk serious consequences as well as possibly blow the entire investigation.

I played things real cool as I said, "Horse listen, right now it's not about that, obviously I know what the hell I'm doing and I know what I can do and what I cannot do. And I'm going to shoot straight with you because I like you and I respect you and although I was investigating you I'm still human and I really do care about you."

Horse looked at me and smirked.

"Horse, what I'm saying is this, you need to forget about all of the code-of-the-streets bullshit and cooperate with us on this investigation," I said.

"Who the fuck is us?" Horse arrogantly asked. "The government?"

"Yes," I replied.

"Jessica . . . Paula, or whatever your name is, there ain't no way. I mean if I'm going down, then I'm going down. It's as simple as that. But I ain't ratting on my niggas," Horse confidently stated. "And if y'all got shit on us then y'all got it, what do you need me to rat on my people for?"

"Horse, stop with the street shit! For once just let it go!" I yelled. I knew that I had to be beyond convincing with the lies that I was getting ready to tell.

"Your *people*, your *boys*, your *niggas*, Horse, come on!" I said as I ran my hand down my face. "Here you are laying here and you can't even get out of bed on your own and walk across the room to the goddamn bathroom and take a piss! And you know why, Horse? Let me tell you why, it's because your *people,* your *boys,* your *niggas* weren't as live and as real as you thought they were. They didn't want this war with the Calvinos as bad as you did. They wanted to end the shit and they resented that you wanted to keep it going. So you know what? Your *people,* your *boys,* your *niggas,* they rolled over on you and that's why you are laying in this condition right now, paralyzed for life and having a pity party!"

Horse stared at me in order to read me and my body language.

"Look at me, Horse. Look at me all you want and try to see if I'm bullshitting you, but I'm not. And deep down inside you know I'm not. Horse, do you really think that it was a coincidence that Supreme and I were not sitting down near the lane that you were bowling in when the shots rang out? Horse, look at it for what it is and call a spade a spade. But Supreme was nowhere near that lane when the shots rang out because he knew that the shots were about to be fired because he had set you up!" I said very convincingly.

Horse didn't respond.

"With Horse out of the picture, the war with the Calvinos is over, you would be dead—or that's at least how it was supposed to go down—and Supreme would get another hungry business-minded producer to come in and replace you. Gun Clap would continue to flourish and make all kinds of money," I said as I lied and continued to sound very believable.

"Horse, if you don't cooperate then you're going down and the people responsible for your paralyzed condition will get far less time than you're gonna get. They'll never be held accountable for initially breaking the code of the street. They broke the rules first, Horse, not you."

Horse nodded his head. I seemed to be getting through to him.

Then I added, "Horse, listen to me, all that you have ever strived for will be snatched away from you in a heartbeat by the government, including your son. Horse, you know first-hand what it's like growing up in a group home and being abandoned by your mother and the people who were supposed to be caring for you and looking out for you. Is that what you want for your son? Do you want him handed over to the state while you do your bid in prison? I know it's not what you want because of what you were telling me the other day. But Horse, I can tell you this: if you and I can't come to an agreement within the next couple of minutes, then I can promise I will be on to the next investigation and probably shipped out of New York and placed in another city to fight crime. But the thing is, my career and my life will go on, and I'll eventually have to testify against you and send you away probably for twenty-five years. And pretty much everyone's life will go on relatively the same, everyone except for you, Horse."

Horse finally spoke. "So if I cooperate, what type of guarantees do I have? Put it in writing, get my lawyer involved, and if the guarantees are there then I can roll with it. But I can tell you this right now, I don't want no jail time, and I wanna keep some of the things that I worked for, like my house and my cars."

"Well Horse, if you cooperate, then you would go into the witness protection program and while we'll work to get you the best deal, your life can pretty much be the same, only it will be in a different state and you'll have to assume a whole new name and identity, and social security number and all of that. But Horse, it will be what you had wanted. It will give you that opportunity to leave all of the nonsense and drama alone, and just raise your son and spend time with him and be there for him," I stated.

"Jessica, that's all good. And it sounds nice. But get in touch with my lawyer. Get my guarantees down on paper and if the guarantees are there for me then I'm wit' it," Horse boldly said.

"Okay," I replied as I dialed Sherry on my cell phone and summoned her back to the hospital room so that she could place Horse under arrest. And although he wasn't a flight risk because of his being paralyzed, we still would have to hand-cuff one of his wrists to the railing of the hospital bed.

CHAPTER THIRTY-ONE

*S*herry returned to the room rather quickly.

"Is everything all right?" she asked.

"Yeah, everything is all right. Sherry, I need for you to place Horse under arrest. I spoke to him and he's willing to—"

Before I could finish my sentence I felt my hair being grabbed very violently and pulled back and I then heard the sound of a gun being cocked and I felt what had to be the barrel of a gun being pressed against my skull.

Sherry turned and saw what was going on.

"Bitch, if you even flinch, your girl is dead!" the strong deep-sounding voice stated.

Sherry immediately held her arms up in the air to show that she was surrendering full control to the person that had the gun to my head. My heart immediately began pounding as I knew that this was now something serious.

"Horse, whatever you do just don't say my name," the man instructed.

"I ain't gonna say your name, nigga, I just wanna know

what took your ass so long to come from up outta that bathroom?" Horse stated.

The guy didn't give Horse an answer as he brutally yanked me to the ground by my hair.

"Test me if you want to and see if I don't spill this bitch's brains all over this floor!" he yelled at Sherry. "Keep your hands up in the air!" he instructed Sherry as he reached and felt all over me for my gun.

After he took my gun and my cell phone he rammed my head to the floor and kicked me in the head. I felt like I was gonna pass out but I willed myself to stay conscious because a big part of me knew that if I had blacked out that I probably would never have opened my eyes again.

"I said keep your goddamn hands in the air!!! Bitch, you think this is a fucking game?" the dark skinned short, and stocky guy asked Sherry as he walked in her direction. I was finally able to see his face. He definitely didn't look familiar and I had no idea who he was.

Whack!!!

The guy slapped Sherry with his gun and he must have knocked out the entire top row of her teeth, or at least it looked that way as Sherry fell to the ground with pools of blood spilling out of her mouth.

"Where your gun at?" the guy asked as he searched Sherry until he found it along with her cell phone.

"Horse, what's the deal? Speak to me, nigggga!" he nervously asked as he went and locked the door of the hospital room.

"Get me the fuck up outta here! That's what's up," Horse replied.

"Nah, I'm saying, you was just fronting with all of that talk about cooperating with the feds, right?" the guy asked.

"Yo, Haz, come on, nigga! I knew you was in the goddamn bathroom! You know I ain't a rat! Come on now. Just get me the fuck up outta here!" Horse replied as he desperately tried to move his weak and crippled body with no luck.

"Why the hell you saying my name?" Haz asked. He made it over to Horse's bed and yanked at the rails as he attempted to move the bed.

"A'ight this how we gonna do this. I'm calling for a nurse and me and y'all two are gonna be behind that door, so when she comes, I'll unlock the door and let her in and then lock it right behind her. And if y'all scream or talk or try something slick, that nurse is gonna be wiping up your brains from off the floor!"

As Haz held the gun on us he pressed the button near Horse's bed in order to summon a nurse to the room.

"A'ight, move!" he yelled at us as he grabbed me in sort of a yoke hold and held the gun right at my cheekbone.

Many thoughts were running through my head. For the first time in a while I thought about my fiancé and family and wondered if I would ever see them again. I thought about how desperate Haz and Horse must have been feeling and I knew that criminals were at their most dangerous when they feel a sense of desperation. I also thought about trying to grab at Haz's balls to yank them from his body in an attempt to subdue him and save myself and Sherry.

In all of the training that I had received and with all of the experience that I had gained over the years, I knew that one of the biggest mistakes that Sherry or I could make was to allow another person to come into a hostage situation. Haz already had me and Sherry and we couldn't risk another innocent person coming into the mix.

"Listen," I struggled to say as the force of Haz's yoke hold made me cough.

"Yo, did I tell you to talk?" Haz asked as he whacked me in the head with the butt of the gun.

My legs became very wobbly and I almost passed out from the blow. Haz had to grip me very tightly to keep me from falling to the floor. It felt as if my head was bleeding but I wasn't sure. The only thing that I knew was that I was seeing stars and I quickly nixed the plan of preventing another hostage from coming into the room. Haz acted and seemed as if he meant business and I knew that staying alive was more important than preventing another hostage from coming into the fray.

"Get behind the door! If either one of you opens your mouth there's gonna be a bunch of muthafuckas catching a slug up in this hospital!" Haz warned.

As we were positioned behind the hospital-room door, Haz loosened the grip that he had on me and reached to unlock the door. We waited for the nurse to arrive.

"Horse, we'll be up outta here in a minute!" Haz stated as he returned me to the yoke hold.

As we waited for the nurse to arrive it was as if you could hear every heartbeat of every person inside the room. I wondered what Sherry was thinking. I wondered if she would make some type of attempt to spring us free. She also knew that it was a no-no to allow anyone other than law enforcement into a hostage crisis.

As we waited in fear I heard what sounded like my cell phone ringing. The sound of it distracted everybody and just at that moment the doorknob to the hospital room started to turn. I guess that Sherry sensed that Haz might have been distracted and she let out a yell as she grabbed for Haz's gun.

Haz completely let go of me. I lost my balance and fell to the ground as Haz and Sherry battled over the gun. The nurse that walked in didn't have a clue what was going on.

"Excuse me! Hello! People, this is a hospital!" she yelled at Haz and Sherry.

At that point Haz kicked Sherry in the midsection. She quickly doubled over in pain and gave up her struggle for the gun.

"I'm calling security!" the nurse shouted as she must have seen the gun for the first time.

Haz quickly ran over to the door and closed and locked it before the nurse could exit. The nurse yelled for security. She screamed at the top of her lungs until Haz was able to grip one of his hands around her mouth. Even with her mouth covered she continued to try and yell as she made inaudible muffled sounds.

Haz threw the nurse to the ground and she landed on her back. He stood over her and put the barrel of the gun inside her mouth. That move finally made her take notice and she stopped resisting.

"Listen to me!" Haz instructed. "There is only one way that we are doing this. And that way is my way! You see that bitch over there with the wind knocked out of her and her teeth missing? She didn't wanna do things my way! Now let me explain this to you and I'm only explaining it once. I'm gonna stand you up, you gonna unplug whatever tubes you gotta unplug for my man over there, and you are gonna wheel him outta of this room and out of this hospital all together. You got me?"

The nurse nodded her head in agreement.

"If you open your mouth I swear on my life that I will murder you and not think twice," Haz said in a very convincing manner.

"Horse, you a'ight man?" Haz asked. Horse replied that he was.

At that point what sounded like my cell phone began to ring again.

"Yo, who is that calling y'all?" Haz asked.

No one replied.

"Haz, come here real quick," Horse instructed.

Haz went over to Horse and he whispered something into Haz's hear. Haz nodded as if he agreed with whatever was said.

"Aight, I asked y'all who was that calling y'all. And I'm still waiting on an answer! And don't say that y'all don't know!" Haz screamed.

"Can I look at the caller ID or can you tell me what number it is that was on the phone?" I asked.

Haz ignored me and unreasonably demanded to know who it was that was calling me.

"You don't need to see no caller ID! Tell me who the hell is calling your phone!" Haz demanded to know.

I didn't know what to say or do but I knew that I had to give some kind of an answer. "It might be my boss," I said.

Haz looked at Horse but they didn't say anything.

"Where is your boss at?" Haz asked.

"He's outside with a bunch of other agents," I lied.

"Muthafucka!" Haz yelled.

He paced back and forth trying to figure things out.

"Listen, he's probably calling to check on me. And I can tell you that if he doesn't hear from me real soon that he will be on his way up here if he isn't already," I said in an attempt to rush Haz into making some kind of mistake.

"Haz, we gotta call Supreme and tip everybody off to what's going down," Horse stated.

"Nah, we gotta get up outta here first. They probably got the nigga's phone tapped or trailing the nigga or something," Haz stated.

He then asked the nurse if she could get access to an ambulance or a similar type of vehicle. And she stated that she could.

At that point there was a knock on the hospital room door. Everyone in the room froze.

Haz held up one finger to his mouth, signaling for everyone to be quiet. Then he motioned for the nurse to go by the door and he went with her. He held a gun to her back as he said some things into her ear that only she could hear.

"Who is it?" the nurse asked.

Someone answered on the other end but I couldn't hear what was being said.

"Oh, okay. Well, this is Nicole. He had called for a nurse and I responded. But I might be a while. Something happened that he is sort of embarrassed about and I don't think you really want to bear the smell, if you know what I mean," the nurse said.

She had done a great acting job, apparently, as the person on the other side of the door bought her story and walked away.

"Haz, let's get up outta here!" Horse stated in his weak-sounding voice.

"Horse, I got this! So can you get this ambulance or not?" Haz asked more aggressively.

"Well, the ambulances are run by the city. This hospital doesn't have its own ambulances but we do have ambulettes which we use to transport patients and I am sure that we can get one of those," she responded.

"Okay listen. We're gonna wheel my man outta here. But when we do, I don't want no kinds of tricks," Haz stated. Then he looked at Horse and Horse nodded to him.

There was a pause for about thirty seconds and no one said anything.

After snapping out of his trance, Haz walked over to the nurse and frisked her. "You ain't got no cell phone, do you?" Haz asked.

When she replied that she didn't Haz instructed the three of us to all go into the bathroom and wait for him. We did as we were told. And as I made it into the bathroom I felt uneasy like I never had before. I hated the fact that Haz held so much power over us. It is not a good feeling to have your life literally hanging in the hands of someone else and being subjected to their every beck and call.

"We're gonna be okay," I assured Sherry and Nicole even though I didn't sincerely believe that.

"Nicole, if it will assure you any, Sherry and I are both FBI agents," I stated.

"What?" Nicole asked in disbelief. "I know I'm gonna die today. I know it! Why did I come to work today? I knew I should have kept my black ass home!"

Sherry still looked to be in a ton of pain. Her lips had ballooned due to the swelling from being hit in the mouth by the gun. She didn't say anything and I could tell that she, like me, hated that feeling of desperation and powerlessness that was surrounding us.

"Nicole, he has our cell phones on him and they have this global tracking device. We'll cooperate and go with him but once we are gone for too long or the Bureau finds out that Horse is missing or they can't get ahold of me they will track us through the phone and send an army to come get us. But it's key to remain calm and do whatever he tells us to do," I whispered as Sherry nodded in agreement.

Haz walked into the bathroom and closed the door behind him.

The room was deathly silent and I didn't like what my senses were telling me. Haz looked at us with one of the coldest stares I had ever seen in my life. He didn't say a word, just opened up the door and walked back over to Horse. He took the pillow that Horse was laying on and handed Horse the remote control to the television set that was hoisted in the air.

"Yeah, turn that shit up as loud as it will go," Haz instructed before coming back into the bathroom and closing the door behind him.

He was holding a white pillow in his hands and had instructed Horse to turn up the volume on the television. It didn't take a rocket scientist to figure out what Haz was thinking and I needed to break that train of thought.

"Haz, you don't have to do anything drastic, especially if it's not necessary," I said.

Haz ignored me. He commanded us to turn around and face the toilet bowl.

"Kneel down!" he barked.

I did as Haz instructed but I was beyond nervous as hell. I blew out some air as I sighed.

"Mister, please. I have two little babies at home," Nicole attempted to say. She too was fearing the worst.

"Everybody shut the fuck up!" Haz screamed, which almost caused me to violate my underwear. "This is what y'all don't understand! I'm running this show. Now turn around and kneel at the toilet bowl!"

We all nervously did as he said.

Haz then placed the pillow over the gun and put that combination at Sherry's head and pulled the trigger without hesitation.

"Oh God!" Nicole screamed as Sherry's blood and brains splattered all over the bathroom.

I remained silent, wanting to throw up from fear and the gruesome sight.

"Y'all see that?" Haz asked. "That was for that little stunt that she pulled when she tried to grab my gun!"

Nicole and I remained silent as we kneeled at the toilet bowl expecting the worst. I could see chunks of Sherry's skull and patches of her hair along with her blood floating in the toilet bowl. Sherry's motionless, lifeless body didn't say a word as it lay limp on the cold, hard bathroom floor.

Like a cold-hearted psychopath, Haz proceeded to talk. "Now this is what we're gonna do. We are gonna calmly walk out of Horse's room and wheel him to that ambulette thing that you were talking about. But I want y'all to look at this chick right here," Haz said, referring to Sherry.

"She tested me and look at her ass now! I'm telling the both of y'all this one more time. Test me if you want to and see if y'all don't end up like this bitch! Cooperate with me and y'all will have no problems."

Neither Nicole nor I said a word. We both knew that Haz meant business and therefore our only option was to cooperate.

"When we're making our way out of here I want everybody looking as calm and as normal as possible. A'ight?" he asked.

Nicole and I nodded our heads. Haz then instructed us to both get up and make our way out of the bathroom as he held his gun on us. Horse turned down the volume on the television.

"Nicole, take us to this ambulette thing. You better know where you're taking us and don't play no games!" Haz commanded as Nicole and I made our way over to Horse's bed and began to prepare to roll him and his bed out of his hospital room.

CHAPTER THIRTY-TWO

as we wheeled Horse out of his room and into the tenth-floor hospital lobby, Haz held close by me and Nicole. If either one of us had tried anything we would have definitely caught a bullet in our backs. So we were certain not to make any false moves. There were doctors and hospital staff walking around but since Nicole was with us, nothing must have looked out of order.

I was trying my best to make eye contact with someone so that I could rapidly blink my eyes at them and try to alert them in some way. But unfortunately the opportunity did not present itself.

After the one-minute walk, which seemed more like an eternity, we had reached the elevator. Nicole pressed the down button and no one said a word. We didn't even look at each other. I was sure that all of our hearts were pounding very rapidly due to the anxiety that we all had to be feeling, including Haz.

As we waited for the elevator, two nurses and a doctor

walked past us. One of the doctors seemed to do a double-take and he stopped.

The elevator reached our floor and the doors opened up. Just our luck, the elevator was empty.

"Excuse me! Nicole!" the doctor who had done the double-take yelled.

"Don't pay him no mind, let's go!" Haz commanded.

Nicole looked at the doctor but then turned her attention back to the elevator and proceeded to press the button of our desired floor.

"Nicole!" the doctor yelled again.

The doors to the elevator began to close.

But just before they were fully closed the doctor stuck his foot in the door.

"Nicole, didn't you hear me calling you? Where in God's name do you think you're taking him?" the doctor asked in a pissed-off manner.

All of us froze.

I had two choices. I could have either tried to blow up Haz's plan, but that would have been risky and it could have caused us to bring another hostage into the situation. Or I could have played things off in an attempt to limit any bloodshed or loss of life. I opted for my second choice and I knew that I had to speak before Nicole spoke.

Sir, it's okay. I'm with the FBI. This is official FBI business. We will be bringing the patient right back."

"Well I wasn't informed of any of this!" the doctor emphatically replied. "I'm responsible for this patient!"

"Sir, if you do not move your foot from the door, I'll have

to place you under arrest!" I stated with a very authoritative voice.

"Place me under arrest for what?" the doctor asked.

At that point our loud conversation began to draw the attention of others and I knew that Haz would get antsy and do something desperate and irrational if the situation escalated. So I pushed the doctor back out onto the hospital floor and he fell backward as the door closed.

"A'ight, where the fuck is this ambulance thing gonna be at?" Haz asked, sounding very nervous.

"There should be one right near the emergency-room entrance," Nicole replied in a nervous tone of defeat.

"A'ight. Yo, if anybody tries anything I want you to run that same FBI shit on them so that we can get the hell up outta here," Haz commanded me.

As we reached the ground level of the hospital and wheeled our way toward the emergency-room entrance I desperately wanted to disrupt our getaway. We had always been trained that if at all possible, never let ourselves or a hostage be taken to another location. The chances of surviving such an ordeal are very poor.

I scanned the floor, looking for someone to alert.

Suddenly the sounds of cell phones ringing started coming from Haz. From the ring tone I was certain that it was my phone.

"Eh, sir, excuse me. Cell phones must be turned off in the hospital, sir," a security guard stated as he appeared out of nowhere.

"Keep walking!" Haz instructed. "Nicole, where is this fucking ambulance thing at?" Haz muttered under his breath.

"There should be one just past that door," Nicole stated as we all picked up the pace.

"Haz, I think you should answer the phone," I said in an attempt to add some confusion to the tense atmosphere.

"Sir, did you hear me? Cell phones are not allowed inside the hospital," the persistent guard restated.

Haz looked as if he was attempting to reach for his gun as he stopped and turned to confront the security guard.

"Money, why are you stressing me? Am I using the phone? I didn't even answer the call!" Haz stressed as he clearly intimidated the security guard.

The guard stopped in his tracks and fortunately for everyone involved, the cell phone stopped ringing.

"Okay sir, please have a nice day," the guard calmly stated before walking off.

At that point, almost simultaneously, all of the cell phones that Haz was carrying started ringing. I knew that it had to be my superiors at the FBI trying to contact both me and Sherry. Someone had probably found Sherry's body and alerted the police. I could have been wrong but that was my wish.

We finally spotted the ambulette. To me it looked just like a regular ambulance, an ambulance whose engine was running and was sitting idle with no one inside.

"What's up with this one?" Haz asked Nicole.

"That's a city ambulance, it's not one of the hospital ambulances. The paramedics probably just dropped someone off in the ER and will be right back," Nicole replied.

Haz checked the back door of the ambulance and it was open.

"We're taking this one," Haz said. He commanded Nicole and me to get inside the back while he hoisted Horse to us.

Getting Horse inside the ambulance wasn't the easiest thing but somehow we managed. Horse was in obvious pain but I think his thoughts were more focused on getting to a new destination.

"Y'all are riding up in the front with me so that I can see y'all," Haz instructed as he led us out of the back door and into the front.

As Haz gripped the handle to the front door we heard an alarm sounding off from the hospital.

"Code Red! Code Red! Code Red!" a very loud-sounding computer voice kept repeating as a siren blared in the background.

"Hurry up and get in!" Haz shouted as he hustled to the driver's side and jumped in the ambulance.

Just as Haz was pulling out to get away, security guards from inside the hospital emerged from every door and were frantically looking around. I was certain that they had been informed of Sherry's death and Horse's disappearance.

The cell phones that Haz was carrying all began ringing simultaneously.

"Shit!" Haz screamed in frustration. He ignored the cell phones, which wouldn't stop ringing.

"How do you turn on this goddamn siren?" Haz vented. He pushed any and every button and flicked every switch that he could find. He eventually hit the correct switch because the ambulance's siren came on and it gave Haz a license to speed and blow lights.

All of the cell phones continued to ring until finally Haz picked up one of them.

"Yo, where y'all at?" Haz asked as he continued to recklessly maneuver the ambulance through the city streets.

"Hold on, hold on, I gotta put you on speaker so I can drive this thing," Haz yelled into the phone while barely missing a pedestrian and almost sideswiping a parked car.

He pressed buttons on his cell phone and began speaking into the phone. With the siren blaring in the background and the other cell phones continuing to ring, Haz was growing increasingly agitated and antsy.

"Yo, 'Preme, you ain't gonna believe the shit that just went down, kid!" Haz yelled into the phone's speaker.

"Why you got me on speakerphone and what the hell is all of that noise?" the person on the other end asked. I was sure that it was Supreme, but with all of the noise I wasn't 100 percent sure that Haz had said Supreme's name.

"Kid, I'm in a fucking ambulance trying to get the fuck outta Dodge!" Haz replied.

"What?" Supreme questioned.

" 'Preme, I'll explain everything to you in a minute but—"

Supreme cut Haz off. "Haz, what's up with Horse? Are you hurt? What the fuck are you doing in an ambulance?"

" 'Preme, Horse is in the back of the ambulance and I'm driving this bitch!"

"What!" Supreme yelled.

" 'Preme, just listen to me, nigga! Round everybody up and do whatever you gotta do but bounce right now! The feds is on to y'all niggas real heavy," Haz yelled into the speakerphone as he appeared to be maneuvering his way toward Queens.

"Haz, you had a job to do and it sounds like you fucked it up!" 'Preme yelled.

Haz appeared agitated as Supreme seemed to be totally ignoring Haz's words.

"Haz, you was supposed to *pose* as security for the nigga and merck his ass and get the fuck up outta there! How did you mess that up?" Supreme asked as I listened in disbelief.

I had a very extensive slang vocabulary and I knew that "merck" was a synonym for murder. I could not believe that Supreme had actually planned to have Horse murdered! Immediately I started questioning myself and wondering if the shooting at Chelsea Piers had in fact been orchestrated by Supreme. That was ironic, because I had lied about it to Horse in an attempt to get him to cooperate with us and from the sounds of things it seemed like that really may have been the case.

" 'Preme! I gotta disrespect you for a minute just to get your attention! Please shut the fuck up and listen to me, nigga! Goddamn!" Haz yelled.

"Do you know a light-skinned chick named Jessica?" Haz asked.

"Yeah, why? She—"

Haz cut Supreme off and continued on, "She's sitting right here next to me, Supreme! Do you know that this bitch is a fucking federal agent?"

There was dead silence and my heart began to race.

Even Nicole, who didn't know all of the details, could put two and two together and sense that something just wasn't right. She squeezed her hand around my right thigh. I was sitting in the middle between Haz and Nicole and I made sure not to respond to Nicole's nervous gesture. But like Nicole probably knew, all Supreme had to do was give the word to Haz and the two of us would have been taken out in a heartbeat.

"A fed? Get outta here! She ain't no fed. Nigga, I fucked that bitch and even nutted all up in that!" Supreme stated through the phone.

Nicole released her grip from my thigh after that comment and I could only imagine what she was now thinking.

"'Preme, I'm telling you the bitch is an agent. I saw her badge and all of that! She was trying to cut a deal with Horse to rat y'all niggas out!" Haz yelled.

There was silence. Supreme must have been contemplating what he should do.

"Haz, tell me I'm not getting set up!" Supreme stated.

"Supreme, if you don't get ready to bounce, your ass is getting locked up! This ain't got nothing to do with no setup. I just murdered an FBI agent up in the hospital about fifteen minutes ago and Horse is with me, missing from the hospital. Them niggas' next move gotta be to come calling for you."

"A'ight, yo, I'm gonna get on the horn with my people right now. What I want you to do is meet me at my mom's old crib in Rosedale, it's over near Snake Road and One-forty-seventh Avenue," Supreme instructed.

"A'ight, I'll be there in about fifteen minutes. Yo, what you want me to do with Horse?" Haz asked.

"That nigga is dying tonight! Just bring him and Jessica to the crib and I'm gonna have Jessica pull the trigger so our hands will be clean!" Supreme stated like the devil that he was.

I knew that Horse couldn't hear any of what was being said and I was certain that when we got to our destination he was gonna be in for the surprise of his life. But I also knew that there was no way that I could pull the trigger and kill him.

But then again I had been known for bending the rules . . .

CHAPTER THIRTY-THREE

hen we arrived at the location in Rosedale, Haz parked the ambulance and waited for Supreme to show up.

"You should be a'ight, ma," Haz said to Nicole.

Nicole didn't respond. She looked as though she were living through the worst nightmare ever.

"Ain't nobody gonna get hurt that ain't gotta get hurt. Just as long as you don't do nothing stupid you'll be a'ight," Haz reiterated, for the first time showing signs that he was actually human.

"Yo, that's them!" Haz stated as he quickly opened the driver's side door.

He was instantly greeted by Supreme and his entourage of four beefy and intimidating-looking men, none of whom I recalled ever seeing before.

"Where's Horse?" Supreme asked, speaking in a rushed tone.

"He's in the back of the ambulance," Haz answered.

"Listen. You was right about me possibly getting locked up

tonight. My cell phone started ringing nonstop with my people telling me about the feds running up on everybody and raiding everybody's crib and all that shit! So we gotta be in and out. I already called Jet Networks and chartered us a plane so that we could just get outta town and figure out what we gon' do. You feel me?" Supreme asked.

"I feel you," Haz answered.

"Okay, y'all help him get Horse outta the ambulance and bring him into the crib right there across the street," Supreme ordered and then he quickly turned his attention to me.

Snatching open the passenger-side door of the ambulance, Supreme stood as stiff as a statue and peered at me.

"Jessica, I gotta give it up to yo ass. You had a nigga fooled," Supreme said with a disgusted frown on his face. "You did E pills, you drank, you even fucked a nigga, and all this time you was a damn agent?"

I didn't know how to respond so I kept my mouth shut and just shook my head no.

"Get out of the ambulance!" Supreme yelled as he dragged me out of the seat and threw me onto the floor.

"Who the hell is this?" Supreme asked, referring to Nicole as she also made her way out of the ambulance. Haz left Supreme's underlings to attend to Horse and he ran over and quickly explained who Nicole was.

"A'ight! Yo, just get everybody in the crib. Bring Horse to the basement. I don't even wanna see that nigga," Supreme explained.

Everyone followed Supreme's orders. We entered the tidy single-family home. It appeared to be lived in but no one seemed to be home at the time.

Haz had been instructed to take me and Nicole into two separate rooms and to handcuff us to the radiator in each respective room. And as we were being handcuffed I could hear Horse yelling from the basement, asking for Supreme to come downstairs. Horse was in tons of pain and considering that he didn't have painkiller medication dripping into his veins like he had in his hospital room, he was probably feeling double the pain he had felt just hours ago.

You could even hear the sounds of pain in his voice as he helplessly yelled out for Supreme to come downstairs to his aid.

"Fuck that nigga!" Supreme stated as he yelled to the basement for the beefy bodyguard-looking guys to come back upstairs. When they arrived he instructed them to keep an eye on me and Nicole while he and Haz went to the adjacent room to talk.

Horse was still screaming out in pain. Through the thin walls, Haz could be heard talking extremely theatrically and loud. I could hear him describing to Supreme everything that had gone down in the hospital. But I guess it was all an attempt to make himself look good, because he did a horrible job of accurately describing what had gone down between Horse and myself at the hospital.

" 'Preme, word is bond! Maybe dude thought I was some freelancing off-duty cop that you paid to serve as his bodyguard or something. I don't know. But like I said, I go to the bathroom, I'm taking a shit, right, then I hear this chick in the room. So I crack the door open and I didn't just walk out on them 'cause I didn't know what was what but I knew she wasn't no nurse or nothing like that. And then boom! The bitch pulls out a badge and the whole nine and starts saying that she's a muthafucking federalee! And Horse got silent. And at that point I reached for my gat and was ready to just come out the bathroom blazing, right! Then I hear Horse bitchin' up, talking about the witness protection program and all of that. And I couldn't believe the shit! So I thought about the situation and I was like a'ight, cool. I'll just play it like everything is everything. You kna'imean? But I knew that I had to just get everybody up outta that hospital and get things relayed to you," Haz stated. Supreme listened as Haz went on to describe how and why he murdered Sherry.

After having heard enough, Supreme came into the room where I was and asked me point blank whether I was an agent or not.

My heart was in my shoes and I was feeling numb all over. When you think you're about to get beat or killed there probably is no other way to feel. With my left wrist attached to the base of the radiator like I was some dog chained to a fence, I knew that I wasn't in a position of power and if I wanted to stay alive I would have to do some serious fast talking. But for some reason the words just were not finding their way to my mouth.

"Answer me bitch!" Supreme yelled as he slapped the taste out of my mouth.

"Yes, Supreme but you don't understand!" I replied through tears.

"I don't understand what?" Supreme hollered as he pulled out his gun and cocked it back.

"You just don't understand!" I replied again.

"I understand that you about to get your brains splattered

all along that wall right there. That's what I understand!"
Supreme yelled.

Through my tears, I pleaded. "Supreme, yes I'm an agent,
but I'm dirty! You think I love working for the fucking FBI?
It's just a job that pays the bills. But what went down with me
and you, that's real! That's me! I crossed that line with you
and I don't have to go back to the FBI side. And I can prove it."

"Bitch, yo ass is a fucking liar! You just saying that to save
yo ass right now!" Supreme yelled as he appeared to be raising
the gun toward my head.

"Supreme no!" I pleaded. "Listen to me. I was at the hospital placing Horse under arrest. If I had wanted to we could
have easily been taking you down. But I never pulled the plug
on you."

"Bitch, you lying to me!" Supreme yelled. He now had the
gun at my forehead.

At that point I just knew that I was gonna die, and I was so
scared that I almost pissed on myself right there on the floor.

"Supreme, please just listen to me. I came at Horse and
told him to cooperate but that was just to bring down the
Calvinos. That's what I wanted him for. If it was to bring you
down, that would be stupid. Supreme, I fucked you. I did
drugs with you. There would be no case against you because
all of the evidence would get thrown out and then my ass
would have ended up in jail. All I wanted to do is show the FBI
that I got something out of the investigation, which would
have been the Calvinos, and they would have been happy
about that. And I figured that if Horse ever turned around
and talked bad about you and tried to bring you down that

you and I could just bounce together, because like I said, with the shit that I did, I would get fired and locked underneath the jail for that," I pleaded.

Supreme finally relaxed the gun.

Haz stepped in the room and totally threw a monkey wrench into the program.

"'Preme, kill that bitch! She's lying! I was at the hospital and she was talking real slick and greasy about you. She ain't never said shit to Horse about taking down the Calvinos!" Haz stated.

I knew that I had to take drastic action or I would be killed immediately. Just as I was about to jump right back in and verbally defend myself, Horse started with his pleas from the basement. But thank God that he did because it triggered my way out of my predicament.

"Supreme I'm not lying, and I'll show you I'm not. I overheard what you said to Haz when we were in the ambulance, and if you loosen these handcuffs and bring me downstairs I swear to you that I'll kill Horse myself!" I stated, shocking even myself.

Supreme looked at Haz.

Then they both looked at me.

"Uncuff her ass," Supreme instructed. "I'm gonna test her gangstress."

As the handcuffs were being unlocked I stated, "Supreme, if I do this, you still can kill me and be gone. But at least let this prove to you that I'm willing to go to the other side with you. I know the system and how to get around it. Just don't kill me. Let me bounce with you and I promise you we'll be okay," I begged.

"Bitch, you talking too much for me! Get the fuck up! We going to the basement and I swear on my grandmother's grave that if you don't kill this nigga or if you try something slick, I'm gonna take you out!" Supreme threatened.

I could hear Nicole's sobs coming from one of the locked bedrooms on the first floor as 'Preme, Haz, and I made our way to the well-lit basement.

"Supreme, what the fuck is up, man?" Horse asked as he laid sprawled out on the ceramic-tiled basement floor. He looked as if he was unsuccessfully trying to do push-ups and he grunted from the pain and anguish of not being able to move.

"You know what they do to horses that break their leg?" Supreme calmly asked Horse as he stood next to me.

Horse didn't immediately answer him.

"Supreme, we been through too much together—" Horse eventually blurted out before being cut off by Supreme.

"First it was not wanting to squash the whole Mafia beef! Then a nigga didn't wanna pay G-Baby's ransom money! Now I find out a nigga wanna become a rat? Horse, you tell me what the fuck I am supposed to do!" Supreme barked.

Horse remained silent.

"And you see this bitch right here? Remember it was you who introduced us to this bitch! You, Horse! And now we see that Chris was right when he said she was a cop. But you ain't believe him and you set the nigga up. You believed this bitch over Chris. And Chris was your man!" Supreme recited as he paced back and forth.

"Jessica, since Horse don't seem to be able to recall anything, why don't you tell me what it is that they do to horses that can't walk or horses that have a broken leg?"

"They shoot 'em," I calmly replied with a rapidly beating heart and sweaty palms.

Supreme handed a gun to me, while Haz pointed his gun at me to check me.

"That's right. They shoot 'em in order to put them out of their misery," Supreme stated. "Horse, look at you, man! You can't live like that, nigga! All crippled and shit."

"So this is what it all comes down to?" Horse asked as he lay humbled and helplessly sprawled on the floor. "All this money that we made together, all these hit records, the company we built, and this is what it comes down to?"

Supreme didn't respond to his question.

"Jessica, come on. Please. I got my son to look after. I'll take the rap for all of this shit. I'll sign my name to a confession right now. Just don't kill me. Please," Horse begged. At that moment he was as far removed from the cocky, confident, always-walking-with-swagger person that I had come to know. But I guess you'll get like that when you are staring death in the face.

"Man, fuck all that! You didn't give a fuck when G-Baby was about to get his head blown off or when Chris got killed! Jessica, kill that nigga right now!" Supreme ordered.

I raised the gun and Horse stared at me with a look of fear that I will never forget. Everything seemed to go blank as things got unbelievably quiet around me. In fact it was so quiet that I don't even recall the sound of the gun blast as I pulled the trigger.

But I do remember the way Horse's blood-splattered head slammed to the ground after the bullet from my FBI-issued 9mm handgun ripped through his skull, killing him instantly.

CHAPTER THIRTY-FOUR

*i*f you had asked me when I began my career as an FBI agent if I thought I would have stooped this low and done the dirty things that I've done, I would have thought you were insane or delusional. And yet, I had done drugs while on the job, I had had unprotected sex with the criminals that I was investigating, and worst of all I had actually murdered one of the men that I was investigating.

What was sick was that I felt remorse, I felt huge remorse and sorrow, but I felt a bigger sense of power. The badge that I had literally gave me the power to do whatever the hell I wanted to do. And I knew that as long as I covered my ass and played my cards right, I could in fact get away with murder and all sorts of other crimes.

But with the investigation right at the point of ending, I knew that I was playing a real risky game. Risky in the sense that I could have been killed at any moment by Supreme and his crew. I also knew that I could go to jail for life if any of the dirt that I had done came to light.

Exploiting this investigation to my financial benefit had

always been in the back of my mind and I had planned for it. Those plans had escalated ever sense I had been set up by some of the discriminating male FBI agents and I almost ended up dying as a result of that discrimination. Just like I had carried the cocaine around with me and it helped me get out of a jam in the past, I had set some things up that I knew would be necessary to help me possibly get rich from this investigation if the opportunity presented itself.

So as Supreme left Horse dead on the basement floor and Nicole handcuffed to a radiator, I hoped like heck that he wouldn't kill me. I knew that if I could just stay alive that I would be able to pimp the investigation and come out on top.

"We gotta hurry up and get outta here!" Supreme instructed as he grabbed me by the arm and led me toward the front door.

"Yo, put her in the truck, I gotta check the house real quick and then we out," Supreme stated.

I was quickly brought outside and put inside of a black SUV. I sat in the backseat between two of Supreme's Hulk Hogan–size henchmen that I didn't know. The driver of the SUV looked familiar, I wasn't sure if it was O-Water, but I doubted it. I couldn't exactly recall his name or where I'd seen him before. He sat with the truck in park and the engine running and he appeared a bit nervous.

I turned my head just slightly and I could see a Mercedes-Benz also idling just to the left of the SUV.

Supreme finally came out of the house and he made his way to the driver's side of the Mercedes-Benz. He spoke for about thirty seconds to the driver and then he hastily made his way back to the SUV and hopped in the passenger seat.

"We gotta get to Republic out in Farmingdale," Supreme instructed the driver.

"Aight," the nervous-looking driver responded as he put the truck in drive and took off.

There was a moment of silence in the SUV. Even Supreme appeared to be a bit anxious. He hadn't even turned to the back of the truck to look at me.

"What happened to Teterboro? I thought we was going there?" the driver asked Supreme.

Supreme sat slumped in his seat and he seemed like he was deep in thought. He ran his left hand down his face and blew out a gust of air from his lungs.

"Nah, I just found out that we would have had to catch a dead leg at Teterboro and I ain't trying to depend on that. But they got us at Republic," Supreme stated.

I couldn't fully decipher what he was saying but I knew that he was referring to Teterboro Airport. I just wasn't familiar with "Republic" or with the term "dead leg."

" 'Preme, what's up with shorty? She was a cutie. She ain't rolling wit us?" the guy on my right asked.

"Nah, I left her in the crib. We don't need her slowing us down," Supreme replied.

My guess was that they were referring to Nicole. From the sound of things, I could only guess that she was okay. Supreme was the last one in the house with her so only he knew if he'd left her physically safe.

"So this plane is chartered, right?" the driver asked, again sounding nervous.

"What the fuck? I got this! What's with all the questions?" Supreme responded.

We had made our way onto the Southern State Parkway and we were heading east going toward Long Island. The car was eerily quiet. There was no loud rap music being played and no one was saying anything. I could only guess that everyone, including Supreme, was in shock that Horse was actually dead.

"Jessica, what's the deal?" Supreme asked without turning around to face me.

"What's the deal? You tell me," I said, trying to come across as normal as possible, although I was nervous as shit.

"You murdering cats, you do drugs, you sexing niggas? Is that what they teach y'all at the academy?" Supreme asked sarcastically. Everyone in the truck began smirking and laughing a bit. "Shit, get me a job with the FBI!"

"I make my own rules," I stated. I hoped that Supreme was still carrying my cell phone or Sherry's cell phone.

"Yeah, I can see that you make your own rules. All y'all cops and feds is corrupt. Word is bond!" Supreme retorted.

I kept quiet.

"So tell me the truth, what's up with this whole hip-hop police shit. Y'all really trying to take down hip-hop or what?" Supreme asked.

I didn't answer Supreme's question. He wasn't acting hostile at the moment and I had to take advantage of that.

"So what's the story, 'Preme? Where are you taking me to?" I asked.

Supreme didn't respond.

"If you wanna make it through this, Supreme, I can help you," I stated as we passed exit 25 on the Southern State Parkway.

After having shot Horse I had built up enough credibility with Supreme for him to take me seriously.

"Help me how?"

"I can help you keep some money and make it outta this country with the money. And 'Preme, honestly, your only option is to bounce outta the United States," I said rather frankly.

"We already got a plane to take us to St. Barts," Supreme replied.

"St. Barts?" I asked with sarcastic curiosity.

"Yeah," Supreme responded.

"Supreme, listen to me. Doctors save lives but I'm sure on the flip side that if they wanted to kill you painlessly they would know how to do it. And it's the same thing with me being a fed. I lock people up and put them away for years, but on the flip side I also know how those same people that I lock up could get away with just about any crime conceivable," I stated.

"So whatchu saying?" Supreme asked. From his tone and from his body language I could tell that he was game to hear what I had to say and game to trusting me.

"What I'm saying is if you go to St. Barts, you will get caught and extradited back here to the United States," I replied. "They know that's where all of y'all rap cats vacation at."

"But we got a crib out there and we got a stash out there," Supreme replied as we exited the parkway.

"Supreme, you could blow my brains out right here if you want to and get on a plane and take your chances. But you can also listen to me, and I'll get you out of this jam, and my life will be my collateral," I stated.

There was silence as we turned to enter into the airport.

"Okay, Supreme, here's the deal. Whenever you see those major drug busts on TV, where they have the wads of cash alongside the bricks of cocaine and the illegal guns that were seized, what no one knows is that a lot of times the DEA and FBI agents take a lot of that cash for themselves. But they don't spend it here in the United States. They arrange for it to be wired to offshore accounts that they have set up in countries like the Cayman Islands, or to Swiss bank accounts," I said.

"Yeah, drive right over there. We can park the truck here and walk over," Supreme instructed the driver. Then he turned his attention back to me. "So what exactly are you saying?"

"I'm saying you need to transfer as much money as you possibly can into one of my offshore accounts that I have set up, and we—"

Supreme cut me off. "Get the fuck outta here! How the hell would I know if I was wiring my dough to a fucking government account?" Supreme asked. "I could wire the shit to my St. Barts account."

Supreme was right, he could have done that, and he was also correct in being cautious about wiring funds to a bank account that he had no idea who controlled. But I knew I had to quickly convince him otherwise, because I really wanted the loot in my account. There was no other way to pull off my plan.

"Supreme, two things. Number one, you gotta fly to Mexico. And then from Mexico you could fly into Cuba. And in Cuba you could do whatever the hell you want to and not worry about getting extradited because the United States doesn't mess with Cuba on any level. And not a lot of countries do business with Cuba, but with my Swiss bank account you could have the money wired even to Cuba. And that way everything would be untraceable and you would be good. The real players go to Cuba and hide out. Not to St. Barts or any island like that," I stated. It was a lie but I knew that it sounded accurate and believable.

"'Preme, don't fuck with this bitch!" one of the henchmen stated.

"Yo, let's hurry up and get on this plane," Supreme instructed as he exited the truck with his boys following his lead.

"Supreme, I'll be with you and you can kill me on the spot if we get to Cuba or Mexico and the money isn't available," I stated.

Supreme walked close to his man and whispered in his ear. The guy nodded and then everyone was silent as we stood in the parking lot waiting for Supreme's instructions. Supreme thought for a moment.

"Jessica, you gonna roll with us because you got that badge. And I'm gonna transfer seven figures into this account that you say you got set up. And when we get to Mexico, if that money ain't there—"

"Supreme, it will be there," I said, cutting him off.

Before long we all boarded an exquisite, custom-made, eight-passenger private Lear jet. Supreme spoke to the pilots and worked out the details of the changes to the flight itinerary. In no time we were taxing onto the runway, getting ready to take off to Mexico. The pilots explained to Supreme something that I already knew before I offered up the suggestion that we fly to Mexico. If we wanted to make it safely to Mexico, we would have to stop over in Texas in order to refuel the plane. Most small planes couldn't make it directly to Mexico without refueling. Supreme thought nothing of it and he agreed to making the stop wherever we had to make it. His only insistence was that it only be *one* stop. And the pilots assured him that it would be.

As five of us sat in the passenger seats of the plane, Supreme and I talked. We prepared to transfer money into my account before any of his assets were frozen. From one of the phones on the plane, we would be able to access all of the necessary bank accounts and transfer the funds to and from the appropriate accounts.

I knew there was one thing that I forgot to let Supreme in on. My cell phone, which he had, was a government-issued cell phone, as were all FBI-agent equipment. And the cell phone had a global positioning system tracking device in it, which meant that no matter where we went, the FBI would be able to track us down with pinpoint precision.

The fact that my cell phone had not rang in some time was my confirmation that the FBI knew that something was up. Part of their procedures was to stop calling the cell phone to avoid any unnecessary suspicions and to immediately monitor the whereabouts of the phone via the GPS tracking system.

I knew that once we landed in Texas or wherever, that an army of law enforcement authorities would more than likely be waiting to make a surprise appearance. I just hoped like hell that I would not get killed before we landed and that I would actually be able to get Supreme to successfully transfer the money into my accounts.

CHAPTER THIRTY-FIVE

*a*fter we had been in the air for about forty-five minutes or so, the mood on the airplane seemed as if it had become much less tense than when we first boarded the plane. That was in part because of the liquor that was offered up to everyone and passed around. And it was also due to Supreme probably feeling as if he was free and in the clear.

I wasn't in the mood to drink, especially considering how my mood got drastically altered whenever I drank. But I didn't want to seem out of character or raise Supreme's suspicions in any way so I accepted an eight-ounce bottle of Beck's beer when it was offered to me.

"We'll be in Texas in a few hours, but now this nigga is telling me that he can only fly us to Mexico!" Supreme shouted to his cronies, referring to what the pilot had told him.

"Yo, 'Preme, I'm telling you, fuck this whole Cuba thing. We need to go to St. Barts and do what you wanted to do from the jump," one of the bald-headed henchmen said.

Supreme thought for a minute.

" 'Preme, it's not a big deal. We fly to Mexico and then we board a commercial plane and take that to Cuba," I said, breaking Supreme's train of thought.

Supreme looked at me without saying anything.

"Supreme, don't sweat this. Matter of fact, what we can do is transfer the money now before my people realize what's up and try to freeze your accounts, and when we get to Mexico we can double-check and you can see for yourself that I transferred the money to where I'm telling you I will," I stated.

Supreme just ignored me. He went to the back of the plane by himself with his drink in hand and thought in silence for about fifteen minutes.

"Yo, 'Preme! The pilot wants to talk to you again," Supreme's boy shouted to the back of the plane, finally breaking Supreme's train of thought.

Supreme took his time as he made his way to the front cabin.

I knew that I had to hurry up and get Supreme to transfer the money because I was starting to get a bad vibe all around. It just seemed as if Supreme was gonna change his mind about my plan, and if he did then I was surely gonna get killed.

Two minutes later I heard, "Fuck this! Yo, hand me my heat!" Supreme stated, sounding pissed off like he had just been disrespected or something.

"What's up? What happened?" his boys asked.

"Now this nigga is telling me that we gotta make an emergency landing in St. Louis!" Supreme barked.

"For what?" I asked, trying to appear like one of the boys.

"Just hand me my gat!" Supreme demanded. "This mutha-fucka is going where I say he's going!"

Trying to be the voice of reason, I stood up and walked over to Supreme and said, "Supreme, listen, first find out why they want us to make this emergency landing. And just remember that you gotta be careful because if you start threatening them and carrying on, the next thing you know they'll alert the authorities."

"'Preme, handle your business!" his crony said as he handed Supreme the handgun.

"Supreme, you're with me. I got FBI credentials so you don't gotta worry about nothing. But if you start blowing shit off the handle then there ain't shit that I can do to help any of us," I said rather convincingly. "Find out why he's landing the plane and then let's take care of this money."

"Yo, why you keep stressing me about the money?" Supreme shouted.

"I'm stressing you because at this point every law enforce-ment agency in the country is probably looking for you! There is a dead agent in New York, Supreme! The FBI will shut all of your shit down, and all of Horse's assets and Gun Clap Rec-ords' assets will be shut down if they ain't already! I know how they operate, Supreme! My God!" I said, trying to come across as if I was getting pissed off.

Supreme looked at me. He knew that I had made a clear and convincing point.

"Yo, Haz, go in there and find out from these pilots what's up 'cause if I go in there I'm a flip on somebody!" Supreme said.

Haz quickly followed Supreme's instructions.

Supreme finally sat down next to me.

"Jessica, I'm telling you, you better not fuck up my money!" Supreme stated.

"I got you, 'Preme."

"So what do you need to get this done?" Supreme asked.

"I need the bank name, the name of the account, the routing number, the account number, and you should have some kind of swift code or password for wire transfers," I stated.

"Jessica, I don't have all of that on me! I don't normally do this kind of shit!"

Yeah, most people were not like me, in that I had all of my necessary account info embedded in my memory.

"Well, can you call somebody who can get it for you?" I asked.

"Yeah," Supreme stated as he took the phone and prepared to make his call.

Haz was still up front with the pilots and I was wondering what was going on. I was hoping that he had not done anything confrontational.

"Yo, pass me a piece of paper or something to write on," Supreme said as he instructed the person on the other end to hold on a minute.

Just as Supreme began to write down the information, Haz came back from the front cabin.

"'Preme, these cats is bullshitting! Something ain't right!" Haz stated.

Thankfully Supreme ignored him and continued to write down the pertinent bank info. When he was done talking on the phone, Haz was still in his ear, which was kind of good because it distracted Supreme and he just handed me the piece of paper without even acknowledging me.

"'Preme, they bullshitting me! They telling me there's a mechanical problem wit' the plane, but they don't know what it is," Haz stated.

Supreme instructed Haz to call the private jet company and get someone on the phone who could tell us what was up.

"Can't none of us fly no plane, so if they saying it's mechanical, then let them land this muthafucka," Supreme stated, finally sounding somewhat rational.

Haz took the phone from me and asked for the number to the private jet company. At that point a light went off, and I knew that the FBI had tracked the plane with the GPS device that was in my phone. They had more than likely notified the private jet company to tell the pilots to land the plane as soon as possible.

Haz did get someone on the phone real quick, and after a three-minute tirade of cursing and ranting and raving, he finally hung up the phone.

"They saying that they don't really know what the problem is either, and that is why they wanna get the plane on the ground—so that they can have the plane looked at. But they promised to have another plane there waiting for us and ready to take us to wherever we need to go," he explained.

Supreme didn't seem too happy about that arrangement, but what was he gonna do? None of us had any wings so we had no choice but to submit to the pilots' commands.

I didn't want to seem overly anxious, but I was very nervous as the plane started to descend. I wanted to get the money transferred before we landed. But I had to play things cool.

"Supreme, can you pass me another Beck's?" I asked.

Supreme looked at me and he nodded for one of his henchmen to get me the beer.

When the beer arrived, I sipped on it for a few minutes, and then I took the initiative of picking up the phone so that I could get connected to my bank overseas and make the wire transfer.

Supreme looked at me kind of closely and I whispered out loud to him, "The bank . . . I'm on the phone with the bank."

He nodded his head in my direction and made sure that he kept his eyes fixed on me.

My heart began racing a mile a minute. I was so close to transferring the money, yet looking out the window I could see that we were close to landing. I was praying that there were no glitches in the account info that Supreme had given me. There was no doubt that this was gonna be my last chance to get this money. I was also hoping and praying that none of the bank accounts had in fact been frozen.

I finally connected to the bank and I began relaying information to them.

"Yes," I spoke into the phone's automated system.

"Yes," I said again.

"Yes," I said for the third time.

Then I was instructed to start entering my bank account info and routing numbers.

" 'Preme, how much do you want to wire out?" I asked.

Supreme buried his face into his hands and thought for a moment.

"Transfer one-point-five," he instructed.

It was wild how he spoke about millions the way the average Joe would speak about fifties and hundreds.

"Okay," I replied.

With such a large amount being wired, I was routed to a live representative who, after grilling me with security questions that I had to get the answers from Supreme, assisted me further. But after another two minutes or so, one and a half million dollars had been wired into my Swiss bank account. I now controlled more money than most people would ever see in a lifetime. In fact, if I worked for the FBI for more than twenty-five years I still don't think that I would have been able to gross one-point-five million dollars!

"So we good now," I said as I ended the call. "Even if they freeze your accounts this money will be safe."

"Jessica, I swear to fucking God! If you fuck up my money I will torture your ass to no end!" Supreme threatened.

I gave a sinister smile, as finally I was able to relax just a bit. I sipped on my Beck's beer and said, "Supreme, I got you. Don't worry about it."

CHAPTER THIRTY-SIX

⁓

*W*hen we finally landed in St. Louis, you could sense a high level of anxiety and uncertainty in Supreme and his boys. Haz was going from window to window of the plane, looking for something out of order.

" 'Preme, you need to keep an eye on those pilots. I don't trust something about them dudes," Haz stated.

Supreme was also looking out of the airplane's windows as he replied, "Nah, shit is cool. We'll be a'ight."

Being that we were on a private plane, we didn't have to taxi to the terminal gate. It seemed as if we were right in the middle of the runway when the pilots brought the plane to a complete stop. In no time the doors to the plane were being opened and the pilots informed us that we could soon exit the plane.

At that point I hadn't seen any movement that looked out of the ordinary so I began to wonder if the FBI had tracked the plane at all. *Maybe there really were mechanical problems with the plane.* I didn't know for sure but I definitely didn't want to board another plane with Supreme and his crew.

"We just have to wait for the ladder to be positioned and then we can exit," the calm-looking copilot explained as he stood next to Haz.

"So where is this other plane?" Supreme asked.

The pilot told him that the other plane was being refueled and should be ready for boarding in no time.

"Someone on the ground will escort you there. Don't worry," the copilot reassured.

Five minutes later the ladder was in place and we all began to make our way down the steps of the airplane. Supreme made sure to keep me close by as I walked in front of him. We were quickly picked up in what looked like a golf course type of cart.

In no time we had reached the other plane. *Where the hell is my FBI team?* I remember thinking to myself.

I couldn't believe that we were getting ready to board the other plane and no local authorities or anyone had come to aid me. *That GPS system didn't work,* I remember thinking to myself. Then I remember hoping like hell that the FBI wasn't still on some sexist, racist bullshit and had left me out to dry.

Supreme and Haz didn't say a word to one another until Haz finally spoke up and asked Supreme what he was thinking.

"I think we good," Supreme replied. "I don't see no under-covers. Ain't nobody on the rooftops. Let's just board this bitch and get the fuck up outta here."

In no time we were all on the other plane and we were greeted by the pilot and the copilot. They greeted us with warm, customer-service-friendly smiles and handshakes.

"Sorry about the situation on the other plane," one of the pilots said. "We'll do our best to get you guys to Mexico as fast as we can. I'm Captain Foster, and this is my copilot—"

"Exactly how long do you think it will take us to get there?" Supreme asked, rudely interrupting the pilot.

"Well, we don't have to stop over in Texas like things were originally planned, so as soon as everyone is seated, I will check the flight pattern and let you know. In the meantime, Dawn will be your flight attendant and she will get you guys whatever it is that you may need," the pilot stated, referring to the gorgeous, young, black flight attendant.

As the pilot turned to walk back toward cockpit he looked at me and winked. At first I didn't understand it, but it quickly hit me that the wink wasn't just an ordinary wink.

I played my position and finally felt a sense of relief because although I wasn't 100 percent sure who the pilot was, I felt confident that someone was alerted to what was going on.

The flight attendant asked us to all sit and fasten our seat belts so we could prepare for takeoff. Haz wasn't paying the flight attendant any mind as he whispered something in Supreme's hear.

Supreme, who was already seated, nodded his head one time and Haz sat down.

"I know that you guys have been through this drill over and over again, but it's a federal rule that I go over certain things with you guys before we take off," the flight attendant said.

As she was talking Supreme unbuckled his seat belt and came in my direction.

"Excuse me, sir. I need everyone to have a seat until takeoff.

We should be in the air any minute now. Please just give me a minute," the flight attendant politely asked.

"Jessica, I told yo ass that if you was playing games with me that I would fucking murder you! Right?" Supreme barked as my heart skipped. I didn't know what had spooked him but he had suddenly become highly agitated.

"What?" I asked as I held out my palms to show a sign of surrender.

At that point Supreme violently grabbed a fistful of my hair and proceeded to ram my head against the headrest of the plane's leather seat.

I screamed in pain as I asked Supreme what I had done.

"Supreme, you're hurting me!" I screamed.

"Sir, excuse me, sir, is there some sort of problem?" the flight attendant asked.

"Mind your business, lady!" Supreme barked.

"We won't be able to take off until everyone is seated!" the helpless-looking flight attendant screamed.

Supreme paid her no mind. He continued to grip my hair so tightly that I was certain he had yanked some of it from the roots.

"What the fuck was that winking shit about, Jessica?" Supreme demanded. Again he rammed my head into the headrest.

I knew not to play stupid so I gave Supreme the best answer that I could come up with.

"I think he was flirting with me! Supreme—" I replied before having my words cut off by him.

"Flirting with you? What if you was my girl?" Supreme asked, behaving like a jealous abusive boyfriend. All of his crew stood up and looked as if they were waiting for direction from Supreme.

"'Preme, she's lying, she know that nigga!" Haz stated.

"No I don't!" I yelled, still being detained by my hair.

While all of the commotion was going on, the flight attendant Dawn had maneuvered herself about four feet from Supreme and myself.

"FBI!" she yelled. "Everybody on the ground!"

Supreme and his crew looked stunned.

"On the ground!" the undercover FBI agent yelled as she pointed her gun directly at Supreme.

The two pilots then quickly emerged from the cockpit with their guns drawn and they also ordered everyone to the ground. Everyone had complied except for me and Supreme.

"Put your hands out where I can see them!" the male agent ordered. "You! I said get the fuck on the ground!" he barked. Supreme was still standing and now had me in a headlock with my back to his chest.

"I ain't getting on the ground!" Supreme yelled. "Y'all flying this fucking plane or else this bitch is dying!"

Supreme was poking me in the back with his free hand, and from my angle I couldn't see exactly what he was poking me with. It didn't feel like a gun but I wasn't certain and I didn't want to take any chances. From the angle that he was holding me, even the other agents didn't have a good enough view to be able to determine if in fact he was holding a gun or not.

"I'll splatter her guts all over this plane if we don't get this muthafucka up in the air right now!" Supreme commanded.

The agents didn't respond to Supreme. Two of them kept

their guns aimed at Supreme's crew and the other agent aimed his gun at Supreme.

"Jessica, where is my money?" Supreme yelled. I could feel the rage in his tense muscles as he screamed. From experience—just like the episode with Angela Calvino—I knew that when a suspect gets angry they are capable of doing anything.

"It's safe, Supreme. The money is where I told you it would be," I stated.

Supreme tightened his hold on me and I felt like I was going to pass out. I looked out of the window and I could see all kinds of law enforcement activity going on. The authorities scrambled to get in place and surround the plane.

"Jessica, you called these muthafuckas! You set me up, Jessica!" Supreme barked as I desperately hoped for some air.

"Supreme, drop your weapon and let her go!"

"Fuck you!" Supreme shouted.

"Supreme, look outside, you see all of those agents and officers?" the agent who was aiming his gun at Supreme asked.

Little did Supreme know that that was one of the oldest hostage-situation techniques in the book. The question was designed to distract Supreme for split second and it worked.

I could feel Supreme's grip on me loosen just a bit as he focused his attention on the police activity taking place on the runway.

Boom!

The gun blast was deafening as Supreme and I both fell to the ground. Fortunately for me I was still breathing and I hadn't been hit by the slug from the agent's .357 Magnum.

Supreme wasn't as lucky. He had been hit right between the eyes.

"Jessica, are you okay?" my fellow agents asked.

"I'm shook up a bit but I'm okay. I didn't get hit," I said.

Instantly the plane was raided by federal agents. The agent who shot Supreme felt horrible after it was quickly determined that Supreme had just been bluffing. He never had a gun in his hand. All he had was a cell phone which lay next to his lifeless body.

"You had to take the shot," the female agent, Dawn, assured our fellow agent as Supreme's crew was being handcuffed and hauled off the plane.

As I rubbed my throat I tried to get the blood circulating in that area of my body. I walked over to Supreme and shook my head. He had a gaping hole in his forehead but the lack of blood that flowed from the wound proved that he died instantly.

I stared at Supreme's lifeless body and wished that what I was witnessing wasn't true. Unfortunately it was. Supreme was dead, Horse was dead, and Gun Clap Records would probably suffer the same fate.

Never in my wildest dreams did I imagine that the White Chocolate investigation would have taken the twists and turns that it did. And never in a million years would I have predicted the collision course that the investigation took.

CHAPTER THIRTY-SEVEN

*i*stayed in St. Louis for two full days in order to sort things out with the St. Louis office. The fact remained that Supreme had been shot dead by the FBI and he had no weapon on him. There had been mounting momentum in New York about "hip-hop police" waging war against the hip-hop community. So part of my two-day stay in St. Louis was spent in closed-door sessions where we repeatedly went over the details of the shooting and what prompted it. This way everybody would be delivering the exact same well-rehearsed details about the shooting.

When my stay in St. Louis was over I boarded a government plane and made my way back to New York. The New York office, along with the FBI headquarters, wanted to quickly shape the public's perception of the White Chocolate investigation. When I arrived in New York I was immediately whisked to numerous press conferences that were held to praise the success of the investigation. Each press conference was carefully orchestrated to build and create a celebrity status for me. We felt that my new "celebrity status" would be the only smokescreen that we could use and we definitely needed a smokescreen when you consider that Horse had been killed with an FBI-issued handgun and Supreme had also been killed by an FBI agent. Regardless of what the facts were, people are people and we didn't want it to seem like the government had murdered the black targets of their investigation before letting them get their due process, while the white targets in the Mafia had not been murdered.

Each press conference that was held elevated me to a higher status in the mind of the public. And it took the attention off of Horse's and Supreme's deaths. I was being billed as "what was right about America." The media loved the fact that I was a young black girl originally from Compton, California who managed to risk her life and infiltrate the seedy underworlds of hip-hop and the Mafia. But we made sure that we kept most of the focus of the press conferences on the Mafia side of the investigation so that we wouldn't have to explain any of the hip-hop deaths.

To the media, here I was, a young, beautiful lady who had been kidnapped, and witnessed all sorts of barbaric violence and had survived. And in the process I had done something that no other agent had ever done before: getting so close to a Mafia don via his daughter! Instantly there was talk of book deals and movie deals about my investigation.

I played along with the script at the press conferences but things didn't sit right with me. All my life, since my incestuous childhood, I had been conditioned to be someone that I wasn't in order to hide the real truth. I guess that is why I was so good at it. I had tons of guilt but there was no way that I was gonna expose all of the scandalous things that I had done as far as the drugs and the sex were concerned. And of course there was no way that I was gonna mention the money that I had wired into my secret bank account.

The fact was, that with Horse and Supreme dead, any type of prosecutor would have had a hard time proving any allegations of wrongdoings on my part and I knew that. If it ever came to it, the only person that the prosecution would have on their side was the Gun Clap Records crony O-Water. But being that he was an ex-convict with a lengthy rap sheet I was certain that he would be the absolute last person that someone would want to use as a credible witness.

All sorts of thoughts ran through my mind, especially thoughts of just disappearing to another country with the money I had taken from Supreme. But that would have been too much work and it would have also made me a worldwide fugitive for life. However, I did strongly consider that option. That was up until the big news came. When that news came down, I knew that I would be safe.

Angela Calvino had decided to turn against the mob. She agreed to enter the witness protection program and turn State's evidence and testify against her father and anyone else that she needed to testify against. She did that as an act of vengeance against her father who had already turned his back on her. To add to the matter, her father found out that she was carrying Horse's baby and had put a contract out on her life even though she was behind bars.

. . .

When I had silent time to sit alone and think, I wondered if my investigation had really done any good. In essence I had managed to end Horse's life and thereby ruin his son's life in the process. Supreme was a bad apple but even his life was over and I was sure that his family would never be the same again. There were numerous people, such as S&S and Tech-9 and G-Baby who had lost their lives as a result of the Gun Clap Records and Mafia feud. An FBI agent had gotten killed. Gun Clap Records would cease to exist, meaning many jobs would probably be lost and record careers would be ruined. Angela Calvino would be separated from her family forever in the witness protection program. My relationship with my family and my former fiancé was ruined beyond repair. The mob had put a million-dollar contract out on my life so I really had to change my identity for real. I had to get a new social security number, driver's license, as well as minor plastic surgery. Those were the things that I would think about as I asked myself, was it all worth it? Yeah, Paulie Calvino Sr., and his cronies would get locked up and it would put a major dent in organized crime, but I would still ask myself, was it all worth it?

I knew that eventually, when the time was right, that I would access the money that I'd taken from Supreme, and with the toys that money could buy I was sure that it would help to justify the entire investigation in my mind.

But one thing was certain and that was that money could never help to perfectly re-engineer my self-esteem. When I looked back on the course of my life I knew that I had created double personas and was so good at being someone else, simply because I found it less painful and more enjoyable than facing who I really was.

I knew that I would have to do some deep soul searching to correct the character flaws that I had. And I also knew that I wouldn't be able to change my character flaws until I was willing to face the incest demons from my past head on.

What was really wild is that the book that came about as a result of the major publishing deal was titled *White Chocolate,* and it went on to sell three million copies worldwide. The movie, titled *Jessica Jackson,* debuted at number one and stayed there for four consecutive weeks. And with those successes I was labeled the poster girl of what can happen when hard work is mixed with relentless ambition.

What I would say about the White Chocolate investigation is that it enabled me to experience things that I would have never experienced otherwise. But the price that was paid as a result of the investigation—it certainly was not worth it.

I've come to learn that we must look at the root causes of why we are the way we are and why we are motivated to do the things that we do, even though they are harmful to us and those around us, yet provide pleasure. It is easier than disguising what we don't want to deal with or disguising who it is that we don't want to be.

I can say that my disguise, like the disguises of many people, was in the name of ambition and accomplishment. Ambition and accomplishment are never worth it when it takes an emotional toll on yourself, your morals, your ethics, or those around you who love and trust you.

Unfortunately I realized that after the fact.

EPILOGUE

*P*aulie Calvino Sr. and Paulie Calvino Jr. each were sentenced to twenty-five years behind bars for conspiracy, money laundering, and racketeering. In all, fifteen members of the Calvino crime family were sent to prison on various charges. However, all of the members of the Calvino crime family pleaded guilty to the charges they faced without going to trial. They didn't want to give the government the satisfaction of having Angela Calvino testify against them and in the process bring down more mobsters than necessary.

Angela Calvino entered the witness protection program and she lives under a new identity in Oklahoma. She eventually gave birth to Horse's baby boy. The positive side of Horse's legacy continues to live on through his children.

Gun Clap Records folded and a whole host of Gun Clap Records' and Supreme Team associates were tried and convicted on charges of conspiracy, money laundering, murder, and racketeering.

With the fall of Gun Clap Records, White Lines went on to sign with Roc-a-Fella Records, where he found multiplatinum success.

Jessica Jackson retired from the FBI two years after the White Chocolate investigation ended. She never told anyone about her misdoings while conducting the investigation, nor did she ever tell anyone about the money that was wired into her account. She relocated to the Bahamas, where she lived off the one and a half million dollars and made a new life for herself while finally trying to deal with the incest demons of her youth.

An **unforgettable urban tale** of a young girl
who gets **caught up** in the game—but will she
be able to get out before the game claims her?

a novel

Lady's Night

M A R K   A N T H O N Y
Essence Bestselling Author of *Paper Chasers*

After Lady cries rape on her mother's boyfriend, she is kicked out of
her home. A young girl on the streets with nowhere to go, she gets
recruited to a notorious gang's prostitution ring. Lady has no
intention of working the streets forever. In fact, she plans to run
the show. Soon, Lady finds herself deep in a game she can't control.

www.markanthonyauthor.com
www.stmartins.com

St. Martin's Griffin
Available wherever books are sold

ORDER NOW!

Qty	Selection	
____	**Lady's Night** • Mark Anthony • 0-312-34078-8	$14.95
____	**The Take Down*** • Mark Anthony • 0-312-34079-6	$14.95
____	**Eve** • K'wan • 0-312-33310-2	$14.95
____	**Hood Rat*** • K'wan • 0-312-36008-8	$14.95
____	**Hoodlum** • K'wan • 0-312-33308-0	$14.95
____	**Street Dreams** • K'wan • 0-312-33306-4	$14.95
____	**The Bridge** • Solomon Jones • 0-312-30725-X	$13.95
____	**Ride or Die** • Solomon Jones • 0-312-33989-5	$13.95
____	**Criminal Minded** • Tracy Brown • 0-312-33646-2	$14.95
____	**If I Ruled the World** • JOY • 0-312-32879-6	$13.95
____	**Nasty Girls** • Erick S. Gray • 0-312-34996-3	$14.95
____	**Extra Marital Affairs** • Relentless Aaron • 0-312-35935-7 . .	$14.95
____	**Inside the Crips*** • Colton Simpson • 0-312-32930-X	$14.95

*Available November 2006

TOTAL AMOUNT	$_____
POSTAGE & HANDLING	$_____
($2.50 for the first unit, 50 cents for each additional)	
APPLICABLE TAXES*	$_____
TOTAL PAYABLE	$_____
(CHECK OR MONEY ORDER ONLY—PLEASE DO NOT SEND CASH OR CODs. PAYMENT IN U.S. FUNDS ONLY.)	

TO ORDER:

Complete this form and send it, along with a **check or money order,** for the total above, payable to V. H.P.S.

Mail to:

V.H.P.S.
Attn: Customer Service
P.O. Box 470
Gordonsville, Va 22942

Name:_____

Address:_____

City:_____ State:_____ Zip/Postal Code:_____

Account Number (if applicable):_____

Offer available in the fifty United States and the District of Columbia only. Please allow 4-6 weeks for delivery. All orders are subject to availability. This offer is subject to change without notice. Please call 1-888-330-8477 for further information.

*California, District of Columbia, Illinois, Indiana, Massachusetts, New Jersey, Nevada, New York, North Carolina, Tennessee, Texas, Virginia, Washington, and Wisconsin residents must add applicable sales tax.

🦁 **St. Martin's Griffin**